THE YELLOW HAIR

A NICK DRAKE NOVEL

DWIGHT HOLING

JACKDAW PRESS

The Yellow Hair

A Nick Drake Novel

Dwight Holing

Print Edition
Copyright by Dwight Holing 2026
Published by Jackdaw Press
All Rights Reserved

ISBN: 979-8-9938220-1-3

For More Information, please visit dwightholing.com.

See how you can Get A Free Book at the end of this novel.

In Memory of Dwight Mitchell Wiley

1

———

Potholes on a road I'd never traveled before grabbed at the wheels like a bad conscience seeking redemption. It led to a ranch east of Burns surrounded by withered hayfields scratched out of a dead sea of sage scrub. Tumbleweeds hung on rusty strands of sagging barbed wire. The wind-scoured house and barn looked ready to give up the ghost. If the call that brought me out proved true, the owners already had.

A brand new 1980 Cadillac Sedan de Ville was parked out front. The color made me think of the old saw about red skies in the morning. The driver's door opened and released a cloud of cigar smoke followed by a big man wearing a pearl snap-button shirt and stockman boots. He set a summertime Stetson atop his crew cut and eyed the seven-point gold star on the door of my rig.

"I take it you're the new sheriff," he said. "I heard Harney County had a special election to fill the boots of the old one who got hisself killed."

"Nick Drake," I said. "And you are?"

"Red Caldera." He chuckled. "Yup, I know, heckuva moniker. My folks' idea at being clever. Pleased to make your acquaintance, though the situation inside is none too pleasing. Couple been dead a week, be my guess."

When I didn't make a move toward the house, he clucked his tongue. "I woulda thought you'd charge right in, but maybe you don't know you're s'posed to on account you're new to sheriffing."

"If they're dead like you say, what I need to know first is why you went inside uninvited."

The straw cowboy hat reared back as he aimed his double chin at me. "Now, hold it right there. I didn't do nothing wrong. I'm the one called it in and I'm the one been cooling my heels on a hotter than a firecracker morning waiting for you to show up."

Caldera took a suck on his cigar and waited for an apology. The smoke and stink were akin to a big rig slamming on the brakes.

"Okay, okay, have it your way," he said. "I knocked. Didn't get no answer. Hollered a hello. Still nothing. Thought they might be round the back so went to have a gander. Glanced in the window as I passed by and saw what I saw."

"Which was?"

"Both of 'em in the kitchen. One still sitting at the table, the other sprawled on the floor."

"And you went inside to see if they needed help," I said.

"No, I knew they was dead. The bloat. Like a cow swole up in a pasture before the buzzards get to it. You follow? I went in to use the phone but it was as dead as them. Had to use the CB in the Caddy to get patched through to your office."

"Touch anything else in the house?"

"Hell no. Only the phone. Couldn't wait to get out of there." His jowls flapped when he feigned a shudder.

I asked what brought him to the ranch.

"Business." Red Caldera blew a smoke ring. "I'm a commodities broker. That's a fancy title for a middleman with farmers and ranchers on one side and wholesalers on the other."

"Your car has Idaho plates."

"'Cause I live over in the Treasure Valley. Richest soil in the Great Basin. Rich dirt makes rich farmers and that's paydirt for me."

"But now you're here," I said.

"My business is the same as farming and ranching. It's grow big or go under. I been signing up Oregon customers in Baker and Malheur Counties and now here in Harney."

I made a point of looking at the ramshackle spread. "What made you think there was any money in it for you here?"

"Why the third degree, son? I didn't do nothing wrong. How long you gonna take before you go in and see about the dead folks?"

"Let's get something straight, Mr. Caldera. I'm not your son. I'm the sheriff. I ask the questions and you answer them. We can do it here or back in Burns."

"Okay, okay. I know the place don't look like much, but from where I sit, a percentage of a lot of somethings is a whole lot better than nothing of nothings," he said. "Fact is, this is my second visit here trying to seal a deal. I admit it's in piss-poor shape. Even more so than last time."

"When was that?"

"Couple months back." The straw Stetson waggled. "Looks like they ran out of patience on their spread making it and shut it down themselves."

"What do you mean?"

"Well, you'll see for yourself if you ever bother to go inside. Both been shot in the head. Gun lying on the table between 'em. Either a murder-suicide or double suicide. Who went first and was it voluntary be your job to figure out. You follow?"

I asked him if he picked up the gun.

"Hell no. Already told you, only the phone. Nothing else. And I mean nothing!"

Dispatch had told me the name of the rancher's owner, but I asked Caldera anyway.

"Daniel Hardward. Ol' Daniel, I called him, like in the 'Book of.' Lotta farmers over in Idaho straight-up Mormons like him. They're always a tough sell. His wife? Mail-order bride."

"What makes you think so?"

"She's twenty, thirty years younger than him. Chinese-looking gal but I don't know if she was. Definitely not Paiute or any other tribe. Could be Japanese, I s'pose. Maybe Korean. One of them places overseas, take your pick. I never been."

"Did she ever speak to you?"

"You mean in American or her lingo?" he said.

"Either."

"I don't recollect she ever said anything in hers. Had a soft voice with an accent when she did talk, but it wasn't big in the words department. More like, 'Tea? Cookie?'"

Caldera patted his sizable gut and smacked his lips. "Stuffed pastry sort of thing. If she gave it a name, I didn't hear it 'cause I was too busy scarfing 'em. Man oh man, were they good. And sweet?"

He puffed his cigar some more. "I got other customers up in their years who finally get the itch to wed and do it like they're ordering something out of the Sears Roebuck. The brides? They always seem to be named Kim. Ol' Daniel, he introduced her as Mrs. Hardward, but I heard him call her Kim once."

"I'm going to have my look-see now," I said. "You stay put. Two of my deputies are en route. They're going to need a statement from you. Fingerprints too."

"Hold on, goldurn it. I didn't do nothing wrong. I been hanging round here long enough. I got customers waiting on me."

"They're going to have to wait a bit longer. We need your prints when we dust the place."

Caldera rocked back on the heels of his Stockman boots. "You think it's something other than suicide?"

I stepped in close and gave him the hard eye. "I need you to keep your opinions to yourself. Don't breathe a word about this matter until I say so. That's an order. The Hardwards deserve respect, not rumors, not gossip, not speculation. Understood?"

"Sure, sure, Sheriff. 'Course I won't say nothing. Wouldn't anyway. Bad for business people got wind I had customers die like that."

As I headed for the house, he called after me. "Best put a kerchief to your beak. Gets plenty dry out here in the high desert, but not dry enough. You follow?"

The knob squeaked as I twisted it and toed the door open. The front room was clean and tidy. A crocheted Afghan draped the back of a brown sofa. Twin rocking chairs faced a potbelly stove. Pictures cut from magazines and pasted on cardboard were tacked to the walls. One was of a green field dotted with blooms of purple lupine, orange mallow, and pink mariposa lilies. Another was a clear-water brook streaming through a glade surrounded by conifers.

The kitchen was just as quiet, but the scent of wildflowers and pines ended at the doorway. In their place, the stench of overcooked cabbage, sour milk, and rotting meat took hold. The odor wasn't coming from something left on the stove or in the sink. It was a stink I'd smelled before, both on battlefields during the three tours I served in Vietnam and the ten years I patrolled wildlife refuges that had been used as dumping grounds by killers.

I fished a blue bandana out of my jeans and tied it bandit-style.

Daniel Hardward's bibbed overalls and long-sleeved shirt

were bursting at the seams, but the bulges hadn't come from overeating. He was seated in a Shaker-style wooden chair with his head thrown back and arms hanging straight down. The mustacheless beard on his waxy face was white like his hair and the pupils of his eyes that were open but unseeing. The hole in the middle of his forehead had the color and texture of a crater in black lava.

Mrs. Hardward was curled on her left side on the floor across the table from him. The wound in her right temple was ringed by gunpowder burns.

The bloating didn't mask her Asian features and made me blink away flashbacks of dead women and children in bombed-out hooches and farmers floating face down in rice paddies. A teapot and a plate in the middle of the table triggered another memory. Despite a coating of mold, I recognized the shape and flaky pastry of *banh pia*. I'd bought the sweet mooncakes from street vendors while on leave in Saigon.

Tires crunching outside and slamming doors snapped me back to the moment. I took another look around the killing room before going outside.

Chief Deputy Orville Nelson had already slid from behind the wheel of his rig and into the seat of his custom wheelchair, his biceps pumping like pistons as he sped toward me. Close behind was Deputy Trace Wakefield. My predecessor, Sheriff Pudge Warbler, had hired him shortly before his death. The young deputy was a recent graduate of the police academy in Salem. Before that, he'd played two seasons as a tight end for the Seattle Seahawks until a shoulder injury ended his pro career.

"I have some information on the Hardwards," Orville said, letting go of the chair's push rims to wave a sheet of paper as he skidded to a stop. "I must warn you it is as stark as this ranch appears to be."

He glanced at the red Cadillac with the driver sitting behind the wheel. "I take it that is the man who called it in, a Mr. Red Caldera."

"He says he's a commodities broker from Idaho," I said.

"That comports with the preliminary backgrounder I have on him."

I asked Orville if he had a printout of it.

"Negative," the chief deputy said. "I was unsure how long his records search might take and so I entered his name into my computer and left it running. When it completed, Jazz, er, dispatch, read me the results over the radio while I was driving here."

"Any red flags on him?"

Orville said none to speak of. "He has a slew of speeding tickets in Oregon and Idaho, which fits with his occupation as a traveling salesman. He was also arrested for a DUI when he failed the walk-a-straight-line and touch-your-nose tests. The charge was dismissed. His lawyer convinced the judge Mr. Caldera had trouble keeping his eyes open while driving, pulled over to take a nap, and self-administered a dose of prescription cough syrup."

"Smoker's cough," I said. "The cigars."

I beckoned to Deputy Wakefield. "Print Caldera and take down his statement. Remind him he's under strict orders not to talk about what happened here. Make sure he knows we're serious about that. He's free to leave afterward. Then take a walk around and see what you can find."

"Q witness, eye ranch," Trace said in a low voice as if he were back in a huddle repeating the play to let the quarterback know he understood his blocking assignment and pass route.

Orville handed me latex gloves, put on a pair himself, and then donned a surgical mask from the crime scene kit balanced on his lap. It wasn't that long ago the county coroner would've conducted the prelim, but since Pudge Warbler's death, Orville had thrown himself into studying forensic science and crime scene investigation techniques.

Even the curmudgeonly old sawbones had to concede that the chief deputy's boundless inquisitiveness and embrace of new technology made him ideally suited for the task. "That doesn't mean I'm about to hand my scalpel and rib spreaders over to him," Doc had told me.

I led Orville into the house and tugged my kerchief back up as we entered the kitchen.

The chief deputy's head mimicked an owl's as he took in the scene. Then he clicked on a cassette recorder and began describing every detail as he repeated the survey, right down to the color of the dead couple's clothes, skin tones, and positions of their bodies. Next, he took out a camera and began snapping away.

"Make sure to get a close-up of that bun on the plate before you bag it," I said. "Get a sample of the tea in the pot too."

"Do you suspect they were laced with a sedative?" he said.

"I don't know about that, but the bun's a Vietnamese pastry. I believe Mrs. Hardward could be too."

"Perhaps, but I found no record that can either confirm or deny it. In fact, I found nothing about her at all." He paused. "Yet."

I asked what he'd found on Mr. Hardward.

"Daniel Hardward. Middle name Joseph. Age sixty-one. He purchased this land in the winter of 1945."

"End of the war. Maybe he used a GI loan. Did he serve?"

"I do not know. I will initiate a search with the National Archives as well as the Veterans of Foreign Wars when I am back in the office."

"Caldera called Mrs. Hardward a mail-order bride. You didn't find a marriage license?"

"Negative. I asked Jazz if she could do a records search at the courthouse while I am here."

"In between her dispatcher duties."

"Correct. Only a week on the job and she is already proving to be quite capable of multitasking. You made an excellent choice hiring her."

"We'll see. She's young and green," I said. "Ol' Daniel, as Caldera called him, no record of a previous marriage or any children or kinfolk?"

"None that I could find." Orville paused again before delivering another "Yet." "I was able to locate the deed to the property and a vehicle registration. A 1972 Ford pickup." He read off the license plate from his notes.

"There's a Church of Latter-day Saints in Burns. Could be he was a member and others will know something about him. Maybe he and Mrs. Hardward were married there."

"The church's street address is actually next door in Hines. I already entered a meeting time with the bishop on my scheduler. I programmed it to send me a reminder thirty minutes ahead of time."

Orville took a breath. "If only you would take up my offer to teach you computing. It would simplify organizing and managing your daily schedule in fifteen-minute increments."

"Daily? I wish. I'd need a scheduler with just as many slots for nights."

2

I left my chief deputy in the kitchen and searched the rest of the house. Beyond the indoor bathroom, I found two bedrooms. The larger of the two held a double bed, neatly made with a floral spread tucked in at the corners. Hanging above the headboard was a framed print of a Christlike figure walking through a wheat field followed closely by a woman wearing a blue headscarf and robe. A *Book of Mormon* sat on one of the nightstands.

A handheld stretcher with a nearly finished needlepoint lay on the other. I recognized the colorful subject by its crane-like body, crested head, and outstretched wings. It was a *Chim Lac*, a mythical bird that represented the Vietnamese's spirit, connection to nature, and hope for a brighter future. Though the North had won the war, the jury was still out on how bright a united Vietnam's prospects would be.

The smaller of the two bedrooms had a single bed made up like a couch, a desk and chair, and bookshelves. It was clean and orderly like the other rooms. A telephone was on the desk. I picked up the handset and put it to my ear. Nothing. I clicked the plungers a couple of times and spun the dial. Not even static.

The desk's top drawer wasn't locked. A folder lay on top. It was filled with bills, past-due notices, bounced checks from the bank, and dunning letters from collection agencies. Beneath it was a checkbook register. The last entry had been made a month ago.

The side drawers were empty. No file folders. No shoebox filled with tchotchkes, old keys, and spare buttons. No correspondence with a marriage broker and letters between a prospective husband and wife, much less a marriage license, immigration documents, passport, and visa.

The bookshelf held copies of *Farm Journal* and *American Cattlemen*. The most recent issues were months old. It was the same for the back issues of *Bulletin* and a slick monthly called *Ensign*. Both were publications issued by the Church of Latter-day Saints. I thumbed through an *Ensign*. The contents were devoted to faith-promoting feature stories and reports about the church's worldwide operations. One double-page spread was dog-eared. It was a map of Asia. Vietnam was circled in blue ink.

There were no framed wedding photographs on the shelves or hanging on the walls—no photo albums, either. I searched for a family tree book or even a simple chart. I didn't know much about the LDS faith, but I was aware of its emphasis on genealogy and the expectation for families to maintain detailed records. My search came up empty.

I stood back and took in the room. It was a little too neat, too orderly, too absent of any personal effects.

Orville had finished examining the kitchen and was dictating notes into his cassette recorder when I rejoined him. He recited the exact distance between the two bodies that he'd measured with a carpenter's tape and gave an estimate of how long they'd been dead based on the rate of decomposition. Six to seven days.

"What's your gut tell you happened here?" I said.

"Given both bullet wounds and presence of gunpowder burns on the female's temple, it would appear that Mrs. Hardward shot Mr. Hardward from across the table and then turned the weapon on herself."

I picked up the plastic evidence bag holding a Smith & Wesson .38 Special with a four-inch barrel.

"A cop's gun," I said.

"Affirmative. The revolver is a popular model and caliber among both rural and urban law enforcement agencies."

"Military as well. Lot of Navy and Air Force pilots carried them in 'Nam in case they got shot down. They carried tracer bullets for signaling rescuers. Tunnel rats also used them. They could put a silencer on it, plus a revolver wouldn't jam like a semiautomatic."

Orville glanced at the weapon riding in the holster strapped to my hip. When I was with Fish and Wildlife, I packed a Smith & Wesson .357 Magnum revolver like all my fellow rangers. I swapped it after being elected sheriff for my father-in-law's .45 semi that he'd been issued as a Marine in World War II and carried as a lawman for thirty-five years.

Pudge had bequeathed it to me, along with the badge now pinned to my chest, in a handwritten note urging me to run for sheriff upon his death. The gun shot as straight and true as he'd been, and I was betting my life it would do the same for me.

"We still have to run ballistics on the .38 to positively ID it as the killing weapon," Orville said.

"I see you bagged Mr. and Mrs. Hardwards' hands," I said.

"To protect them from contamination so Doc can test them for GSR." He paused. "Gunshot residue."

"I'm up on the terms," I said.

"My apologies. I have gotten in the habit of explaining criminal investigation and forensic science acronyms to Jazz."

"So long as it doesn't interfere with her dispatcher duties."

"I will make sure of that."

We stared at the bodies. Orville looked up at me. "Your expression—or more accurately, your absence of one—suggests you do not believe either of the Hardwards fired the weapon."

"Doubt everything until proven otherwise. Pudge used to say that. Of course, his choice of words were a helluva lot more down-to-earth."

"Your father-in-law was unique. It was an honor to serve under him."

"You have to wonder what a farmer is doing with a cop's gun," I said. "A shotgun or a deer rifle, that makes sense. Maybe a .22 pistol for dispatching rats in the barn. But a .38?" I shook my head.

"And then there's Mrs. Hardward here. Holding a revolver that weighs a pound and a half steady while aiming and firing it from across the table and hitting her husband right here." I tapped my forehead an inch above right between the eyes.

"Then pressing the barrel against her temple and squeezing the trigger and dropping the gun so it lands square on the table for all to see as she falls to the floor without knocking over a chair."

"Precisely," Orville said. "It is in my notes. The one thing I cannot do is provide an irrefutable degree of the angle of the gunshot from her side of the table to his. Was she standing or sitting? Was he sitting up straight or slouching? All I can provide is a range based on a trigonometric equation."

"Will your equation also be able to tell us if there was a third person involved?" I said. "Either sitting or standing next to Mrs. Hardward? Maybe even shooting them somewhere else and staging the bodies?"

"I put that possibility in my notes as well. Dusting for fingerprints could confirm it unless the third party was gloved. There is always a chance they left clothing fibers or shoe tracks behind.

I did notice there were only two teacups on the table. I dusted them as well as the ones in the cupboard."

"In case a third party washed the one he used and put it back."

"Correct. The *banh pia* is in an evidence bag and a sample of the tea in a vial," he said.

"Thorough as always. Do you need my help dusting and searching?" I said.

"It would be more comprehensive and accurate if I do it myself to conform with the execution pattern I have plotted out."

"Too many cooks in the kitchen will spoil your recipe? Or are you worried I'd wind up painting myself into a corner?"

"I better plead the Fifth."

"Smart man," I said. "Make sure you dust the telephone in the office. Caldera said it's the only thing in the house he touched."

"Except for the front doorknob coming in and going out," Orville said.

"Yeah, but he didn't name it both times I asked what he'd touched."

"Aha!"

"Exactly. See if you can turn up his prints anywhere else. I'll go check on Trace. Give a holler when you're ready for us to carry out the bodies."

Back outside, I rounded the house. The sun was glinting off something shiny outside the kitchen window. It was a twenty-gallon galvanized tub. The inner walls were ringed like a dirty bathtub. Dried pond lily leaves and flower petals were clumped on the bottom.

I grabbed a handful and gave a sniff. The smell was earthy but still sparked a memory from Vietnam of ponds filled with lotus flowers. I bet the tea the Hardwards were drinking when they died was homegrown. Lotus and jasmine were both Vietnamese favorites.

Looking at the surrounding fields, I could see reflections of the sky hovering right above the ground as sunlight bent passing through temperature layers to create the mirages. Red Caldera was also passing through quickly. He didn't appear concerned he might knock his new red Cadillac out of alignment by hitting the potholes as he sped away.

I surveyed the flat, desolate patch of the High Lonesome in all directions. The Hardwards had it all to themselves. I couldn't see any other ranch houses before the horizon was lost to the curvature of the earth.

Deputy Wakefield was poking around the barn when I caught up to him.

"Find anything?" I said.

"Too much nothing," Trace said.

"Meaning?"

"I grew up on a ranch outside of Madras. Where's the tractor, the tools? Bags of seed, hay bales, and such?"

"Any sign of a '72 Ford pickup with Oregon plates?"

He shook his head.

"According to their checkbook, they were going under. Maybe they sold it along with everything else they owned, including their livestock."

While Trace had bright blue eyes that even the gloaming inside the barn couldn't dull, they didn't seem to move when he signaled no. It was another holdover from his days as a tight end; linebackers could never get a read on who he was targeting to block or where he was going to run to catch a pass.

"Does that mean you found their stock?" I said.

He spun on his bootheels. I followed him outside, through a corral that was missing rails, and across a pasture of cracked, dry earth that resembled jigsaw puzzle pieces. Ten, twenty, thirty, forty yards. A half a football field. The ground sloped down and then ended abruptly at the edge of a gully. The bottom was littered with carcasses.

"Their cattle," I said.

"I make out no more than a half dozen. A few sheep and a couple of hogs too," he said.

"Not much in the way of a herd."

"Not much in the way of graze here either."

"Could be Ol' Daniel put them out of their misery for lack of feed and dumped them down there. Either that or he did it after some kind of disease got to them."

I waited for the young deputy to offer an opinion, but he didn't.

"You know my wife, Gemma, is a large animal vet, right? She also does work for Oregon Department of Ag. She'll need to investigate this to determine if it was disease. If so, she'll have to see if it's spread to other ranches."

"Bad news for them if it did," he said.

"Could've been the other way around," I said. "The disease came from another herd and that rancher wanted to keep it quiet."

"Meaning worse news for the Hardwards." Trace scanned the dead animals. "Your wife, she'll need protection if she goes calling on the neighbors."

"Gemma's always prided herself on being able to handle whatever's thrown her way. When she first started off, she had to convince all the ranchers in Harney County a woman could treat large animals as good if not better than any man."

He looked past me at the house with the dead couple inside.

"I'll talk to her," I said.

When Trace nodded, I could tell he was already visualizing the rushers he'd block, the would-be tacklers he'd level when he ran point for Gemma.

"This whole thing strikes me as off," I said.

"How so?"

"There's an office inside that's cleaned out like the barn. There's nothing personal, only a stack of unpaid bills that help point the way to explaining why the couple's dead. No photos, no marriage license, no nothing that shows how and when they met, who Mrs. Hardward is, and where she came from."

"Someone take it?" he said.

"More likely put themselves on shit-burning detail," I said. "What grunts who got demerits in 'Nam were assigned. Emptying the latrines into a pit or fifty-five-gallon drums, dousing them with diesel, and tossing in a match."

Trace's blue eyes finally narrowed.

"Yeah, it stunk that bad."

We walked to a desiccated pasture on the other side of the barn. The incinerator was in the southeast corner like I figured it'd be because of the prevailing winds that'd carry the smoke away from the house.

It was like the fuel drums I remembered in country, only this one had a metal grate on top to lessen the risk of embers escaping. Harney County's sagebrush steppe was prone to burning and had a long history of deadly and devastating range fires. The young deputy hoisted the heavy grate and we stared down at a mound of ash.

"Unlikely there's anything legible in there," I said.

"Could be something at the bottom," he said.

Orville called from the kitchen window. "All set."

"We'll leave it till later," I said. "Let's go help Orville."

By the time Trace and I got to the kitchen, the chief deputy had already retrieved two body bags from his rig. Lucky for us they were the new kind made of PVC and not the old canvas ones prone to leaking.

Despite the bloating, rigor mortis had come and gone in

both bodies. That made it easier to move Daniel Hardward from the chair and into the bag. Once zipped up, Trace grabbed the head and shoulders and I took the feet. He didn't break a sweat lifting, but I felt a twinge in my back and knew where I'd be aiming the showerhead when I got home that night.

That is, if I did get home.

Bagging Mrs. Hardward was easier since she was smaller and already on the floor. After we placed her in Orville's rig alongside her husband, I tacked a sheriff's "Do Not Enter" notice to the front door.

"There's a fork in the road a mile or so back," I said. "It likely leads to another ranch or two. Trace, you go check out their herds and see what kind of condition they're in. If anyone asks, don't say anything about what we found here. We need to keep this under wraps as long as possible. Orville and I'll head straight to Burns."

"Set left, eye ranch," he said.

"What about the district attorney?" Orville said. "You are required to inform him in a timely manner."

"I know and I will," I said.

"And Bonnie LaRue?"

I pictured the longtime editor and publisher of the *Burns Herald*. She was getting up there in years, but still as fiery as her red hair.

"That's another thing Pudge taught me. Always better to deliver the news yourself than let someone beat you to it and put their own spin on it. I'll tell her, but I won't give her the names and location yet, only a promise I will as soon as I can."

"She will not like that," Orville said.

"I know, but we need time. I'll tell her she'll be the first person I okay to release the info to the public. When I do, she'll know she can trust I'll play square with her the next time."

"And the one after that," he said. "There always seems to be another next time."

I couldn't argue with him there.

"We do have a significant vulnerability attempting to keep this quiet," Orville said. "Specifically, Doc is required to register anyone brought to the morgue. The DA and *Burns Herald* will be able to find the Hardwards' names."

"But without being able to match fingerprints to records, how do we know for certain they're the Hardwards?" I said.

Orville grinned. "You did learn some tricks from your father-in-law. John and Jane Doe it is."

We moved out with Trace taking point, Orville in the middle, and me sweep. It reminded me of driving in a convoy back in country. Seeing Mrs. Hardward was triggering memories of my time there. Though the war had technically ended for me the moment I stepped on the Freedom Bird home, it was only the beginning of a long struggle to come to grips with Vietnam's aftermath—my drug addiction, flashbacks, guilt, and anger.

I owed my life to a stint in Walter Reed's shrink unit and getting a job as a wildlife ranger through a special program for veterans. Falling in love with Gemma Warbler and having a family sped my recovery by teaching me life was worth living no matter my past.

While my memories of Vietnam hadn't disappeared completely, what I'd never allow myself to do again was wallow in them. That became especially important after Gemma and I adopted our son.

Johnny was the orphan of an unknown GI father and Vietnamese mother—a *bui doi* as they called him and other mixed-race foundlings, a child of the dusty streets. His mother's murder by a pimp had sent Johnny on an unfathomable journey that took him from the back alleys of Saigon to the jungle as a child soldier to stowing away on a US cargo plane to an orphanage to our home in No Mountain.

I worked hard to teach him to be proud of his cultural heritage, which would help guide him on his path to manhood. Seeing Mrs. Hardward made me realize I'd fallen short. Outside of giving Johnny books about Vietnam, I hadn't gone looking for other Vietnamese people to introduce him to.

I should've tried harder. Just before Saigon fell, tens of thousands of South Vietnamese who worked for the American war effort were airlifted to the States to prevent them from being slaughtered. Hundreds of thousands more fled the country and eventually emigrated too. While most settled in large urban areas, it was no excuse for my blunder.

Smacking the steering wheel, I vowed that as soon as this business with the Hardwards was settled, Gemma and I'd take Johnny to Portland to visit the city's own version of a Little Saigon. Maybe the Hardwards' deaths would turn out to be some kind of double suicide after all and I'd have the case closed in a couple of days and we could go the coming weekend.

Maybe.

I could still hear my DI in Basic all these years later. "Hope is not a strategy," he'd scream red-faced. "Maybe means you're already dead."

3

———

Deputy Wakefield turned left at the fork and Orville and I continued to Burns. He took the Hardwards straight to the morgue while I drove to a squat pink building that housed the sheriff's department. It was still taking some getting used to calling it my office after a decade using an old lineman's shack at the edge of No Mountain for one.

It was even more unsettling to see a pickup parked out front that was identical to the one I used to drive, right down to the US Fish & Wildlife service emblem on the door and a gun rack behind the front seat.

Its driver was sitting at my desk talking on my phone.

"Make yourself right at home," I said.

Loq ignored me as he listened some more, muttered, "I'll let you know," and hung up.

"I ate lunch at the Pine Room just now," my former partner said. "They're still cleaning up the bar. Looked like a stampede went through it. Barkeep said it was a biker's doing after losing a game of eight ball to a local cowboy. Began swinging a cue and touched off a brawl."

"Yeah, Trace Wakefield took the call," I said. "He's the newest deputy and was handling night shift on his own."

"What'd he do?"

"He went to break it up and the biker chucked a chair at him and rabbited out the back. Jumped on his chopper and took off."

"So, the biker got away?" Loq said.

"For a couple of blocks. Trace gave chase and tackled him," I said.

"On foot?"

"He's plenty big and even faster. Used to play pro ball."

"Sounds like a worthy addition. Having a young guy working the heavy bag for you gives you more time to deal with all that." The Klamath's unwrinkled face gave nothing away, not even a hint of a grin, as he chinned at the pile of paperwork on my desk.

"Funny," I said. "Who were you on the phone with?"

"Your old district supervisor," he said.

"What'd Liz want, try to convince you to talk me into quitting the sheriff's and ask for my job back?"

"She wanted to know why I rejected her latest candidate as your replacement."

Loq had been hired as a ranger through the Vietnam veteran program around the same time as me. While I lived in Harney County and he made his home 150 miles west in Klamath County, we were supposed to split the sprawling territory between us, but more often than not wound up working together. Force multipliers is what our boss Liz Bloom always called us.

"How come you nixed this one?" I said.

"Kid's never been west of Ohio," Loq said. "He asked me what there was to do here on the weekends."

"And you told him there's no such thing as a day off."

"Kid said the employee manual guaranteed it. Also read me the part where it says all rangers are entitled to a week off during the holidays."

"And you told him that's our busiest time of the year. What with busting poachers hunting geese at Malheur to sell for Christmas dinners and pronghorn at Hart Mountain for New Year's feasts."

"Kid said he and his family always go to Florida for Christmas."

I shrugged. "He eighty-sixed himself."

"What I told Liz."

"You know you're going to have to accept somebody to fill my spot or you'll be back spending even more time behind the wheel when that beautiful tribal cop you fell in love with returns home."

Up until a couple of months ago, Loq had been making the five-hour drive from his house in Chiloquin to the Umatilla Reservation to spend time with Officer Bina Mantioc. Shortly after I was elected sheriff, Bina was given a temporary assignment to help the Burns Paiute Colony start their own tribal police force. Gemma and I had invited her to stay with us and use the apartment we'd built above the stable. Loq became a frequent visitor, shortening his drive time to be with Bina by two hours each way.

"I met your new dispatcher," he said.

"Jazz," I said.

"She's good with computer stuff."

"How do you know?"

"The printouts she had on her desk. She told me you and your deputies were called out to investigate a murder."

"Jazz may be new, but she's smart enough not to have told a stranger anything like that. You're fishing."

"I was and you just bit. Who's dead and how?"

Loq and I were brothers, bound by a blood oath, bound by mutual trust formed over years of working together that was deeper than the water in Giiwas, the lake sacred to the Klamath people that later became known as Crater Lake.

"A husband and wife," I said. "Could be a double suicide or a murder-suicide."

Loq looked down his high cheekbones. "Could be?"

"Or made to look like it."

"Mm," he said.

"There's more. The wife? She's Vietnamese."

That elicited another "Mm."

"I know. A long way from home," I said. "Apparently it was an arranged marriage. A mail-order bride sort of thing."

"You need my help?"

"I'm telling you, aren't I?"

His long mohawk rippled. "Now it makes sense why I came here today. I woke up this morning but was still partly in dreamworld."

"What was your dream about?" I said.

"I was back in 'Nam but also here in Harney. Two people were talking to me. One was this cagey VC guerrilla we were hunting who'd been ambushing our recon teams. Another was a local woman we used as a translator. Both were speaking to me at once, but they were talking backward."

"You mean they were saying the words backward?"

"No, the Charlie was warning me that the translator was hiding on the trail up ahead to ambush me. The translator was telling me how the Charlie was going to save her country by killing me and my men," he said.

"Were they speaking in their own voices or the other person's?"

"Neither. It was another woman's voice. She spoke for both."

"What do you make of it?"

"I don't know yet. I'll have to go back to dreamworld and try to find Talking Woman and ask her." Loq leaned forward. "You want your desk back?"

"You know I prefer standing to sitting, running instead of walking."

"You miss rangering, don't you?"

I didn't need to close my eyes to see the beauty and wonder I'd seen every day I was on patrol. Endless seas of purple sage. Clear, cold rivers cascading down mountainsides. *Vs* of waterfowl embossed against the sky as they winged their way north in spring and south in fall. Cougars caterwauling and bears growling. Bighorns butting heads and pronghorns racing. Steens Mountain glowing red from the setting sun. Camping atop its summit so I could be even closer to the stars that shone, streaked, and pinwheeled overhead to remind me I was but another piece of cosmic dust.

"Sure, I miss working outdoors," I said, "but I've managed to find a little time here and there to saddle Wovoka and ride the old trails."

"Your buckskin's always been a good horse." Loq grunted. "Almost as good as my spotted pony."

"Almost?"

He looked at the stack of paper again. "Do you have to read every page and sign them all?"

"Goes with the job. Pudge always told me he was more likely to die from a papercut than a bullet." I paused, thinking of his last day on earth. "Well, it was just something he said, you know."

Loq started singing a tribute song in Maklak, his native tongue. I recognized some of the words. Strength. Courage.

Tribe before self. A welcome to the spirit world from fellow warriors and ancestors.

When he finished, he said, "The sheriff was a good man."

"He was."

"You show him much honor taking this job."

"We'll see. I've only been at it a little while."

"Tell me more about the dead couple at the ranch," Loq said. "If it wasn't their choice to die, then you'll find out soon enough if you're cut out to be a sheriff."

"Both had bullets to the head," I said. "His in the middle of his forehead. Hers in the right temple. She had powder burns. He didn't."

"And the weapon?"

"A Smith & Wesson .38 Special. It was on the table between them."

"Two-inch or four-inch barrel?"

The two-inch was favored by detectives because it was easier to conceal. Beat cops favored the longer barrel because it gave the round more muzzle velocity and heftier stopping power.

"Four-inch," I said. "You can find them in every sheriff's office and police station in Oregon. Every state for that matter."

"Not only the ones here," Loq said. "South Vietnamese MPs and civilian cops in Saigon, Hue, and Da Nang packed them too. They were so common you could buy a .38 on Tu Do Street for three flip-top boxes of Marlboro Red. You get a serial number off it?"

"Orville bagged it and took it to Doc's for ballistics. He'll run the number while he's at it."

"Unless it was filed off." Loq stood. "Give me the location of the ranch and I'll go have a look. I'll tell you what I find at supper tonight."

"If not supper, then breakfast. No telling how long it'll take me to get through all those reports."

"I'll ask Girl Born in Snow to leave a plate for you," he said.

"Better if you ask Gemma to leave a little patience for me," I said.

He eyed the stack of paperwork again. "Hope you know what you got yourself into, brother."

4

———

Pudge Warbler had always insisted his office open on to the tiny lobby and be the closest to the front door. "I'm the sheriff and I aim to be the first person anybody sees either coming in asking for help or looking to settle a grudge," he explained.

It was sound reasoning and I saw no reason to change it when I pinned on the star. I was sitting at my desk shuffling papers the day after I placed a classified ad for a new dispatcher when a woman's voice caused me to look up.

"I'm Jazz," she announced.

Taking in her dark mascara, spiky black hair, and dressed all in black from her leather jacket to her combat boots, I pegged her for the girlfriend of the biker locked in a cell upstairs.

"Wrong office," I said. "You need to talk to the bailiff at the courthouse next door."

"No, I'm in the right place. I'm here about the dispatcher job you posted."

The young woman promptly began reciting her résumé. She was born and raised in San Francisco, had been an outside hitter on the girls' varsity volleyball team, and just graduated from Oregon Tech in Klamath Falls.

"My name is Jasmine Flambeaux, but I go by Jazz, though my tastes definitely run more Patti Smith and Joan Jett. Have you heard of them?"

"I'm more Bob Dylan and Neil Young," I countered. "You heard of them?"

She laughed. "Of course. My dad listens to them."

"Wait, Flambeaux? San Francisco? Is your father Detective Torch Flambeaux?"

"Right on."

Harry "Torch" Flambeaux was a robbery homicide detective who was a legend in law enforcement circles. While his nickname was a play on his French last name, it also reflected his hard-nosed tactics that spawned stories, including one where he locked a suspect in a car and threatened to light it on fire if he didn't get a confession. Some claimed he was the model for a Clint Eastwood movie.

"So, you're here about the job because your father wants you to go into police work," I said.

The spiky hair shook. "No, it's because he doesn't want me to."

"You're trying to prove something to him?"

"Of course I am. All kids try to prove themselves to their parents." She trained her heavily made-up eyes on me. "Didn't you?"

I hadn't needed the shrink at Walter Reed telling me the reason I'd enlisted in the Army and volunteered for long-range reconnaissance patrols was that my father was a lifer.

"Why did you go to a little college like Oregon Tech instead of Stanford or Berkeley?"

"My father wanted me to go to his alma mater." Her pert nose wrinkled. "Too Jesuit. Too close to home."

"If you thought K Falls was small-town compared to San Francisco, Burns is even smaller. Much smaller," I said.

"San Francisco's population is thirty times greater than Klamath Falls and Klamath has eight times more people than Burns. See, I'm already used to downsizing."

"You just did that calculation in your head?"

"I have a thing for numbers," she said. "Would you like me to tell you how much larger Harney County is land-wise compared to San Francisco County? By the way, SF is both a county as well as a city—not many people know that. The answer is two hundred twelve times larger."

"I'll take your word for it. Your father aside, why do you really want to take a job here and not go back to California? It's called the High Lonesome for a reason. The middle of nowhere. The back of beyond."

"That's exactly why I do."

Jazz started counting off on her fingers. The long nails were the same color as her eye makeup and hair.

"One, the sheer size of Harney County. Two, the fact there are only seventy-five hundred people living in it. Three, the great distances between places. Four, the limited number of sheriff's deputies. Five, the statistically high rate of crime."

"It's not that high," I said, making a stop sign with my palm. "Harney isn't Portland."

"Proportionally, the rate is—" She let it go. "Statistical aberration aside, the reason I want to be your dispatcher is that it'll be a challenge and I'll be good at it. I see myself as a kind of air traffic controller."

"A what?"

Jazz mimed holding a microphone. "Dispatch to Deputy Wakefield. 10-65 in progress. Green's Market. Crane. Take 78 east. Exit Crane-Venator Road. Left on Harney Avenue. Right on Third. Right on Fairmount to reach the back door to the store out of view of the three perps inside. Two males, one female. One is wielding a knife, another a broken bottle. The female is cradling a baby, but it's not a baby. It's a sawed-off shotty wrapped up like one."

She took a breath. "Dispatch to Deputy Nelson. 187 at T Cross T Ranch. Three miles northeast of Wagontire. Take 20 west to Riley. Then 395 south. Proceed thirty point nine miles. Look for the T Cross T overhead on the left. Avoid right-hand side of the cattle guard. Has a broken rail. Suspect is armed. Proceed with extreme caution. Backup is fifteen minutes out."

"How do you know my deputies' names and how do you know those codes?" I said. "Heck, how do you know the fastest way to get to a blink-and-you'll-miss-it town like Wagontire?"

Jazz smiled. "It's what I do, Sheriff."

"Hey, Orville," I yelled down the hall. "Come meet our new dispatcher."

The wheelchair's rubber tires screeched as he came barreling around the corner and skidded to a stop in my office.

"Who is it, sir?"

"Meet Jazz Flambeaux. She's from San Francisco by way of Oregon Tech."

He sized her up. "What was your favorite class there?"

"Coding," she said.

"You know BASIC?"

"Of course, but I'm more into C now. You can do so much more with it."

Orville's face lit up. "I know. Have you tried C+?"

"Totally tubular. A game changer."

"Affirmative. When I started off coding, there was only Fortran."

"Ugh." Jazz made a face.

"It was so—"

"Neanderthal?"

"Precisely." Orville turned to me. "When does she start?"

"When can you?" I asked her.

"How about right now?" Jazz said.

"Do you have a place to stay in Burns?"

"I'll find one."

"My mother-in-law owns a boarding house that has a vacancy," Orville said. "Do you like Basque food?"

"Of course. San Francisco has lots of great Basque cafés in North Beach. They're all close to my favorite clubs."

"My wife and her mother are going to love you," he said.

Now, Jazz was ringing through to the phone on my desk.

"What do you got?" I answered.

"Deputy Wakefield radioing for you. Should I patch him through?"

"Go right ahead."

The buzz of static and then a *bing-bing* was soon followed by the deputy's voice. "Sheriff?

You were right about ranches up that road."

"How many?" I said.

"Two. Both were in a lot better shape than the Hardward spread."

"Did you see their herds?"

"The one nearest to the fork, the Big D, had healthy-looking Black Angus. Least the hundred or so I saw grazing on either side of the road."

"And the second?"

"The Triple Triangle. Saw a dozen or so horses, but no cows."

"Doesn't mean they aren't grazing somewhere else," I said. "Anybody stop and talk to you?"

"No, but I had eyes on me from the front porch of the Triple Triangle," the young deputy said.

"I'll ask Orville to take a look at their land records, see how big both the spreads are and where the Triple Triangle's stock might be."

"Should I go back to the Hardward ranch and check the incinerator?"

"Yeah, and Trace? My former partner's also on his way over there to have a look-see. His name's Loq."

Static filled my ear for several seconds.

"Is he going because you think it's a Fish and Wildlife crime?" Trace said.

"No, but Loq can see things others can't and, well, we may end up needing someone who can operate outside this office's purview. Understand?"

The static returned for a few seconds. Finally, the young deputy said, "I'll run any play you and he call."

"Good man. Report back what you find."

I hung up and stared at the stack of paper crowding my desk. "The trees you came from are long forgotten and the Hardwards will be too if I keep sitting here," I said.

The paperwork didn't argue and so I fast-stepped to Orville's office. He was sitting behind an assemblage of tables pushed together that he called the Bridge in a tip of the hat to his favorite TV show. The tops were crowded with monitors, keyboards, and metal boxes containing who knew what.

"How long till Doc gets back to us with something?" I said.

"He said he would be able to share his preliminary findings in twenty-four hours. Blood work will take longer. But he did make a couple of observations."

"What?"

"The weapon has a front sight at the tip of the barrel, but it did not leave a mark on Mrs. Hardward's temple. I mean, Mrs. Jane Doe's."

"Could be she didn't press it hard against her skin or it got hidden by gunpowder burns."

"Doc also noticed there was no blood spatter on it or the tip of the barrel."

"I'm assuming he's going to run ballistics on the weapon."

"I will do it for him." Orville gave a keyboard a flurry of taps. "Right now I am putting in a search order on the serial number with the National Tracing Center at the Bureau of Alcohol, Tobacco, Firearms, and Explosives. That should help if the weapon was manufactured and sold after 1968. Before then, manufacturers were not required to put serial numbers on their products, though many did."

"If the weapon's origins were military, either issued to GIs or supplied to South Vietnamese cops, it'll have one," I said. "Everything military gets a number, including soldiers. Our unis, our dog tags, our blood types stamped on cards we carried inside our helmets."

"If I do not receive anything from BATF, I will file a request with the Department of Defense, but my initial research revealed that accounting for weapons is largely left up to the armorers at all the military bases and National Guard armories."

"That's a helluva lot of haystacks," I said. "I take it you dusted the gun for prints at the scene?"

"Affirmative."

"And you'll run ballistics on the slug you took from the wall behind Mr. Hardward and the one inside Mrs. Hardward's skull? I noticed it wasn't a through-and-through."

"Of course, but Doc said something interesting about the latter. Given the force of a .38 Special round fired from a four-inch barrel pressed against the temple, nine times out of ten it would have exited the skull. This one did not."

"Maybe Mrs. Hardward has a particularly thick skull."

Orville shook his own. "Doc measured it. Hers is average for a female. Precisely .28 inches. Males average .25 inches. Depending on load, the muzzle velocity of a .38 Special round ranges from seven hundred and fifty to nine hundred feet per second. Depending on the targeted material, the average penetration can be—"

"And I'm sure you'll put all those numbers in your report," I said, "but what I need to know ASAP is will your ballistics be able to prove she shot her husband and then herself or did someone else?"

"I could speed up the process with some help," he said.

"You know I don't have a budget for any more computers."

"I meant personnel help. Jazz could code a program that—"

"Done, so long as it doesn't interfere with her dispatcher duties. And Orville? Remember, she's not qualified for fieldwork no matter how much she wants it. I can't take that risk."

"I know," he said.

"Good. What about fingerprints you lifted at the scene?"

"I am still processing all the ones I took. Not surprisingly, everything so far matches those of the deceased."

"None from any third party yet?" I said. "What about Red Caldera?"

"As soon as I have a definitive report, I will let you know."

"Okay, but I need to give the DA something fast or he'll take the easy route and chalk it up to a marital spat. Case closed."

"Does that mean you have already scheduled a meeting with him? I can set a reminder of the date and time on my computer for you."

I tapped the side of my head. "Already put it on mine."

It took less than a minute to walk to the district attorney's office on the first floor of the courthouse, but I had to spend an additional ten waiting outside his closed door. The delay was intentional, partly Sidney Sessions's way of showing how important he was, but mostly to reinforce his ongoing resentment.

"Make it quick. I'm very busy," he said when I was finally ushered inside.

He stayed planted in a black leather chair positioned behind a desk that was crowded with snow globes. It was set on a four-inch riser to give him a height advantage over anyone who sat across from him.

When I didn't start talking, he scowled.

"You know, Drake, no one's buying that strong, silent type you try to put on. You don't deserve that star you're wearing and you know it. Everyone does. Why don't you admit it's a big mistake and go back to writing parking tickets at the Malheur Refuge?"

"Don't recall I ever wrote one," I said, "but I'll never forget punching the former regional sheriff's ticket to the State Pen after Pudge died. How's Bust'em Burton faring over there?"

Sidney jabbed his stubby finger. "We'll see who gets the last laugh. Do you know you're about to be recalled? Signatures are already being gathered. Harney County will have a new election for sheriff before summer's over."

"You planning to run your nephew again?"

"Go to hell."

"Don't have time. Consider yourself officially notified that my team is investigating two suspicious deaths. I'll keep you updated."

I started to leave when he slammed his fist on the desktop. Blizzards swirled in all the snow globes.

"Dammit, Drake, hold it right there. I'm the DA. Give me the particulars. Who's dead, how'd they die, and how'd you find out about it?"

"A John and Jane Doe. Gunshots to the head. Could be a murder-suicide. Could be a double suicide. Could be a double murder. Won't know for sure until I complete my investigation and won't know their names until we can match fingerprints to any on record."

More snow flew. "I demand you give me their real names and the location this instant."

"Can't risk it," I said. "Since it's still not clear the Does died by their own hand, that means there could be a killer on the loose. I'm under no obligation to give out information that could spread and cause the perp to flee."

"What legal code says that?"

"Common sense law."

Sessions's face turned crimson. "I'll have Judge Manton sign a court order demanding you give me the details within the hour!"

"If you think he will," I said.

"You dumbshit," the DA said. "You don't get it, do you? Whose idea do you think it was to recall you? Judge Manton says your election was an embarrassment to the entire county. All of Oregon, for that matter. You have no experience. Zero. You're utterly unqualified."

"And your nephew does? He's a rookie patrolman in Bend."

"He went to the academy; you didn't. It makes all the difference."

"The voters disagreed," I said. "Maybe they'll recall you and Manton for trying to overturn the will of the people."

Sessions started sputtering, but I was no longer listening. I left his office and kept on walking right out of the courthouse to a brick building on Broadway that housed the *Burns Herald*. Unlike the DA, Bonnie LaRue maintained an open-door policy to her office. I closed it behind me.

She looked up from her desk and peered through a pair of periwinkle cheaters perched on the tip of her nose. "Good afternoon, Nick. Or should I call you Sheriff Drake?"

I hooked a thumb at the badge on my chest. "This doesn't change a thing, Bonnie."

"We'll have to see how long that lasts." She took off the

cheaters and set them on the desk. "The look on your face tells me this is important and it's something you feel obliged to tell me, but you really don't want to."

"Pudge always said you could read people like a book."

"And he said to me right before he died my paper should endorse you if you decided to run."

"But you didn't," I said.

"No, the *Burns Herald* didn't endorse any candidate," she said. "I thought it prudent to take a neutral position given my long and public friendship with your father-in-law."

Bonnie and Pudge's on-again, off-again relationship had simmered then flamed then cooled then rekindled more times than a branding fire on a cattle ranch. They had always set tongues wagging at beauty parlors and barber shops alike.

"You didn't need it anyway, especially not after Judge Manton and DA Sessions put up that paper tiger." The newspaper woman tilted her head. "You do know the two are orchestrating your recall."

"Pudge always said a sheriff who spends his time politicking instead of policing isn't worth the spit used to shine his boots. Another thing he told me was it's always best to be straight with you when it came to news," I said.

Bonnie LaRue's eyes brightened. "What do you have?"

"Two suspicious deaths. A John and Jane Doe. My team's investigating now. Until it's concluded, I can't give you any more details than that. I told DA Sessions the same thing a minute ago."

"I would've loved to see the look on his face when you did that," she said. "But Nick, the press has the right to know. If there's a killer on the loose, we need to inform the public so they can take the necessary precautions."

"We don't know if this was a homicide. From all appearances, it looks like a murder-suicide or double suicide."

"I'm reading that book again. You don't believe that one bit. Can you at least tell me where you found the bodies?"

"Sorry, Bonnie, but that's the way it has to be. We haven't positively identified them. I promise I'll give you the particulars as soon as I can."

"After you give them to Sidney Sessions first so he can grandstand and make it look like he solved it himself," she said. "If you do that, he'll use it against you to further Judge Manton's campaign to have you recalled."

"When I'm ready to share the details, I'll give you a call to meet me at Sessions's office and give them to you at the same time. My money's on you getting the word out before he can."

Her eyes narrowed behind the cheaters. "The dead don't talk, Nick, but someone had to have called it in. There's no way they won't blab to someone no matter how much you threatened them to keep their mouths shut. Humans aren't wired to keep secrets. It's only a matter of time before word gets out."

"I know. Why my team and I are running flat out to get answers."

"And you trust I won't have my reporters out searching who's dead and how they died right now?"

"No, I trust you'll set them loose," I said. "I believe in freedom of the press, but I can't help your reporters do their job right now. All I'm asking is for your people to stay out of my people's way and that anything you do find out, you hold off running it until you run it past me."

"That's not the way journalism works," Bonnie said. "My job is to keep people informed in a timely fashion."

"And my job is to keep people safe and deliver justice."

"Oh my," she said, adopting a Southern accent and fanning herself. "Aren't you something right out of the movies."

I left and figured in the few minutes it'd take me to walk back to my office, Bonnie LaRue would've called an all-hands-on-deck meeting and was dishing out assignments to a reporter and photographer and having the editor mock up a front page with a screaming headline about a double murder on the High Lonesome.

Passing in front of Bella's Café, I had to break stride to keep from running into a pair of kids attempting to fry an egg on the sidewalk. They were squatting around it, their eyes glued to the clear albumen and pale yolk.

"See, it's not working," one said.

"Give it time," the other said. "My mom always sets a timer when she fries 'em. Three minutes. Dad doesn't like 'em runny."

"But it's already been five. Sidewalk's not hot enough."

"Mom said it'll work. Why she asked Bella to give us an egg to come out here and fry it."

"Aw, they just wanted to talk girl stuff without us hearing." He made kissing noises.

"Hello, boys," I said.

Both looked up. Their eyes widened when they saw my holster and badge.

"We're not doing nothing wrong, Sheriff. Mom said so."

"And your mother's right. Only wanted to give you a little tip. Something I learned when I was your age. Move back some. You're shading the sidewalk, cooling it down."

Both boys saw their shadows and scuttled backward like a pair of crabs.

"Thanks, Sheriff."

As I resumed walking, one boy said to the other, "That was awful nice of him."

"It was," said the other, "but Dad says he's not cut out to be sheriff and won't be one much longer."

5

———————

Despite my pickup being new, it still rattled when I crossed the cattle guard at the entrance to the Warbler ranch. It was closing in on ten o'clock and sunset was a half hour gone, but the changing of the light made the surroundings even more beautiful.

The black-capped buttes to the west were etched against deep purple. The sea of sage scrub that rolled east all the way to the Stinkingwater Mountains looked more marine-like than ever. The top of the brooding hulk of Steens Mountain to the south had already joined the heavens.

Even the darkened windows of the house reflected the color of a ripe eggplant on its way to indigo, but I was glad to see one still shone yellow.

I took off my boots so I wouldn't thump up the front steps, eased the door open, and padded to my home office where I stored my sidearm in the top drawer of the file cabinet. Then I went to the bedroom. Gemma was propped on pillows reading a thick book in the glow of the lamp on her nightstand.

"Like a moth to the flame," I said.

She laughed. It was the best laugh in the world. "Just be happy it's not the sun and you're not Icarus."

"I'd take the chance anyway." I bent over and planted a kiss.

"Slow down, hotshot. I'm still trying to adjust to these late hours of yours."

"I would've thought you'd be used to them growing up with a sheriff for a father."

"Operative word there. Father, not husband."

I returned her smile. "The kids in bed?"

"They better be. School may be out, but they both have jobs to be at in the morning."

Hattie was working at Lyle Rides Alone as she had for the past few summers. She'd graduated from cleaning out stalls to helping the horse breeder break and train a new crop of cutting horses. Fifteen-year-old Johnny worked at Blackpowder Smith's Dry Goods. He'd started out as a box boy, but was now head cashier and in charge of inventory.

"What about Loq and Bina?" I said.

"What about them?" Gemma said.

"They must've turned in early."

"So?"

"It's not like they haven't seen each other for a while."

"Frequency's never been a damper for us," she said.

"No, it hasn't," I said, "but I meant I was hoping Loq would wait up and tell me what he found about something I asked him to look into."

Gemma's eyebrows arched. "You're saying you'd rather be talking to Loq right now?"

"That came out completely wrong, babe. I've been on the run all day. Give me a sec so I can take a shower."

"After you go to the kitchen. November made a plate for you and you know she won't go to bed till she makes sure you eat every crumb."

I nodded at the book. "What are you reading?"

"A medical reference on livestock diseases. I need a refresher."

"Loq told you?"

"Uh-huh. I didn't know the Hardwards, but it sounds awful. I'll go out tomorrow and examine the stock."

"What's left of them," I said.

"There should be enough to take tissue samples," she said.

"Think you can hold off telling the Ag Department the exact location? I need to keep this on the QT until I figure out if the couple died by their own hand or someone else's."

Gemma blew a wisp of hair that had fallen across her cheek. "I can wait until I get the test results, which should take a day or two. But if the findings point to an epidemic, I'll have to sound the alarm immediately. I can't risk a deadly disease spreading. Livestock is Harney County's number one industry."

"And time's number one for me determining if someone else is responsible for the Hardwards' deaths," I said.

"Go eat your supper, then come back and we can talk about timing."

"Only talk?"

Gemma pretended to throw the book at me.

I heard the rocker rocking even before I pushed open the kitchen door. November was sitting in the dark, lit only by the low blue flame burning beneath a covered cast-iron skillet atop the range.

"Good evening, Girl Born in Snow," I said in her native tongue using her birth name.

The old healer tsked. "Speaking in Numu does not earn you respect," she said in English. "What you do tomorrow for the dead couple will."

"Sounds like Loq told everybody about what I found today."

"He asked me to help him understand a dream he had."

"The two Vietnamese people talking to him. Were you able to interpret it?"

"Talking Woman is the only one who can tell him what it means. But if he asks her, he puts himself in danger because she may want the dream to become real and will make it so if she can."

"She lives in both dreamworld and this world?"

November harrumphed. "It is only those who are too frightened to that do not."

"The couple at the ranch, I think someone tried to make it look like something it wasn't. Does it have anything to do with the woman in Loq's dream?"

"Perhaps. Or perhaps you will learn Talking Woman has to do with a dream you have not dreamt yet."

Trying to find meaning in the old healer's words was always difficult, but now the day started to feel a lot longer. My back was hurting from when I'd strained it lifting Ol' Daniel Hardward; it was grumbling louder than my empty stomach.

The old Paiute woman started rocking again. "Eat your supper, Nick Drake. Take a shower. Go to bed. Dream of Gemma. Leave the dream of Talking Woman until daytime because you will need all the light there is if you are to see what you must see so that you can see what is right and what is wrong, what is good and what is evil."

I left my clothes in a heap beside the shower and turned the hot water up high and aimed the spray at the small of my back. I tried to let the drumming of the water drown out the memories of Hanoi Hannah on the radio telling GIs about the antiwar protests back home and how we'd already lost, the same as Tokyo Rose and Seoul City Sue had done in Far East wars before. I closed my eyes and tried not to see women wearing conical hats and black pajamas spraying AK-47s at Loq and me.

I jumped when hands grabbed my shoulders and pulled me close and lips found my ear.

"You've been in here so long, I thought you'd fallen asleep," Gemma whispered over the spray of the water.

"No, just—"

She pulled my hips against hers. "Ah, so you are awake."

We started kissing and before long our breath was adding to the steam already clouding the shower glass and any thoughts of a sore back or memories of Vietnam or concerns about Talking Woman in dreamworld and this world swirled down the drain.

Afterward, I carried Gemma to bed and when we were still clinging to each other beneath the sheets, she whispered, "Good night, Icarus."

Before I could laugh, I was already snoring.

When dawn painted the sky gray outside the bedroom window, my first thought was the color matched the ash in the burn barrel at the Hardward ranch. That made me recall the two bodies with bullet holes in their heads. What had I missed spotting? What was I getting wrong?

Slipping out of bed without waking Gemma, I went in search of coffee. Loq and Bina Mantioc had already beaten me to it. They were seated at the dining table drinking from mugs and eating fry bread.

Bina wore her long hair pulled back in a bun held in place by a beaded comb. Beaded earrings the shape of tiny birdwings dangled from her earlobes. Her khaki uniform matched the color of mine, but her badge sported images of crossed lances and a pair of eagle feathers.

I poured myself a mug and asked her how the training was going.

"Slow but steady. You know the history of the Wadadökadö here," she said, using the Numu word for Wada Root and Grass-

Seed Eaters, what the local Northern Paiute people called them-selves. "They fought long and hard for federal recognition, but didn't receive it until twelve years ago. Getting financial assistance to start a tribal police force or operate a health clinic for their people has always been a challenge."

"I'm sure the tribal council appreciates you helping out," I said.

"They may be Numu and I'm Umatilla, but all First Nation peoples share blood and history. I'll do what I can to train cops here until my police chief needs me back home patrolling our rez."

I turned to Loq. "Find anything at the Hardward ranch?"

"It would've been better if I'd been there when the bodies were still in the kitchen," he said.

"Is that Maklak for you came up empty?"

"It's for how did a left-handed woman shoot herself in the right temple."

Something stronger than caffeine jolted me. "How do you know that? I searched the office, the desk, everywhere. The only thing with any writing on it was the checkbook and none of the letters or numbers had the telltale slant of a southpaw."

"The *Chim Lac*," he said.

"What about it?" I said.

Loq took a bite of fry bread and chewed it slowly. He flexed his shoulders and rotated his neck as if working out a kink. Then he reached for the coffee pot and topped off his mug. When he started sipping it, Bina groaned.

"Men!" She turned to me. "Loq's met my Aunty Moon, the woman who raised me. She does needlepoint and is a lefty. Aunty always starts in the bottom-left corner and moves up while righties stitch from top-right to bottom-left. The stitches are different too. Righties' stitches lean right; lefties' lean left.

Loq didn't have to point it out. I saw it right away like he had, especially since the *Chim Lac* isn't quite finished."

"You brought it here?" I said.

Loq nodded toward my office. "On your desk. I'm surprised you missed it when you came home last night. Wovoka makes less noise galloping on hardpack, though not as quietly as my spotted pony."

Bina groaned again.

I retrieved the *Chim Lac.* The stretcher frame had black smudges from when Orville had dusted it for prints. The stitches leaned left.

"There's more," Loq said. "Your deputy came and we turned the burn barrel upside down."

"You and Trace find anything?" I said.

"Couple of scraps of paper at the bottom that were pretty smudged and partially burned."

"Could you make anything out on them?"

"Some Vietnamese words. Or at least the parts that weren't charred. It's been years, but I remember what the lettering with all the accent marks looks like."

He handed me a plastic evidence bag. I held it up by the edges and studied the scraps of burnt paper inside.

"It's Vietnamese, all right."

"What's it say?" he said.

I squinted. Though I knew enough words to get by talking with ARVN soldiers and interrogating enemy captives, I never learned how to read Vietnamese beyond words on a map.

"Maybe a word or two, but—"

"What about Johnny? Maybe he can translate it for us."

"I don't want to involve him in this," I said.

"Involve me in what?" Johnny said as he came out of his bedroom.

His eyes went from the plastic bag in my hands to the needlepoint on the table. "Where did you get a *Chim Lac*?"

"A ranch east of Burns," I said. "The people who lived there died. We believe the woman came from Vietnam."

"Like me."

"That's what we think, but we're trying to figure that out for certain so we can, uh, notify her family about her passing."

"Can't you do that by looking at her address book or running her driver's license?" he said.

"Fifteen and already thinks like a cop," Bina mused aloud.

"We didn't find anything like that inside the house," I said.

Johnny poured himself a mug of coffee and added a generous dollop of cream and spoonful of sugar.

"Since when do you drink coffee?" I said.

"Since I started working at Blackpowder's," he said. "I need a cup of Joe to get going in the morning."

Even Loq laughed at that.

"The *Chim Lac* is one thing we have, but also something she may have written or someone wrote to her," I said. "It's only a scrap of paper."

I held up the plastic bag.

"Looks like she used it to start a fire," Johnny said.

"My Vietnamese is pretty rusty. Think you can translate it?"

"I can try."

Johnny began reading silently although his lips moved as he sounded out the words to himself.

"I think it's part of a letter to her from a relative because it mentions '*Bac*.' That means uncle. An old, respected uncle. And then there's something something '*co ay*.' That means missed her. He missed her or someone missed her. And then there's something something '*san lung*.' That means hunting for. Maybe the writer means someone's hunting for her. You know, looking for her. It's pretty smudged and most of the words are missing."

"Is there a name of who wrote it or a return address or a phone number or anything that tells her how to get in touch?" I said.

Johnny shook his head. "No, just the old uncle and the other words and then '*hay can than.*' That means take care. You know, like saying goodbye here."

Hay can than. Hay can than. The words echoed. I remembered the phrase, but it meant something entirely different when the local scouts said it while we were on patrol: "*Take care. Be careful! Booby traps ahead.*"

"This old uncle, he have a name?" Loq said.

Johnny studied the scrap again. "It's burned after *Bac* but I can kind of make out the first letter of what comes next. It's either a T or a K or maybe an H."

Loq's eyes met mine. *Bac H. Bac Ho.* Uncle Ho. It's what everyone in Vietnam called Ho Chi Minh during and after the war.

Gemma and Hattie came in. They both looked at the *Chim Lac.*

"Is that a dragon?" Hattie said.

"A magical bird from Vietnam," Johnny said.

"It's very pretty. Are you going to hang it in your room?"

Johnny looked at me. "Can I?"

"Maybe. I got to hold on to it for a while until I sort some things out."

"November could finish stitching it for you," Hattie said. "You know how good she is with weaving and beadwork."

"Where is November anyway?" I said. "She still asleep?"

"She was already in the kitchen when we got up," Bina said. "She'd made coffee and fry bread, but said she had something to do. Then she put on a shawl, slung a bag over her shoulder, and went outside."

"Was it still dark?"

"Thomas Morning Owl was up."

"Who's he?" Hattie said.

Bina patted her on the head. "White people call him Sirius, the dog star. In Sahaptin, my language, it's Sapnicasi. He is very wise and the keeper of Umatilla culture. Thomas Morning Owl is the brightest star in the sky at night, but doesn't always shine in the morning. When he does like today, it is very special."

"Does Thomas Morning Owl hoot?" Hattie said.

Bina smiled. "If you listen carefully."

Gemma told the kids they needed to eat breakfast and get a move on. "Come on, I have work to do. I'll give you a ride to your jobs on my way."

"Are you going to the Hardward ranch?" I said.

"The sooner the better if I'm to collect decent samples," she said.

"I'll have Deputy Wakefield meet you there."

"I don't need a guard dog."

"Yeah, but I need you to."

The women exchanged looks. "Men!" Gemma said.

"Tell me about it," Bina said.

Everyone finished their breakfast and took off except Loq and me.

"You think we're leaping to conclusions here?" I said. "Mrs. Hardward being Vietnamese. No record of her, at least none that Orville's been able to find yet. A scrap of a letter from a burn pit that may or may not say Uncle Ho is hunting for her."

"What you're really asking is why did a lefty take the trouble to hold a heavy gun with her right hand and shoot herself in the head," Loq said.

"Orville's running tests on both hands for GSR and he's already dusted the trigger and butt for prints. Doc noted the barrel wasn't pressed firmly against her temple. I'll make sure he measures the angle of the bullet's penetration. Hers wasn't a through-and-through, by the way."

"GSR could've been put on her hand after she was already dead."

"If she was shot by someone else," I said.

"Sure starting to feel that way," he said.

"If so, by who? Someone sent by the People's Republic of Vietnam to track her down and kill her? If that's the case, why after all these years? Who was she? Was her marriage to Ol' Daniel just a cover and he wound up collateral damage?"

Loq squinted. "Lot of questions that need answering, but the letter sounds like the writer was warning her someone was after her and to be careful."

"*Hay can than*," I said. "Maybe it's why she had the .38."

"We find who shot her, we'll ask them," he said.

I stared into my coffee mug and wished it were tea and I had the ability to divine leaves. Way too many questions were floating around and way too few answers.

"When I got home last night, I spoke to November. She told me you asked her about the dream you had. November said you'd better watch out if you go looking for Talking Woman in dreamworld."

"After seeing this letter, I'm more likely to find her here in this world," he said.

"Why is that?"

"She wants me to."

"That doesn't mean she'll be any less of a danger," I said.

"Mm."

"November also told me I need to watch out for Talking Woman, that it'd be better if I ran into her during the day because I'll need all the light I can get to tell good from evil."

"Girl Born in Snow is wise," he said. "Best we both heed her advice."

"I'm going outside to look for her. See what she's up to."

"Then what?"

"Find out if Doc and Orville have learned anything more and then check out those ranches near the Hardwards, the Big D and Triple Triangle. I don't want to get so focused on this letter that I'm blinded to what may be a rancher protecting his livelihood by shutting the mouths of his neighbors."

Loq wrapped a couple of pieces of fry bread in a napkin and shoved it into his shirt pocket. He pushed away from the table.

"What about you?" I said. "Got any ranger duties today?"

"None that outweigh curiosity."

6

———

Pudge and Henrietta Warbler were buried side by side atop a knoll overlooking the ranch. A mug of freshly made cowboy coffee was set on his grave and a cup of herb tea on hers. Between them was a woven basket with a black-and-white diamond pattern filled with warm fry bread.

November sat on a hand-loomed woolen blanket beside the two graves facing the rising sun. The rays created a corona around her and turned the smoke from a smoldering braid of sage orange.

She and Henrietta had started off as healer and patient, but soon became as close as sisters. When her medicine couldn't alter the course of Henrietta's cancer, November sang the dying wife and mother a song to heal her breaking heart. She sang of those who'd gone before and would be there to welcome her home. She sang of the lawman who loved her and always would. She sang of her beautiful five-year-old daughter who would grow up to be strong and wise. And she sang a soft but soaring refrain that was a promise to look after them and raise Gemma as her own.

"Nick Drake, I knew you were coming before you left," November said without turning around.

"Spoken like our old friend, Tuhudda Will," I said.

"This is so."

Once again, she used a familiar phrase of the Paiute elder and my spirit guide who'd been born in the same winter blizzard that had earned her the name Girl Born in Snow.

"I'm sure Tuhudda welcomed his old friend Pudge to the spirit world as one warrior to another," I said.

"They will still be talking about the old days even when there is no longer a here but only a there," she said.

"And Henrietta certainly welcomed Pudge for they have much to talk about as well."

November tsked. "They never stopped talking to each other after she made the journey all those years ago, the same as Shoots While Running and I still talk."

I let that sit to give it the respect it deserved. November's husband was Northern Shoshone and he and their baby daughter Breathes Like Gentle Wind drowned in the Snake River decades ago on a visit to see his family at the Fort Hall Reservation in Idaho.

When I didn't respond, the old healer harrumphed. "Do you not believe me?"

"Of course I do," I said. "I was wondering what you talk about."

"Anything and everything. He has been telling me the story about his father who was at the Battle of Greasy Grass. It was a very important battle for all Indian people, regardless of tribe."

"I don't recall that one."

"Because it is the name given to it by the People of the Plains whose battle it was. Lakota, Cheyenne, and Arapaho. White people call it the Battle of Little Bighorn."

Another jolt of caffeine hit me, sharper than the last. "Your father-in-law rode with Crazy Horse? Now *that* is a story I'd like to hear."

"Why? Did your people die with the man the Lakota called Yellow Hair?"

"No. But I wore the First Cav patch in Vietnam. They used the Seventh's ghosts to teach us how to stay alive—showed us exactly where Custer messed up so we wouldn't find ourselves in our own Little Bighorn."

I didn't add that one time when we were pinned down in a firefight, my radioman DJ crawled over and said HQ had intel for us. "Good news or bad?" I said. "Both," he said. I asked for the bad first. "Well, Sarge, Charlie's got us outgunned five to one and reinforcements be two hours out." Then I asked for the good news. "Be glad we ain't Seventh Cav," he said in his laconic way. "If we was, we'd already done lost our hair."

I cocked my head at November. "When they taught us about Little Bighorn, they said Crow and Arikara scouts fought for Custer. They were helping him in exchange for his army driving out the Lakota and Cheyenne who were encroaching on their traditional buffalo hunting grounds. There was no mention of Shoshone warriors with Custer."

"Not every story is simple nor are they always remembered. I will tell you why Shoots While Running's father left home and what he did on his journey to Greasy Grass. Then I will tell you how his journey ended another time so you will remember it when you need to."

And with that, the old healer began her tale.

Shoots While Running's father was born alongside the Snake River on the night of the summer moon. Like all Northern Shoshone boys, he learned how to fish in the big river and hunt for game in the valleys. At night, he listened to the elders tell stories about their ancestors. The ones about the Eastern Shoshone who'd left the tribe's original homeland in the Great Basin and settled on the other side of the Rocky Mountains to become buffalo hunters were his favorite.

The boy told everyone that one day he'd join his Eastern cousins and become a buffalo hunter too. He said it so often, people began calling him Buffalo Dreamer. Some of the older boys made a game of draping elk hides over their shoulders, snorting, and charging, knocking him to the ground. Buffalo Dreamer became the butt of jokes except to a girl who was born the same night as him. Her name was Summer Moon.

Three months before Buffalo Dreamer turned eighteen, a Shoshone warrior from the other side of the Rockies visited the village. He had news about Washakie, the great chief of the Eastern Shoshone. Many of the people listening were distantly related to him, including Buffalo Dreamer's father. Washakie was trying to unite all Shoshone people—Western, Northern, and Eastern—to help drive the Lakota and Cheyenne from his tribe's homeland.

That night, Buffalo Dreamer told his parents he was going to help Washakie. His father said if that is your path, then you must take it, and if it leads you back here, then come home with honor. He gave him his prized repeating rifle.

Buffalo Dreamer was readying his pony early the next morning when Summer Moon appeared. She gave him a small looking glass. When you look at it, she said, see me. When I look into my looking glass, I will see you. We are destined to marry and I will wait for you.

He slid the looking glass into his leather pouch, swung onto his pony, and galloped away. Buffalo Dreamer rode for thirty days, always aiming at the rising sun, singing to himself the steps of the trail the Eastern Shoshone warrior had described to him: Follow the Snake River east, ride up the great mountains, follow a big river down the other side and onto a great plain where the tall grass rolls on forever.

Finally, he reached it and saw his first buffalo herd off in the distance. Buffalo Dreamer galloped toward the beasts, stopping when he reached the top of a hill. Scattered among the grazing animals were hundreds of skinned carcasses and sun-bleached skeletons, the carnage and waste left behind by White hunters who'd only been after their hides. Vultures were feasting on the rotting flesh. Wolves and coyotes did too.

Buffalo Dreamer spotted something crawling through the grass. It wasn't a wolf or coyote. It was a girl about his age. She was naked and bloodied and bruised. He put heels to his pony and rode toward her. When he approached, she cried out and started throwing buffalo bones at him. I'm here to help, not hurt you, he said. She cursed in a language he didn't understand and kept throwing bones.

He pretended to ride away, but then slipped off his pony and crawled back through the tall grass. Catching her by surprise, Buffalo Dreamer pinned her arms. You are hurt and will bleed to death, he said as she struggled. Let me help you. Exhausted, she finally gave in. He wrapped his blanket around her and made camp. Over the next few days and nights he treated her wounds and fed her.

Slowly, she began to trust him. Using sign language and drawing pictures on old bones with charcoal from the campfire, she told Buffalo Dreamer her story. She was Lakota and had accompanied her father and others on a buffalo hunt. A US Cavalry troop saw them and attacked. Many of the hunters were killed, including her father, who was the brother of her village's chief. Two soldiers caught her and carried her off. They raped, beat, and shot her, leaving her for dead.

Buffalo Dreamer told her his name. She said hers was Walks on Clouds and explained how she got it. One day when she was little, there was a big rainstorm. She wanted to go outside, but her mother forbid her to leave the tipi. After the rain stopped, she snuck out and played in a large puddle that mirrored the sky. When her mother saw her, it appeared her daughter was walking on clouds.

I will take you home so your mother can see you walk on clouds again, Buffalo Dreamer said. The Lakota girl shook her long braids. You can't, she said. You are Shoshone and my people's enemy. They will kill you. No they won't, Buffalo Dreamer said, not when they learn I saved your life and brought you home. Finally, she relented.

As they rode double on his pony, Walks on Clouds told Buffalo Dreamer about how the White hunters were slaughtering all the buffalo and making it harder for her people to survive. She described the army of bluecoats that had invaded her homeland and the ongoing war with them, how the cavalry's repeated attacks on Lakota and Cheyenne had forced the tribes to join together into one, big camp that was always moving from place to place to stay ahead of the bluecoats.

A great battle is coming, Walks on Clouds said. Sitting Bull has seen it in a vision. Who is he? Buffalo Dreamer asked. A great chief, warrior, and holy man, she said. Sitting Bull saw an army of bluecoats led by an evil spirit with long yellow hair attacking us and Lakota and Cheyenne warriors fighting back and killing them all.

The morning Buffalo Dreamer and Walks on Clouds neared the joint Lakota and Cheyenne camp, scouts intercepted them. Realizing Buffalo Dreamer was Shoshone, they drew back their bows to fill him full of arrows. Walks on Clouds threw her arms around him and said he'd saved her life. My uncle is Same Knife, she said. Take us to him.

The scouts grabbed the pony's reins and led them to the big encampment at a gallop. It was just as Walks on Clouds had described. The tipis were grouped in large circles as thick and plentiful as trees in a forest. The smoke from all the campfires rose like a thousand funnel clouds. There were more horses than Buffalo Dreamer had ever seen before, more people too.

Instead of welcoming Walks on Clouds home, Same Knife grew angry hearing the news that his brother and other warriors had been killed. He wouldn't listen to her when she told him Buffalo Dreamer had saved her. Same Knife said he'd only done so to trick her. Shoshone warriors are fighting for the bluecoats against Lakota, he said, and Buffalo Dreamer has come to spy for them.

It's true he's Shoshone, Walks on Clouds said, but his people are not buffalo hunters. They are Northern Shoshone and live on the other side of the great mountains and hunt for fish in a big river.

Then he is a Snake Indian, Same Knife said, using a name given to Northern Shoshone when other tribes mistook the meaning of their writhing hand gestures mimicking salmon swimming upriver to indicate where they lived. And so a snake I shall make him, he thundered.

Same Knife ordered Buffalo Dreamer staked out on the ground. Then he drew a shiny blade from its beaded sheath, sliced off his ears, slit the corners of his mouth deep into his cheeks, and lit his hair on fire. Buffalo Dreamer bit his tongue to keep from screaming. When the flames went out, his skull was a patchwork of molten and charred skin. Same Knife grabbed Walks on Clouds and made her look. Behold your protector, he said. He is Buffalo Dreamer no longer. Now he is Snakehead!

November started humming and rocking.

"You can't stop now," I said. "I want to know what happens next. What about the battle between the Lakota and Custer, Yellow Hair? Did Buffalo Dreamer fight in it?"

The old healer said nothing, but held the smoldering braid of sage in front of her with one hand and made a cup with the other to wave the smoke toward her face. Then she held the braid out to me and I did the same. The sweet smoke smelled and tasted a lot better than the stench I'd tried to mask with a bandana in the Hardward kitchen.

"I will tell you the story's end when it is time for you to learn from it," she said. "Now, you must continue to search for who killed the Hardwards. As you do, my son, remember this. See with your own eyes and not someone's who wishes to be blind. Hear with your own ears and not those of people who listen only to lies. Feel with your own heart because not everybody has one."

7

―――――――

I sped to my office in Burns. Jazz intercepted me at the front door.

"Orville called asking for you," she said. "He's at Doc's and said it's important."

"And Trace?"

"He left for the Hardward ranch to meet your wife."

"Radio him to report in the moment Gemma gets there and to report in regularly while she's there."

"She must be awesome," Jazz said.

"She is," I said.

The morgue was only a few blocks away but I drove anyway. I peered through the square of glass in the exam room's door. Orville and Doc were standing shoulder to shoulder studying X-rays on a lightbox. The naked body of Mrs. Hardward lay on a stainless steel autopsy table equipped with gutters on the sides and a drain. Mr. Hardward was in one of the closed refrigerated drawers.

I rapped on the door. Doc looked over and beckoned me in. It wasn't my first time and I knew where the masks and gowns were kept.

"What are you looking at?" I said.

"Mrs. Hardward's skull," Doc said. "Or I should say, Jane Doe's." He gave me a vinegary look. "The image on the left is before I cracked it open and the one on the right afterward."

"What did you find?"

"You tell him, Orville. You did the calculating."

The chief deputy used a penlight as a pointer. "As you can see here on the left X-ray, this line is the path of the bullet from where it entered her right temple and eventually lodged here in the petrous portion of her temporal bone at the base of the skull."

"Looks like it took a downward angle," I said.

"Affirmative. The petrous portion is the thickest part of the skull and protects essential organs for hearing and balance. Petrous is Latin for rock-like."

"Why the slug wasn't a through-and-through."

"More than likely, but the path provides additional information," he said.

"That if she shot herself, then the butt of the gun was higher than the tip of the barrel?" I said. "Awkward and hard on the wrist to fire a heavy revolver like that."

Doc snorted. "I been at this more years than I care to count, but I can count on one hand with fingers left over the number of times someone plugged themself in the head and the bullet went down and not up or straight across."

"Meaning you think someone else shot her?" I said.

He didn't answer but Orville did. "While that is still conjecture at this point without an eyewitness or a confession, it is certainly more than likely despite the fact that she did test positive for GSR on her right hand."

"Which could have been put there afterward."

"It is a distinct possibility," he said.

I asked him what else the bullet path told them.

"The downward trajectory strongly suggests that if she were shot by a third party, then the shooter was either quite a bit taller than her if they were seated next to each other or the shooter was standing."

"What about the lack of a front sight mark on her skin or blood splatter inside the barrel even though she had gunpowder burns on her skin?"

Doc snorted again. "Hell, I've had people on my table who were shot from four feet away and had GSR tattooed on them."

"And the X-ray on the right? What's it show?" I said.

"The hole in her skull where I dug out the slug."

"Anything unusual about it?"

"It got flattened a mite when it hit the petrous, which was a bit surprising considering it was steel-jacketed," Doc said.

"Not copper?"

"You heard me."

"That's unusual since the majority of ammo is copper-jacketed. It was the same for the .357 Magnum rounds issued to rangers when I was with Fish and Wildlife. A running joke was we were bear bait without steel."

I looked away from the X-rays. "It was a different story in 'Nam. Military ammo was full metal jacket for sidearms and rifles alike per the Hague Convention. Rounds that penetrated were considered more humane for killing than ones that flattened out."

Orville made a face. "If there is irony in that, I fail to appreciate it."

"One of many in war," I said.

"Tell Nick what we found out about your trigonometric equation," Doc said. "The revised one."

"The path of the bullet in Mrs. Hardward's skull indicating she was likely seated when shot prompted a revision of the back-of-the-envelope equation I devised at the scene. The entry and exit points of Mr. Hardward's wound were lateral in height, but with a slight right-to-left angle."

"Meaning?"

"The bullet was fired to the right of where Mrs. Hardward was seated based on where her body landed on the floor. It also suggests that Mr. Hardward was looking directly at the shooter who was also seated at the time."

"More reason to think there was a third person there," I said.

"So it would appear. At least mathematically," Orville said.

"Have you gamed out who got shot first, Mr. or Mrs.?"

Doc said, "Can't tell any difference in their TODs considering they'd been there nearly a week, but I'd say him based on Orville's equation and the angles. Way I see it, shooter drilled Mr. Hardward and then jumped up and shot Mrs. Hardward while she was still seated."

"Surprised them both," I said.

"And not the kind of party your family tries to pull off on your birthday," he said.

I nodded toward the file cabinet-like bank of refrigerated doors. "What does the bullet that killed Mr. Hardward tell you outside of the angle he was facing and it going straight through him?"

"I retrieved it from the wall directly behind him," Orville said. "It penetrated the plaster but was embedded in a stud. It flattened somewhat like the one we retrieved from Mrs. Hardward, but appears to be the same caliber and steel-jacketed. I will know more when I complete ballistics on both rounds including the four unspent ones still in the revolver."

"Any luck running down its serial number?" I said.

"I am still searching records."

"We need to know whose it was. If it was the shooter's, why'd they leave it? If it belonged to the Hardwards, how'd the shooter get hold of it?"

"There's something else you need to see," Doc said. He swapped the X-rays for another pair. "The one on the left is Mrs. Hardward's lower left leg; the right one, her right leg. The dark spots you see are bits of metal. I dug them out after I took the X-rays. They're shrapnel."

"How old do you think she is?"

"I'd say early thirties."

"It'd be surprising if she didn't have shrapnel in her considering she lived in a country that was continuously at war for thirty years, first with the French and then us," I said. "Everybody who lived through those times bears scars of some kind, physical and mental."

"From bullets and bombs, I can understand, but from a whip?" Doc held up a photograph. "That's Mrs. Hardward's back."

The raised scars resembled earthworms inching across a wet sidewalk.

"Cat-o'-nine-tails, be my guess," he said.

I breathed in, breathed out. "Let me know what you turn up on ballistics, Orville."

"Affirmative."

As I headed for the door, I pictured a pair of downed pilots my squad rescued from a bamboo cage. Both had been tortured repeatedly by the VC camp's leader who wielded a whip with a short bamboo handle and nine braided cords of hemp tied to fishhooks. Their backs looked like they'd been raked by a cougar with very sharp claws.

The radio inside my rig was screeching like a cougar too by the time I yanked the door open and grabbed the mike.

"Sheriff!" Jazz said. "Deputy Wakefield just reported in. Shots fired. Location is—"

"Don't say it. I know it. Tell Orville. You know where he's at."

I fired the ignition and slammed it into gear. What I didn't do was hit the lights and siren or peel out. It was for the same reason I'd cut Jazz off. Sidney Sessions was likely to have a standing order with the Burns Police Department to monitor the sheriff's radio channel and alert him about emergency calls. The *Burns Herald* always had their police band radio on too and Bonnie LaRue maintained a network of tipsters among the local store owners who she repaid with free advertising.

The last thing I needed was to be the head of a parade.

Once clear of downtown, I mashed the pedal and the big V-8 chewed up miles as fast as the knobby four-wheel drive tires could spin. I didn't slow down even when I hit the dirt road with all the potholes.

To keep from thinking of Gemma being held at gunpoint or Trace shooting it out with gunmen, I concentrated on gaming out an active shooter response plan. After a couple of false starts, I settled on KISS. Come in hot, draw fire, and run over anybody with a gun who wasn't my wife or deputy.

The Hardward ranch came into view. Sun was glinting off windshields and bumpers in front of the house. I counted one rig, two rigs, three rigs, four. Gemma's red Jeep Wagoneer was parked next to a Harney County Sheriff's Department pickup. Two more pickups were parked right behind, boxing them in.

That made me unbuckle my seat belt, undo the retention strap on my holstered .45, and hit the lights and siren. I didn't take my foot off the gas until I saw Gemma and Trace facing off with three men in the parched field near the barn. One man was unarmed, but another held a Winchester at port arms and the third cradled a pump shotgun.

All eyes turned toward me except for Trace's. His never left the two armed men. Nor did his gun hand leave the butt of the service weapon he held at his side.

I braked to a stop, switched off the siren, but left the rooftop light bar flashing to signal I meant business. Like Trace, I kept my hand on the butt of my gun and my eyes on the two gunmen as I got out.

"Put your guns on the ground," I said.

The two armed men glanced at an older man who was wearing a high-crown Stetson creased just the way he liked it. His horseshoe-style mustache was as gray as his hat.

Before he could say anything, I barked, "Do it now and we don't have a problem. Don't and you will."

"Was only a misunderstanding, Sheriff," the older man said.

"Your men don't drop their weapons right now there won't be any misunderstanding on my deputy's and my part."

"Ah, for Pete's sake," he groaned. "You heard him, boys. Do what he says. He's still wet behind the ears when it comes to his job."

Trace and I had already divvied up the two without saying a word to each other. His blue eyes were focused on the man with the Winchester, mine on the shotgunner. Gemma was watching the unarmed man for any tricks. She'd learned more than a few things growing up a lawman's daughter.

When both long guns were on the ground, I ordered the three men to take five steps back and put their hands in the front pockets of their jeans. That earned another "Ah, for Pete's sake" from the older man, but they complied.

"Who fired the shots?" I asked Trace.

"Shotgunner," he said.

"It was an accident," the man with the horseshoe-mustache and high-crown Stetson said. "That's my youngest. Bobby. He had one in the chamber and the 12 gauge went off when he tripped on a rock, which there seems to be plenty of in this sorry-ass field. Only thing got hurt was a chunk of dirt with less life in it than the moon."

"That true, Deputy Wakefield?" I said.

Trace nodded. "I was in my rig reporting in and heard the shot. Told dispatch."

"Per protocol," I added so there'd be no mistake on the older man's part in case he was inclined to lodge a complaint with DA Sessions.

I asked the man who he was and what they were doing there.

"Dill Dillard," he said. "I own the Big D up yonder." He hooked a thumb in the direction where the fork in the road led to the Triple Triangle. "Already told you about Bobby. That there is Manny Hernandez. Hired hand. Been with me for years."

"All your hands carry Winchesters?" I said.

"Damn right they do when they're riding the range. No law against it."

"No, there's not. But pointing it at another person and shooting them is."

"Unless they're rustlers or up to no damn good in general. Why we come down here. See what all the fuss's about."

"You see two rigs, one of them being a deputy sheriff's, and think that's a fuss?" I said.

"Hold on, Sheriff. Lemme explain something. Them rigs, they aren't the only ones been here recently. Why, yesterday, Manny said he saw all sorts of comings and goings on down here to go along with all the ones over the last couple of weeks. His English may be on the extra short side, but Manny knows when something's up and knows when to tell me."

I looked at Manny Hernandez. "What did you see?"

He looked down at his boots.

"*Señor, por favor,*" Gemma said. "*¿Qué visté?*"

"*Ayer en la mañana, un Cadillac rojo. Ese coche es muy bonito. Y más tarde tres vehículos del sheriff.*" He nodded at mine and also Trace's.

"What did you see the other week?" I said.

Gemma translated. Manny responded in Spanish. She asked

him more questions. Again he answered. They went back and forth for a couple of minutes.

I asked Gemma what he said.

"Manny was riding fence a couple of weeks ago—he can't remember the exact day, night actually—he saw a couple of livestock carriers arrive, load up cattle and drive off. Then last week, he saw the Hardwards' pickup driving away. It was nearly dark and he couldn't see inside the cab, but it was definitely their white Ford. The bed had some boxes in the back and was pulling a horse trailer. He thinks it was carrying stuff too because it kept bottoming out in the potholes. *Baches*, he called them."

"*Gracias*," I said to him.

"*De nada*," he said and spoke some more. I recognized *Cadillac rojo* again.

Gemma translated without me asking. "He said you're welcome. That it was his pleasure to remember seeing the pretty red Cadillac all over again because he'd never seen one before and now he's seen it twice."

"Yesterday and a couple of months ago?" I said.

She spoke to Manny. He answered.

"No," Gemma said. "The first time was about three weeks ago. Not long before the livestock carriers came."

"What's this all about anyway?" Dill Dillard said. "Why's your lot here today and yesterday? And where the hell are the Hardwards?"

"My office got a call to make a welfare check on them," I said.

"And you're still checking?"

I didn't answer.

"Well, that's the same thing me and the boys are doing," he said. "Being neighborly. Usually as quiet as a blanket of snow in winter around these parts, but now we got all this coming and going. I'm going ask again. Where are the Hardwards? Their pickup's not here."

"Your spread, it's next door to the Triple Triangle?" I said.

"It is. Has been since my grandpa staked a claim here. You still haven't answered me. Where's Ol' Daniel and his little wife?"

"In Burns," I said. "How well do you know them?"

"Good enough to tip a hat is about it. He's not much for talking over the fence or asking for help, which he sorely needs if you look around."

"And Mrs. Hardward?"

"Never said two words to her. She hasn't been here that long. The road to my spread forks off this one back yonder. Don't have a reason to come this way and don't ride fence no more. Got Manny to do that."

"What about you?" I asked his son.

Bobby looked no more than twenty or so. He shook his head vigorously. "Never met her. She doesn't speak English."

"If you never met her, how do you know that?"

"Uh." He glanced at the ground. "What I heard. She's foreign plus he's Mormon and we're not. We don't go to their church or nothing like that at all."

"What about you, Manny?" I said. "Ever come down here to talk to them or have a cup of coffee?"

Gemma translated. Manny answered rapidly.

"He says he's been here a few times," Gemma said. "Usually after a storm to see if the Hardwards needed any help digging out or have him haul in some firewood for the potbelly stove. He didn't say it, but I'm guessing they gave him a couple of bucks for his labor. Maybe a meal."

I hard-eyed Dill Dillard. "Let me see if I understand this correctly. You and your son say you've never broken bread with the Hardwards or even talked about the weather or the price of cattle with them, yet today of all days you come rushing over here armed to the teeth to see what's what."

"You're jumping to conclusions like a bronc with an extra-tight cinch," he said. "I can see why some folks say you rode into too deep a water wanting to be sheriff and why they're contemplating recalling you."

He traced his mustache with his thumb before continuing.

"Truth is with all the comings and goings, I got to thinking that maybe the Hardwards either are looking to get out or are being forced out 'cause they can't ranch worth a shit. I'm of the mind maybe I can buy their spread to add to my own."

Dillard tilted his high-crown Stetson back toward his place. "Ask around. Everybody knows I been trying to buy the Triple Triangle for ten years but that sumbitch owns it won't give it up. Manny tells me the Hardwards and what's left of their cattle all lit out in the dead of night and then your lot shows up maybe to fix a foreclosure notice on the door; you're damn straight I'm gonna come down and stake a claim before anyone else does."

I glanced at the long guns on the ground. "Staking a claim requires coming armed?"

Dill Dillard snorted. "Hell no, but we got more diamond-backs than tumbleweeds in this part of Harney County and I never let one go to waste."

He hitched his jeans to show off his snakeskin boots.

8

"Find anything?" I asked Gemma once the Big D bunch loaded up and left.

"I'd only gotten started when I heard the shotgun go off and came running," she said.

"Unarmed?"

"Hardly." Gemma pulled a Ladysmith with a pink grip from the waistband at the back of her jeans. The compact revolver was as much a part of her veterinarian kit as forceps, scalpels, and hemostats.

"Always a sheriff's daughter," I said.

I told Trace to radio Jazz and have her call off Orville. "His time's better spent at Doc's."

Gemma and I made the short walk to the livestock graveyard. She slipped the elastic loops of a surgical mask around her ears while I made like a bandit again with the blue bandana. We scrambled down the rocky bank.

The horse doctor's kit was next to a cow carcass. Gemma retrieved a syringe with a long needle.

"I picked this cow because she seems to be the least decomposed. She looks like she died three weeks or so ago."

"Not long before Manny Hernandez said he saw the livestock carrier come and go," I said.

"Hadn't thought about that, but you're right. I'm going to be collecting fluid and tissue samples from her and a hog and sheep," she said. "Go find the freshest two and flag them for me. While you're at it, take a bone saw from the bag and get a sample from each. I don't need that big of one, just as long as it has marrow in it."

"Wasn't that long ago I had to do the same on deer and elk when there was that big die-off."

"It turned out to be chronic wasting disease, if I recall."

"It was. Think all this could be that too?" I said.

Gemma's ponytail swished. "CWD doesn't transmit to domestic livestock."

"But there's got to be at least one infectious disease that kills both cows, sheep, and hogs."

"The most common is FMD. Foot-and-mouth disease. The three species are also susceptible to Johne's disease, though hogs less so."

"You got that skeptical look of yours," I said.

She grabbed the head of the cow, yanked it up, and pried the jaws apart. "Vultures and coyotes haven't gotten her tongue yet. See? It's dried out, but there's no sign of fever blisters on it. That'd be a telltale for FMD."

"And Johne's?"

Gemma felt around the cow's throat. "No sign of bottle jaw."

"What's your gut tell you?"

"It could be one of a couple of other bacterial diseases," she said. "I won't know for certain until I get results back from the samples I'll send in. But right here and now based on what I can see? I'd say they were poisoned."

"Intentionally or unintentionally?"

"I've no way of knowing without lab work. I've seen cattle

who died from botulism eating contaminated feed and also ones that ate rodenticides that farmers put out to kill rats."

"Poisoned by mistake," I said.

"There've also been instances when it wasn't accidental. A rancher in Lake County accused his neighbor of intentionally poisoning his stock by throwing old tractor batteries into his water supply. They'd been fighting over their spreads' boundaries."

"If it turns out these animals were poisoned, then it was deliberate."

"What makes you say that?" she said.

"What Dill Dillard said about wanting to be the first in line to claim this ranch should the Hardwards move on. He must've thought somebody else wanted it too. Also something Red Caldera said about ranching: It's either grow big or go under."

Gemma was wearing a mask, but I knew her lips were tightening. "You know my stance on cruelty to animals," she said.

"Chapter and verse."

"How does that scenario fit with your and Loq's thinking about the scrap of letter Johnny translated?"

"Definitely complicates things. When I was at Doc's, he and Orville all but ruled out murder-suicide."

"All but?"

"They're waiting on ballistics and the provenance of the murder weapon. Orville's running down the gun's serial number."

"Pretty unlikely a killer would've left their gun behind, isn't it?" she said.

"It's happened before. Either out of panic or they were interrupted."

"Or maybe the killer did it on purpose to send a new sheriff on a wild goose chase to buy time to make their getaway."

"Maybe," I said.

Gemma touched my arm. "Don't worry about all that recall nonsense. The election wasn't that long ago. People understand there's always an adjustment period."

"Not when it comes to their safety, they don't. When they learn about this—and learn they will—they'll want an arrest. If not the killer, then me for incompetence."

She gave a squeeze. "Then you're going to have to prove how competent you really are."

A landslide of dirt and rock broke the moment. Trace was surfing down the bank on his bootheels.

"I talked to Orville," he said. "The DA showed up at the morgue with a court order and demanded Doc give him the names of the dead."

"And?"

"Doc told him he'd submitted their fingerprints and was waiting on confirmation from the DMV, FBI, and KMA."

Gemma looked at me. "What's the KMA?"

"Doc's way of saying kiss my ass."

She showed why her laugh was the best in the world. "See, you got people on your side."

"Doc bought us some time," I said, "but it's all the more reason we need to move faster and stay ahead of all these developments. Starting with figuring out what killed these cows and where did the rest of the Hardwards' stock go."

"I can determine cause of death, but how are you going to figure out who took the live cattle and where they went?"

"I'll start by asking Red Caldera why he lied to my face about being here two months ago. As to tracking down the livestock carriers, if Manny Hernandez saw them, then someone else did too. Same with the Hardwards' pickup and trailer."

"I can start looking right now," Trace said.

"No, you stay here with Gemma while I go pay a visit to the Triple Triangle to find out about their herd."

"I'm fine here on my own," Gemma said. "It's better if Trace goes with you if you suspect the Triple Triangle is hiding something."

To buy time before answering, I took a closer look at the cow she was about to sample. "I don't see a brand on it. We're going to need to flip her over."

"No we don't," she said. "She's probably been ear-tagged. Ranchers are doing that more often than hot branding these days. Easier to keep track of their stock. Each ranch has their own numbering system. Lift her head."

I did. "There it is."

"This one's got a tag too," Trace said.

We checked the other carcasses. Same thing.

The sound of Gemma sucking in air and blowing it out echoed in the narrow gully. "If it turns out these cows are infected and not poisoned, then someone out there could be selling diseased cattle to meat packers or mixing them in with healthy herds and spreading the disease even faster. We need to keep these ear tags in case we need to match them."

"Okay," I said. "Trace and I'll help you. I'll start with getting bone samples, and he'll pull tags."

"Uh-uh," Gemma said. "I can do it. You two need to find where the Triple Triangle's stock is and what shape they're in. If the cows here did die from an epidemic, I still need to know where it came from. Time is of the essence."

"It's not safe for you to be here alone," I said. "People were shot. There's a killer on the loose."

"Then leave Trace's rig. Anybody sees it parked out front will think twice before coming in."

I didn't like it, but it wasn't being in deep water that bothered me; it was fast water. I needed to swim quicker, swim harder if I was to have any chance at all of catching a killer and cattle thieves too.

"Okay as long as you keep your eyes open and that Lady-smith close," I said.

"Deal," she said.

Trace and I scrambled up the bank and drove to the Triple Triangle.

As we passed the Big D, the young deputy said, "See, lots of healthy cows on this ranch."

The Dillard house was set back from the road and surrounded by corrals, stables, and a barn. All were painted white. The ranch's brand was painted on a windmill's blades that weren't moving in the still of the day, but the center-pivot sprinklers riding on fat tires irrigating the fields were.

"Dill Dillard must be doing pretty good," Trace said. "That's an expensive way to water grass. My dad could never make that pencil out."

"Is that how you developed the build of a tight end, working on the family ranch?" I said.

"That and a coach in high school whose idea of a workout was dragging pickup tires around the field and pushing sleds weighted with a couple hundred-pound sacks of sand. When I went to Oregon State, it was big rig tires and a half-dozen sacks."

The Triple Triangle was another two miles up the road. The paint on the buildings didn't match, the fence posts weren't store-bought, and the corrals had missing rails.

"Still no cattle and still got eyes on us from the front porch," Trace said as we passed under the overhead that sported the interlocking triangles brand.

"Good morning," I hailed to the man watching us from a rocker as I got out of the pickup. "Sheriff Nick Drake and Deputy Trace Wakefield."

"What d'ya want?" he said, neither getting out of his chair nor beckoning us to join him in the shade.

"To make your acquaintance for starters and also ask you a couple of questions."

"About what?"

"First off, I'd like to know who I'm talking with. Your name is?"

"Simms."

"That your first or last?"

"Only. What do you want?"

I could sense Trace setting his feet next to me.

"Okay, Simms, it's like this," I said. "We got a call to make a welfare check on your neighbors, the Hardwards. In looking around their ranch, we noticed the only livestock on the place were dead."

"That a fact?" he said.

"Know anything about it?"

"Nope."

"What about your stock? I don't see any. Where are they?" I said.

"Why's where my beeves be or not be your concern?"

I patted the badge pinned on my chest. "Because this says it is."

His wrinkled face turned more prune-like. "So's you know, I didn't vote for you and sure as hell never will."

"Answer the question, Simms. Where's your cattle?"

"Up in high pasture. Too damn hot for them down here in summer. I'm not about to waste money irrigating grass like that fool Dill Dillard." Simms hawked a spit. It almost cleared the front porch. "Runs them sprinklers day and night so folks think he's got money to burn."

"Your stock in the high pasture, they healthy?" I said.

"If they wasn't, my foreman would tell me. He rides back and forth every other day," Simms said. "Did say they had a little trouble with a pack of coyotes going after some of the calves, but my boys took care of it. Set a couple of coyote killers. Boom. Boom. No more problem."

I'd come across M-44s before, spring-loaded baited traps that blasted a lethal dose of cyanide into a coyote's mouth when sprung. Problem was, coyotes weren't the only species attracted by the bait.

"Department of Ag may need to check your stock for possible disease," I said.

"Damn meddlers." Simms hawked another spit. Again it didn't clear the porch. "I'll tell you this, I won't bring my beeves down here for them. They'll have to ride up."

I asked him how well he knew the Hardwards.

"I don't," he said.

"You never met them, spoke to them?"

"Didn't say that, did I? Said I didn't know them. Helped Ol' Daniel fix a flat once. He busted down on the road and didn't have a jack. Lent him mine. Lug wrench too. Never said so much as a thank you. That's the kind he is."

"That the only time in all these years?" I said.

"Passed him on the road every so often, but he never even lifted two fingers from the steering wheel to say howdy. The kind he is."

"And Mrs. Hardward?"

"What about her?" Simms said.

"You ever see her?"

"If she was in the front seat with him, I never seen her, she being so small."

"If you never saw her, how did you know how tall she is?" I said.

"Heard she's Oriental. All of them are small, aren't they?"

"Who told you that?"

"About their kind being short?"

"About her being Asian?"

"People talk. Can't recall who exactly," he said. "You got no more questions, I'm going inside. Getting hot out here."

"I got another," I said. "How do you sell your cattle?"

"One at a time for cash money." Simms finally laughed but it sounded more like a cough.

"Do you use a broker or deal directly with meat packers and wholesalers?"

"I wouldn't pay a middleman a damn cent to sell what I spend my own money on for feed and cowboys."

"Ever heard of a broker named Red Caldera? Drives a red Cadillac," I said.

This time the spit did clear the porch.

"Devil in sheep's clothing. Drove up here pretending to be my best friend, telling me how he was going make me rich. I talked to him all right. You want to know what I said?"

"I would."

"Same thing I'm going tell you, word for word. Get. The. Hell. Off. My. Land."

The rocker was still rocking after he went inside and slammed the door.

"We need to speak to Red Caldera and quick," I said.

"Where do you think he is?" Trace said.

"Where folks are ranching because that's where the money is."

Trace's eyes narrowed. "I'll find him and bring him in. Count on it."

"Good. And Trace? Try to keep him in one piece."

9

Gemma was gone when we got back to the Hardward ranch. A note was tucked under Trace's windshield wiper. She was driving straight home to No Mountain to swap her Jeep for her plane and fly the samples to the veterinary diagnostic lab in Corvallis. Results could come as soon as the next day.

"I was hoping for more time, but I understand her obligation to notify Department of Ag if it's an epidemic," I said.

"Two-minute drill," Trace said. "What's the play?"

"Let's hightail it back to Burns. You can start running down Red Caldera's whereabouts by calling the biggest ranches in Harney and see if he's there or they know him. If nothing pans out, move on to the ranches in Malheur and Baker Counties. If he's not in Oregon, then he'll be back home in Idaho."

"That a problem?"

"Caldera told me he lives in the Treasure Valley. That's in Ada County, Idaho's most populous," I said. "The sheriff there has a reputation for being a hard-ass when it comes to cooperating with lawmen from other jurisdictions. He's overly protective of his citizens since they also happen to be his voters."

"Then I better nail him before he leaves Harney," he said.

I led the way back to the office at the same speed I did coming. As our rigs rocketed over the potholed road, I radioed dispatch.

"Anything new from Orville?" I shouted, holding the mike six inches away so it wouldn't bash me in the mouth as the pickup bounced up and down.

"The chief deputy just checked in and wanted to know your ETA," Jazz Flambeaux said.

"Tell him I'm on my way to him. Trace is coming straight to the office. Help him with whatever he needs."

"Awesome," she said. "Real police work. Finally."

"As long as it and you stay inside the office."

I clicked off before I could hear her protest.

Orville Nelson was in a darkened chamber adjacent to Doc's exam room. The interior walls were fitted with thick sheets of insulation and the back wall was hardened with an extra layer of cement blocks. A large tank of water stood beside an iron box stuffed with cotton. Both were used to fire weapons into for ballistics purposes.

The chief deputy's wheelchair was pulled up to a table covered with a sterile cloth. He wore surgical gloves and was examining various parts of the disassembled .38 Special through the lens of a lighted magnifying glass attached to a flexible gooseneck stand. A small tray held six brass cartridges that reflected the glass's light. Two still had bullets; four did not. The slugs lay side by side.

"What did you find?" I said.

"'A riddle wrapped in a mystery inside an enigma.' Winston Churchill said that of the Russians, but it is very apropos here."

Orville lifted one of the slugs with a pair of tweezers. "This is the round Doc removed from Mrs. Hardward's skull." He set it apart from the others. "And this is the one that went through Mr. Hardward and lodged in the wall behind him." He set it next to the first.

He placed a third slug next to them. "This one was unspent in the revolver. I tested it by firing it into water. And the fourth slug here is unfired. I extracted it manually from its cartridge."

"What am I seeing here besides the first two are more flattened compared to the others?" I said.

"Not much more than that with the naked eye, but under magnification you would see a completely different story. I've been able to determine the two slugs that killed the Hardwards have a slightly larger diameter than a typical .38 Special round. Precisely, .008 inches larger or .20 millimeters."

"They couldn't've come from the .38."

"Correct," he said. "The cartridges would not fit unless the .38's cylinder chambers and barrel were adapted. But I have examined both thoroughly and nothing has been altered."

"That leaves a second gun being used and then the shooter fired two rounds from the .38 to leave two spent cartridges in the chambers," I said.

"Affirmative. I compared the two larger slugs to the one I test-fired through the .38. The striations on them do not match. Two different fingerprints, ballistically speaking of course."

"You found something else, didn't you? The Churchill line."

Orville wasn't one for boasting, but he was prone to blushing. "The size of the rounds and makeup of their metal components comport with the specifications of a Russian weapon."

More caffeine-like jolts surged through me. "A 9x18mm Makarov," I said. "We took them off North Vietnamese soldiers. If they weren't firing Makarovs at us, it was Soviet Tokarevs or Chinese Type 54s."

"Indeed."

"Just who the hell is Mrs. Hardward? Why did she own a .38? And who the hell packs a Russian gun used by NVA regulars and VCs, hunts her down and kills her, and tries to make it look like suicide?"

"To quote another famous Englishman, 'To be or not to be. That is the question.'"

"Shakespeare's not going to help us here, Orville. We need a witness, fingerprints, a confession, something, anything."

"I did a thorough check of every part of the .38 for fingerprints, but the only ones on it are Mrs. Hardward's. We can assume they were applied to the grip and trigger postmortem."

"Then the gun's serial number could be our only ticket for finding out more about her," I said.

"I called my FBI contact at Quantico to see what he could do to help speed the search at BATF and the Defense Department. He said he'd try."

"Good thinking, but the last thing we need is for the feds to come swooping in here and take over the investigation and screw everything up."

Orville's head tilted. "I gave my contact the impression the gun was used in a domestic altercation and thus is a local matter."

"Even better thinking." I looked at the disassembled revolver and bullets. "This and the scrap of letter pulled from the burn pit lead one way, but the dead and missing livestock lead another. I don't see how they're related."

"Maybe they are not, only a by-product of intersecting timelines," he said.

"That another one of your mathematical formulas?"

"I could diagram it if you would like, but the fact that both share a common factor—the Hardwards—and both have a start point and are progressing toward an end point, it is only logical they will intersect. How many times and when the next occurrence may be, if at all, is something that I could try to calculate."

"Let's concentrate on the human side of your equation first," I said. "Trace and Jazz are chasing down Red Caldera. While they're doing that, see what else you can dig up on the Triple Triangle and Big D. I've met the owners and both claim they don't know the Hardwards despite Ol' Daniel having lived next door to them for thirty-plus years."

"That sounds extremely unlikely given the nature of remote ranching where neighbors often have to depend upon each other for assistance and fellowship," Orville said.

"Agreed, though neither Dillard nor Simms come across as charitable or likable, especially not toward each other. They could even be competing to buy the Hardward spread."

"A similar goal often breeds conflict."

"That come from another famous Englishman?" I said.

"Actually, it is my observation shaped by a decade in law enforcement under the tutelage of your father-in-law."

"Don't forget you have an appointment with the bishop at the Hardwards' church."

"My scheduler's reminder will not let me," he said.

"Back to the Makarov. What do you think your FBI buddy would do if you asked him if he had any intel on crimes involving one?"

"Since it is a Soviet military weapon, he would be compelled to alert the Bureau's counterintelligence division immediately."

"Then scratch that idea," I said. "What about asking him if other Vietnamese immigrants have been shot and killed on US soil?"

Orville rubbed his chin. "He would want to know why I am asking."

"You could tell him the matter involving the .38 involves a Vietnamese immigrant and though it appears to be a murder-suicide of a married couple, we need to rule out double murder."

"Are you thinking this is not a one-off?"

"I can't rule out it isn't. The scrap of letter. Uncle Ho looking for her. Maybe someone is looking for others too."

"I suppose I could mention Mrs. Hardward's nationality and see if it prompts a reaction from him," Orville said.

"Okay, and drop it if he starts asking too many specifics."

I looked at the tray of bullets again. The flattened slugs looked like shards of scrap metal, but they were anything but junk. They'd killed two people. Whether the Hardwards were innocent or guilty of something, didn't matter. The only thing that did was catching the killer before he killed again.

"Orville?" I said.

"What, sir?"

"Great job on the ballistics."

His still-boyish face reddened again.

"What about fingerprints? Not the ballistic kind, but prints from actual fingers?" I said.

"The teacups on the table matched those of Mr. and Mrs. Hardward," he said. "I dusted the cups in the cupboard. All but one had her prints on them. Probably from washing and drying and putting back on the shelf. One did not."

"The killer's?"

"It had no prints at all. The killer must've been wearing gloves when he dried it and put it back."

"And the tea itself? Was it made from lotus?"

"It was. *Nelumbo lutea.* That's the scientific name for American lotus."

"What color are its petals?"

"Yellow."

"Here's something else for your to-do list," I said. "Call the phone company and check on the Hardwards' incoming and outgoing calls for the past couple of months. Find out when their line went dead and was it because they didn't pay their bill or something happened to it. If you're too busy, ask Jazz to do it."

"Will do."

I returned to the office to check on Trace's progress. He was talking on the phone when I came in and signaled to me with a head shake that so far he'd come up empty.

Jazz was seated at the Bridge in Orville's office staring at a computer monitor. Her eye makeup was even more dramatic than usual. Her matching black-painted fingernails danced on a keyboard.

"I'm creating a call log spreadsheet for Deputy Wakefield," she said. "I've expanded it to include the names and phone numbers of ranches in Malheur and Baker Counties as he is nearing the end of the list of ones in Harney County."

"If you're doing all that, who's answering the phone?" I said.

"Me. I routed incoming calls to the chief deputy's phone."

"And the radio?"

Jazz flicked a fingernail at a black headset that was made nearly invisible by her spiky black hair. "I have both the receiver and transmitter connected to this by a cable extension."

"Have you gotten any calls?" I said.

"The radio, no. The phone, yes. A nonemergency one came in for you several minutes ago."

"Who was it?"

"Tribal Police Officer Bina Mantioc."

"She say what it was about?"

"Nothing specific, only that some tribal alerts were making the rounds of Indian reservations and she believes they might be of interest to you. She said she'd take them home with her tonight and you could read them then."

The day was hurtling toward evening and the odds of getting home anytime soon were fading like daylight.

"I'll catch her at her office before she leaves," I said. "Call me if Trace gets a line on Caldera's whereabouts. I need to be there when he goes after him."

"Can I go as backup?" Jazz said.

"Absolutely not. You don't have the training."

"But—"

"That's an order."

10

———

The Burns Paiute Colony's newly formed tribal police office was housed in a building even more cramped than the sheriff's department. It was stark evidence of how little regard the Bureau of Indian Affairs gave a people who traced their ancestry back ten thousand years longer than anybody whose family came over on the *Mayflower*.

Bina Mantioc's desk was squeezed into a windowless cubicle between a community meeting room and a closet that once held cleaning supplies, but now served as a holding cell.

"I told Jazz I'd bring the alerts home to save you a trip," the Umatilla cop said.

"Doubt I'll get there tonight," I said.

"No breaks in the case yet?"

"A couple." I told her about the Makarov pistol and what Dill Dillard's hired hand had seen at the ranch prior to the Hardward murders.

"A Russian weapon and cattle rustling?" The beads in Bina's hair clip sparkled in the light of the naked bulb hanging from the ceiling as she shook her head. "This'll be one for the books."

"Tell me about the alerts," I said.

"It might be a long shot, but when I read them I immediately thought of your case," she said.

"How so?"

"Back home on the Umatilla rez, we used to get tribal police alerts on a fairly regular basis. These are a first for the Burns Colony, but then again, the fax machine was only installed yesterday. We put out an alert about our new number here and the machine's been spitting out paper ever since."

I asked what kind of alerts tribal cops transmitted to each other.

"Most are be-on-the-lookouts regarding missing women and children." Bina grimaced. "There are way too many of those. And then there are the beware-ofs about con artists going from reservation to reservation peddling one scam or another. Fake life insurance, rip-off car loans, and so on. The worst of the worst are perverts masquerading as doctors offering OB-GYN exams and preteen medical checkups."

"But these alerts," I said. "What's different about them?"

"They're the same in nature, but came from three different tribes. They fall in the category of warnings about people pretending to be Indian and wanting to live on a rez, but there's a twist to them."

Bina explained that during the '60s there had been a steady stream of hippies and back-to-the-landers arriving at reservations thinking the tribes would accept them as one of their own just because they had long hair and wore moccasins. Then there were non-Natives who believed living on a rez would mean they'd never have to work again because the government would provide free food, housing, and medical care.

"A third group are outlaws who figure a reservation will provide them with a safe hideout as well as immunity from arrest because the rez is a nation inside a nation." She smiled. "No one ever said criminals were rocket scientists."

"Tell me more about these alerts," I said.

"The first came from the Tribal Council of the Agua Caliente Reservation in Palm Springs. They reported that a male arrived at the rez a few weeks ago, said he was a tribal member, and asked for residence."

Bina got up, filled two glasses with water from a jug, handed me one, and sat back down.

"I'm sure you know this part already, but federally recognized tribes keep records of enrolled members and have a process for people who want to apply. There's screening because being an official member comes with benefits." She ticked off a list of assistance programs.

"Written records only go back so far, which means a tribal council often has to rely on oral history to verify an applicant's roots. Stories handed down by ancestors. Who married who, who their children were, who they married, who the grandchildren were, and so on."

Bina paused long enough to drink some water. The heat of the day had been trapped in the windowless room. I made a note to myself to look for a spare fan at the sheriff's office and bring it over. If I couldn't find one, I'd give her my own.

"The guy who showed up at the Palm Springs rez doesn't have anything like that, just some cockamamie story about being Agua Caliente," she said. "The tribe being open-minded give him the benefit of the doubt and offer him a trailer to stay in while they sort things out. He's got his own car, moves in, and pretty much keeps to himself. Doesn't attend potlucks or dances or bingo nights. They figure he has a nightshift job somewhere in LA because he drives off in the late afternoon and doesn't get back till dawn."

I asked if he was still there.

"No. After about a week, he drove off one night and never came back."

"He must've given them a name if he was trying to pass himself off as Agua Caliente," I said.

"John Patencio," she said. "It's the equivalent of John Smith. Patencio is the last name of a revered and historic tribal elder. Anybody could've learned that and the ABCs of being Agua Caliente from a trip to the Palm Springs library."

"Does the alert give a physical description?"

"Uh-huh. Early forties. Dark complexion, dark hair. The tribal council member who wrote the alert also noted that he spoke broken English with a pretty heavy accent and looked a lot more Chinese than he did Indian."

"So what prompted the council to issue an alert since he was no longer there?" I said.

"About a week after he left, a female shows up. She says she's looking for her cousin and describes John Patencio to a T. Says he suffered a mental breakdown and the family wants to bring him home and get him some help."

Bina took a sip of water. "Then they ask her if he's really Agua Caliente. She says no, it's part of his condition—he believes he's an Indian. They ask her what her name is and she gives them the equivalent of Jane Smith. When they tell her he left, she asked if he told anyone where he was going next. When they said he hadn't, she asked if she could look inside the trailer where he'd been staying. She did and left right afterward."

"Any kind of description of her in the alert?" I said.

"It says she's mid-twenties, very beautiful with dark eyes and shoulder-length dark hair with blond streaks in it. You know, lightened by the sun or Lady Clairol, more likely."

I finished my cup of water, took hers, filled both, and sat back down.

"What was it about her that prompted the Agua Caliente to issue an alert?" I said.

"Mainly the fact she was looking for him, but also because of the way she spoke English. It didn't seem to be her first language either. One of the Agua Caliente tribal member's wives is Cree. He said they go back to Quebec to visit her family. The relatives there speak French. He said the woman spoke English with a French accent."

"Did she look Chinese too?"

"The alert only describes her as half Asian, half White."

"Any descriptions on what they drove?"

"The male had a late model Chevy pickup. Black with California tags." Bina read off the numbers. "The female was in a blue sedan of some kind. No one wrote down the license plate or remembered it because she wasn't even there an hour."

"What about the two other alerts?" I said.

"The next one came from the Chickasaw Nation."

"Where are they located?"

"The Midwest. About two hours north of Dallas metro. The alert told pretty much the same story. The male shows up, says he's a member, talks his way into a free place to stay, goes to work at night, sleeps during the day, and disappears a few days later."

"Did he go there right after he left Palm Springs?" I said.

"There's no way of knowing for sure, but he could've since it was only a few days later," she said.

"Still driving the pickup?"

"No, this time a beat-up sedan. It had Oklahoma plates." Bina read them off.

"I take it the female showed up too," I said.

"A few days after he left. She gives her cousin looking for a crazy cousin story, asks if he told anybody where he was going next, and then she leaves."

"Same physical descriptions?"

"Pretty much. But a different car. This time a red Mustang, but no one remembers the plates because she wasn't there long."

"And the third alert?"

"This is where it gets interesting," Bina said. "It was issued by the Tulalip Tribes. The reservation is a little north of Seattle. The female arrives first, tells her story about looking for her cousin, his mental condition, and that she's been going from rez to rez searching for him. The tribal council tells her they've never seen him, don't know anything about him. She asks them about other Indian reservations in the area. They say there are several and tell her where. She says thanks and leaves."

"Hadn't they seen the other two alerts?" I said.

"No, not until afterward. Neither alert was marked high priority nor had anyone linked them together yet. They'd both been put at the bottom of the pile at the Tulalip council office. Plus the tribal police there were super busy. The Tulalip were hosting a three-day powwow with other Puget Sound tribes followed by an Indigenous Peoples Summit on the rez."

"What about the male?"

"He showed up two, three days later and starts launching into his story about being a Tulalip and wanting a place to stay," she said. "They tell him they know he isn't one and that his cousin is looking for him. He seemed very surprised by that. Gives them the third degree about her: What name did she give them, what did she look like, what was she driving, did she say where she was going next, and so on."

"They tell him about the nearby reservations like they did her?"

Bina nodded. "Even gave him directions to the closest one. They say he drove off in a big hurry."

"Sounds like the huntress became the hunted," I said.

"If that's true, then why are they hunting each other? I don't buy the cousin line one bit."

"That's what I need to find out. What did the Tulalip do after the man left?"

"Nothing at first, but then someone found the tribal alerts that came from the Agua Caliente and Chickasaw. That's when they sent their own alert around linking them to the others and marked it high priority."

"Same physical description and everything?" I said.

"Not exactly," Bina said. "One of the Tulalip council members served in Vietnam. He said the male was definitely Vietnamese."

This time I could smell the coffee brewing before it jolted me. "No wonder why you thought of my case."

She touched the corner of her eye.

"You learn that from Gemma?"

"All women know it," Bina said.

"And I bet by now Loq does too," I said. "You know where he is?"

"He radioed me earlier and said he was returning to the Hardward ranch to take another look around."

"For anything specific?"

"For whatever Talking Woman told him to look for. Loq didn't say."

"He told you about his dream?"

"Of course he did," she said.

"And he's talked to her again?"

"Yes."

"November told me Talking Woman is dangerous," I said.

"Mm."

"You're not worried?"

"I'm a cop," Bina said. "Lots of things are dangerous. People. Situations. Weather. Driving. Shootouts. I couldn't do my job if I spent my time worrying about what could or couldn't happen. Besides, Loq can take care of himself. He's a born warrior. He certainly proved that when we were looking for his sister."

"That he is," I said. "Can I make a copy of the alerts?"

"I already did. Here you go."

I gave them a quick read-through. "Before you got these, did anyone claiming to be a long-lost member of the Burns Paiute Colony show up asking for a free bed or a cousin looking for a cousin?"

The beads on the hair clip sparkled again as she shook her head. "That doesn't mean they didn't find a place to stay in Harney County all on their own."

"You're thinking the same thing I am. Somehow the man is linked to the Hardwards' deaths."

"It doesn't matter if the department is city, county, or tribal, no cop believes in coincidences, Nick. A man who sounds like he's Vietnamese running around the countryside hiding out on Indian reservations. A woman who looks half Vietnamese searching for him. And now a murdered Vietnamese refugee right here in Harney County."

"And the FBI doesn't believe in coincidences either," I mused aloud.

"Of course not. Why, that'd be a problem for you if they started investigating this?" she said.

"Could be. Before a cattle rustler shot Orville in the back, he had his heart set on becoming a federal agent. Fortunately for all of us, Pudge hired him and the rest is history. Orville's always maintained a close contact inside the Bureau—they bonded over being what he calls computer geeks. He's asked him for help running down the serial number on the .38 Special, but now that we know the murder weapon was a Makarov, I don't want Orville telling that to his buddy."

"For good reason. He'd be compelled to report it to the counterintelligence department and the Bureau would take over our case," she said.

"Our case?" I said.

"Darn right ours. A man pretending to be Indian and using

Indian reservations as a hideout who could be a killer makes it my case too. For all I know, he may be pretending to be Umatilla and staying on my rez right now planning to gun down a Vietnamese refugee living nearby. I have to tell my boss."

When I didn't hide my disapproval, she said, "Don't worry. George Tahamtaham doesn't like interference by the feds any more than you or me. He'd be first to tell you all about Washington's very long history of broken promises."

11

My short career as sheriff took what Chief Deputy Orville Nelson would call a backward quantum leap in the five minutes it took me to drive to my office.

People were gathering near the steps at the front of the brick-sided, two-story county courthouse. A podium equipped with a microphone and speaker had been set on the landing. I pulled over to have a look-see.

That's when the front door swung open and District Attorney Sidney Sessions and Judge Silas Martin Manton came out. The DA stepped to the podium, cleared his throat, and lowered the microphone to match his stature.

"My fellow citizens of Harney County, the land of big skies, big hearts, big ideas, and even bigger ideals," he began. "A land founded by pioneers who came on foot, horseback, and covered wagon. A land where a man's word is his bond, a land of truth, and a land where justice prevails."

Sessions took a breath as he surveyed his audience, striving to make eye contact with each and every person. He lingered on a reporter and photographer from the *Burns Herald*.

"My fellow citizens, a grave injustice has occurred and it is my duty to inform you of a most heinous crime. Two of your neighbors were brutally murdered. Gunned down in their own home."

He let the collective gasp settle before continuing.

"Not only were their lives heinously taken, but their bodies were allowed to lay moldering for a week before their deaths were discovered. But even then, more injustices occurred. The investigation into their foul murders was grossly mishandled from the very start. To wit, their identities were willfully withheld from my office!"

Another pause, another overly dramatic intake of air by DA Sessions followed.

"Who would do such a thing? Who could be so categorically incompetent not to bring to bear the full weight of Harney County's law enforcement and judicial system to solve a double murder? Why none other than Sheriff Nick Drake."

Sessions made a show of raising both arms and patting down the air as if to tamp the outrage he was trying to stoke.

"When I received word of the couple's death from the unqualified and inexperienced sheriff, I demanded he give me their names, implored him to allow me to use the power of my office to bring the perpetrators to justice. But, no, he refused to do so. He purposely withheld them to elevate his own stature at the expense of solving a crime and delivering justice."

The little DA took another deep breath and dabbed at the beads of sweat glistening on his forehead with a snow globe-patterned pocket square.

"Realizing the safety of all Harney County residents is at stake, I took immediate action. I sought counsel from the Right Honorable Judge Silas Martin Manton who rendered an unimpeachable legal opinion in writing. I presented it to the head of the state criminal forensic laboratory that was processing evidence from this crime and demanded I be provided the names of the victims on the spot!"

The reporter started shouting. "What are their names?" "Who are they?" "Where do they live?" The photographer aimed his telephoto lens at the DA and snapped away.

Sessions posed before answering. "I'm saddened to say the victims are Mr. and Mrs. Daniel Hardward, both God-fearing Latter-day Saints and a credit to Harney County's ranching community."

He paused as the crowd gasped.

"Let me be clear," the DA said. "A remedy for this grave injustice is at hand. In fact, it is in your hands. You, the good people of Harney County. You, the good voters of Harney County. A petition is circulating demanding Sheriff Drake's immediate recall and the holding of a special election to elect a new sheriff, one with the experience, competence, and courage to serve and protect Harney County families and businesses."

He took another deep breath. "When—not if—this petition gathers the required number of signatures, an election will be calendared forthwith. You will have a new sheriff by opening day of deer hunting season, I guarantee it!"

Sessions stepped to the side and bowed to the judge.

Judge Silas Martin Manton took to the podium. His hair was silver and his rimless eyeglasses magnified steely-gray eyes.

"Justice," he thundered. "Not retribution. Not vengeance. But honesty. Decency. Righteousness. That is what is called for here, that is what is required, and that is what shall be delivered!"

He pounded the podium reflexively as if wielding a gavel. The microphone picked up the sound and the attached speaker flooded the courthouse grounds with reverb.

"As the Almighty is my witness, the Hardwards will receive their justice and those who committed this grievous crime will pay the ultimate price. Incompetence is no excuse. Cowardliness is neither. Justice must be delivered, and by God, I shall see to it!"

The judge held his piercing stare for the newspaper photographer before wheeling around, sending his black robes billowing, and marched back into the courthouse with DA Sessions scurrying to keep up.

I thought about crossing the grounds, grabbing the mike, and explaining why I'd withheld the victims' names, but Pudge's gravelly voice growled in my ears: "Politicking don't catch killers, son. And it sure as hell don't stop them from killing again."

Pulling away from the curb, I rounded the corner to my office. The front door slammed behind me as I strode to my desk.

"Front and center! All hands. Now!"

Trace Wakefield dropped the phone and sprinted down the hall with Orville and Jazz Flambeaux close behind.

I waved the tribal alerts. "We got a break in the case."

As I told them about the mystery couple, Orville's head started bobbing. "Given Mrs. Hardward's ethnicity, the scrap of letter, and the Russian-made weapon, I estimate the connection between her murder and the man and woman is in the range of moderately strong to strong based on Bayes' likelihood ratio theorem."

"Who's Bayes?" Trace whispered to Jazz.

"Never heard of him, but I get what Orville's saying. It's like he's giving odds on a football game and one team's already got it in the bag," she said.

The deputy squared his shoulders. "Then we go for the upset."

"I don't think the Hardwards are the only victims," I said. "We need to find out if there are other Vietnamese murder victims who live near Indian reservations."

"What's the deal with pretending to be an Indian?" Jazz said.

"He's less likely to leave a trail hiding out on a rez than if he checked into a motel where he'd need to show ID and use a credit card," I said. "He's getting around in different cars, meaning he's probably stealing them. I have descriptions and plate numbers we can run down."

"But he's not killing Indians living on the reservations," she said.

I shook my head. "Not as far as we know, but the reservations he's chosen are close to metropolitan areas with sizeable populations of Vietnamese refugees. The largest are in California, Washington, and Texas. I know this because when Gemma and I adopted Johnny, the agency was leery of us raising him in a small town in a rural area with few if any other Vietnamese."

"Oh, I didn't know your son was—"

"He was born in Saigon. His mother was a local, his father a GI," I said. "The Agua Caliente rez is a two-hour drive from Orange County. It's home to the largest Vietnamese community outside of Vietnam. Chickasaw Nation is a hundred miles from Dallas metro, which also has lots of Vietnamese living there. So does Seattle. The Tulalip Tribes are only an hour away."

"But I still don't get the connection with the Hardward killings," Jazz said. "Harney County's entire population is—"

"A lot smaller than the other places, yeah, I know. For some reason, the killer didn't pretend to be Paiute and ask for a free place to stay at the Burns Colony. We find out why he did come here, we're one step closer to finding him."

"But aren't we forgetting something?" she said.

"What?"

"The chick with the bleached streaks. Who's she? Is she hunting the killer or working with him?"

"The only way to find out is to find her too," I said.

Jazz's lips made a thin black horizontal line when she grimaced. "Unless he catches her first."

"Why we can't slow down. I'm going to hand out more assignments, but before I do, I need to tell you something. Driving by the courthouse, I passed DA Sessions and Judge Manton telling a crowd the Hardwards were murdered and I'd withheld their names."

"How did the DA learn them?" Orville said.

"He forced the forensic lab into giving it up."

"Doc will not like that."

"No, he won't. They're using it to whip up public sentiment against me for the recall. We can't let that get in the way of going about our business and catching the killer. Anybody asks you about the investigation, tell them to talk to me. That includes anyone from the *Burns Herald*. Understood?"

Three heads nodded.

"What about the cattle and Red Caldera?" Trace said.

"We need to keep on that to rule it out as a motive for the Hardward murders," I said. "You and Jazz continue tracking him down. I want him brought back here for questioning. Recheck the records of the speeding tickets he got. Maybe there's a pattern that shows his route.

"Also, go back to the Triple Triangle and check on the health of the herd up in the high pasture. When you're finished with that, drive the potholed road and look for any turnoffs that could take you to other ranches or even a two-lane and beyond. Those livestock carriers and the Hardwards' white pickup may have taken that route. Someone could've seen them. Maybe the carriers unloaded the stock at another ranch or a meat packer. Ask around. Double-check the gas stations too."

"Check Simms. Run route," he muttered.

"Jazz, while Trace is doing that, contact the state troopers and see if Caldera got nailed for speeding recently. Also see if they ticketed anyone driving the Hardward pickup in the last week or two."

"We should also identify who Caldera's wholesalers are and check them out," she said. "If he stole the Hardward cattle, he sold them to someone. The wholesalers could even be in on it."

"Good idea. Now you're thinking like a cop."

She stuck out her chin. "Don't you mean Detective Torch Flambeaux's daughter is?"

"I don't see anyone's dad in this room, only three members of my squad."

That earned a black lipstick smile.

I turned to Orville. "When's your appointment with the Mormon church bishop?"

"Tomorrow morning. It was his first available," he said.

"When you're asking him about the Hardwards, find out if the church works with a mail-order bride business that specializes in bringing women over from the Far East, specifically Vietnam."

"Will do."

"I'll work with Bina and Loq on tracking down the mystery man and woman," I said. "We all keep each other in the loop. We also keep our eyes on each other's backs. There's a killer on the loose. Maybe more than one. Now, let's do our job."

12

———

At ten o'clock I sent everyone home. "Get a good night's sleep. We'll start fresh in the morning."

"With all due respect, that is completely unnecessary," Orville said.

"No, it's an order," I said. "While I know you never sleep more than two, three hours a night like your hero Thomas Edison, the squad needs clear eyes and alert minds if we're going to achieve our mission."

"If I may, I cannot help but notice you have reverted to using military jargon since the discovery of the murders."

"Old habit, I suppose. Haven't been in a position of leadership since 'Nam."

"If I also may, it gives the team, er, squad, a sense of a higher degree of purpose."

Trace and Jazz nodded their agreement.

"One other thing," Orville said. "If we all leave, what about our prisoner upstairs? Someone needs to be here."

I'd forgotten about the brawling biker who'd yet to make bail. I asked if he'd gotten supper.

"He did," Jazz said. "Fried chicken and Tater Tots from Bella's at five thirty per the schedule."

"Then he's good till morning. I still have some paperwork to finish. I'll tuck him in before I leave. Anybody can't be back here by zero-six-hundred hours, raise your hand."

No one did, nor did I expect anyone to.

They filed out and I returned to my desk. Orville's words about taking a military approach to the murders rang in my ears. It also brought back the nightmare of having led the men in my squad into an ambush that cost all of them their lives and sent me into a hellbent spiral and a stint in the rubber room at Walter Reed.

I banged the table with my fist as hard as Judge Manton had done in front of the courthouse and vowed I'd never let that happen to any member of my new squad.

Staring at the blizzard of paperwork, my eyelids started to droop and I was soon asleep. A loud rumbling outside snapped me awake. It was followed by the creak and swish of the front door. I yanked the .45 from the holster and held it beneath the desk. If whoever came in was looking for trouble, they were going to find it among splinters and lead.

The dim light in the lobby backlit a big man. A shadow filled my doorway.

Lucky for him, the silhouette had a long mohawk.

"You here to help with paperwork?" I said.

"No, but if you take that .45 off me I'll take you for a ride," Loq said.

"Come again?"

"I'd be holding a gun under the desk too if I was working alone this time of night."

"I meant, where do you plan on taking me? Home? Can't go. Still got work to do."

"I got your motorcycle out front," he said. "Rode it over from the storeroom you built on the other side of Gemma's airstrip. How come you keep it locked up way over there? You worried that Johnny or Hattie might take it for a spin?"

I didn't tell him the real reason was Gemma and I liked to steal away some nights when the kids and November were asleep. It was parked far enough from the house so the Triumph's engine wouldn't wake them when I kickstarted it. We'd tear across the High Lonesome, me twisting the throttle wide open and she with her arms clamped tight around my waist. We'd hoot and holler and when we stopped in the middle of nowhere beneath the moonlight, the noises we continued making came from a different kind of thrill.

"Where do you want to go?" I said.

"Back to the Hardward ranch. I found a trail needs following," the Klamath said.

"Something you can't do in your rig or on the back of your spotted pony?"

"I followed it on foot a mile, but it leads across country too rough for a pickup, too far for a horse to cover in a single night, even one as fast as mine."

"Be tricky for two of us on a bike to follow," I said. "We could lose the trail in the dark."

"You drive, I'll spot," he said. "I got sharper eyes."

"No, I was thinking it'd be better if we went on two bikes. That way we could run intersecting patterns if we lose the trail."

"Where you going to get another motorcycle this time of night?"

I opened my desk's top drawer and held up a set of keys. "The biker upstairs won't miss it."

"I like your style of sheriffing."

After topping off the motorcycles' tanks from the department's gas pump, we left the city limits behind and sped through the warm night air, the stars and moon bright. Steering around the potholes on the dirt road to the Hardward ranch proved even easier on my British-made Triumph Bonneville than in the pickup. Loq handled the customized Harley Shovelhead as deftly as he did riding the spotted pony he still hadn't named after all these years.

When we reached the ranch, he pulled in front and led us past the barn and incinerator into the desert scrub for a couple of hundred yards. He all but said whoa! as he braked to a stop. I pulled alongside him.

"There," he said, his finger pointing in the same direction as the Harley's headlight. "He rode in on a motorcycle. Parked it there. Walked to the ranch house. Did what he did. Walked back and rode off on the same trail he made coming in."

"He leave any footprints?"

"Only a couple he missed brushing away with a stalk of sagebrush. Lugged soles," Loq said.

"Where did he come from?" I said.

"Some place southeast. I walked the tracks for a mile. Stopped when they went up a rise. From the top I could see they kept on going until the horizon got in the way."

"Not much out there except for some old Basque sheepherding camps, and even those aren't much more than a campfire ring and a flat spot to park a horsedrawn wagon."

"But the shepherds had to get there from somewhere and then take their sheep back to sell," he said. "Jordan Valley's out that way and lots of Basques live there."

"And Highway 95 goes right through it," I said. "From there, you can drive over to Boise or down to the Nevada line in an hour and half, either one."

"And be gone. That is if the killer wants to be gone."

"You're sure he's the killer?"

"As sure as I know we need to keep following this trail and see where it leads," Loq said. "Maybe even right to him."

"Holed up in an old sheepherder's camp?"

"If we're lucky. If we're not, then he's either fallen off his motorcycle and broken his neck and won't be able to tell us why he killed the Hardwards or he got to a rig he stashed near the highway and is long gone."

"Lead the way," I said.

Two headlights along with a lit-up night sky made following the tracks of the killer's motorcycle easier. The few times we did lose them, we'd separate and ride intersecting zigzag patterns. The terrain was mostly unchanging, long stretches of desert floor whiskered by big sagebrush and the occasional stand of junipers. The washes we crossed were sandy but dry. The gullies shallow enough to ride down one side and back up the other. We only had to jump a couple.

I glanced at my field watch without letting up on the throttle. It was going on two in the morning. I figured we'd traveled cross-country sixty, seventy miles, easy. Loq was ahead of me about a hundred yards. His headlight and taillight started pointing up as he climbed an incline. I hunched forward readying to take it on when his brake light flashed and held steady atop a plateau.

"What's up?" I said when I joined him.

"Hundred feet straight ahead," Loq said.

"Looks like an old sheepherder's camp. They must've chosen this place so they could watch over their flocks down below. See the fire ring? The ground next to it has been cleared of rocks."

"It's not that old. Something shiny is reflecting my headlight."

"Maybe it's a beer can."

"Maybe?" he said.

"Right, no maybes," I said. "We leave the bikes here. Circle around on foot. I'll go left."

I didn't have to say it, but we both drew our sidearms and took flashlights before moving out.

There was too much moonlight and too little cover. I kept as low as I could and was ready to take a dive at every step. I blinked away the thought of landing atop a knot of rattlesnakes and dismissed as crazy the image of a black-clad VC jumping up and emptying his Makarov at me. When I reached where I'd calculated I'd be straight across from Loq, I started creeping toward the clearing.

No snakes rattled. No VC jumped up. No one fired a shot.

"Clear," I said.

"Clear," Loq said.

We shined our flashlights.

"He was here, all right," Loq said. He crouched, touched the ground, and held up a finger. "Motor oil. Must've hit a rock and sprung a leak. Not a bad one, though. Bike's gone."

"And the shiny object," I said, training my flashlight on it. "It's a sardine can. Looks unopened. He must've dropped it. I'll bag it for prints."

I was about to pick it up when the wind gusted. It brushed my face and lingered around my ears, the sound soft and lilting. "*Hay can than. Hay can than*," it whispered.

I froze.

"What is it?" Loq said.

"I think I just heard Talking Woman."

"What'd she say?"

"Careful. Booby trap. But not in English. In Vietnamese."

"Are you sure?"

"Sure enough not to want to pick up that sardine can."

We both took several steps backward and trained our flashlights on it.

"It could either be a weighted pressure plate holding down a trigger or it's packed with explosives and attached to a tripwire," I said. "Charlie used beer cans as bait. Cost more than a few cherries their lives."

"Only one way to find out if it's rigged," Loq said. He held his flashlight and .357 in a crossed-wrists grip and sighted down the barrel.

"Wait! Do that and we lose any chance of getting his fingerprints."

"It's better than losing our limbs or lives trying to defuse it and we can't leave it for some shepherd to pick up."

"Then we take ten paces back and crouch." I led the way.

Loq squeezed the trigger. The explosion sent shards of metal and rocks flying as if blasted from both barrels of a side-by-side.

As the dust settled and the echo rolled across the High Lonesome, I raised my chin and said thanks to Talking Woman.

"Now you've met her too," Loq said.

"Doesn't mean she still isn't dangerous," I said. "Could be she's waiting to take us out on her own terms."

"Mm."

"Guy was a Viet Cong for sure. Only now, the Victor Charlies are running the whole country."

"Meaning what?" Loq said.

"That maybe Uncle Ho's successors did send our guy here to take care of Mrs. Hardward and anyone else like her."

The Klamath offered up another "Mm."

"What's that supposed to mean?" I said.

"That if they're looking to settle old scores, it's got to be a long list, and given what you and I both did in country, we're likely to be on it too."

We let the weight of that settle. I found a thin strip of metal from the blasted sardine can and bagged it to take back to Orville for fingerprinting. Then we searched the rest of the sheepherder camp to make sure there were no more jury-rigged explosives.

"He spent at least a night here, maybe two. One coming, one

going," Loq said. "I count a couple of shit piles he tried covering with rocks."

"More booby traps?" I said.

"Only stink bombs."

My chuckle broke the tension.

Our search turned to looking for his exit tracks.

"Over here," Loq said. "He came up and went back down this side of the plateau."

I joined him, located the North Star, and turned a half circle.

"He's not angling southeast to Jordan Valley anymore. Now he's heading straight south to the junction of Highway 78 and 95. Bet you that's where he stashed his rig."

"Why down there? He could've left it a lot closer to Burns."

"Because he stuck to his usual pattern after all," I said. "He's been staying at the Fort McDermitt Reservation south of the junction. That rez is only a two-hour drive by highway to the Hardward ranch."

"Cagey like Charlie always was," Loq said. "He didn't use the Burns Colony because it was too close to his target. Could've been noticed."

"Yeah, and he came by motorcycle because he must've scouted the potholed road to the ranch and saw it was a dead-end trap. Harney County's not the same as stalking and hitting a target in a big city."

Loq looked down his high cheekbones. "You realize we're dealing with someone with a lot of motivation to kill."

"Viet Cong were never short of it," I said.

"How they beat us. We lost ours."

I shrugged. "We never had much to begin with. It wasn't our country we were fighting for like they were."

"We need to figure out who this guy is and fast," Loq said. "He's too good slipping in and out."

"Might be easier finding out who Mrs. Hardward was. That

will tell us why he was so motivated to kill her. Finding out who else he's killed could do that too."

"There aren't that many reasons for killing someone," he said. "War's one. Anger's another. Then there's revenge, jealousy, and—"

"Insanity and money," I said.

"Money? The Hardwards didn't have any. They were going broke if they weren't already. You've seen their ranch."

"But the killer could've thought they had something of value."

"Like what?" he said.

"Maybe gold or jewelry or some kind of family heirloom she brought with her when she came over as a mail-order bride," I said. "Refugees fleeing South Vietnam had to pay a high price to get out, especially by boat. Trouble was, as soon as they shoved off, pirates were waiting for them in the South China Sea to take whatever they had left after paying for their passage."

"And those who couldn't pay got dumped over the side as a lesson to others," he said.

I nodded. "When we were adopting Johnny, the agency said he was lucky the way he got out by stowing away on a US cargo plane instead of a boat. The violence at sea was off the charts."

"Goes with pirating," Loq said.

"Could be Mrs. Hardward smuggled out something extra valuable to warrant so much attention from this killer," I said.

"Like what?"

"I don't know, but the bloodiest battle I ever fought was in Hue during Tet. Not only was the city heavily shelled, but NVA and VC forces ransacked it. It turns out lots of historical artifacts stored in a walled fortress called the Citadel went missing. One was the Imperial Seal. It was solid gold and weighed twenty-five pounds. A cache of ancient figurines made of gold and jade was also looted."

"That could explain why Mrs. Hardward kept a .38 Special," Loq said. "She had something worth protecting from robbers."

"Could be," I said.

"Jewels or no jewels, that still doesn't get us any closer to IDing the killer or knowing how the woman showing up on the reservations figures in. Is she his hunter or spotter?"

"I'm starting to wonder if she's prey trying to turn it back around on him," I said.

"Bold," Loq said. "Makes her even more cagey and dangerous than him."

We stared into the darkness for a while.

"I think she's Talking Woman," I said.

"I was thinking the same thing," he said.

We let the weight of that notion settle over us like the stars blanketing the sky.

"Let's go back to Burns," I said.

"You don't want to ride to Fort McDermitt and see if they have any intel on the guy and know where he's going next? Maybe even be there to intercept the woman in case she shows up?"

"We'd likely run out of gas before we got there. Better is if you retrieve your rig and take the two-lane."

I explained that since the Shoshone-Paiute Reservation wasn't in Harney County and also straddled the Oregon-Nevada line, I'd have no jurisdictional authority and be obliged to notify the local sheriffs on both sides of the border. Loq was US Fish and Wildlife and unbeholden to county and state boundaries.

"I noticed you didn't mention me being Indian and them being Indian would make parlaying with the Fort McDermitt folks easier too," he said.

"Really, you want me to say that out loud?"

"I do."

I started to open my mouth and then saw the twinkle in his eyes wasn't coming from starlight.

"Good one," I said. "You got me."

"What are you going to be doing while I'm talking to my Shoshone and Paiute brothers?" Loq said.

"Figure out where the killer's going next and be there waiting for him."

"Make sure to save a place for me."

"Roger that," I said.

13

The sun edged above the Stinkingwater Mountains and turned gray to purple to red to orange to yellow when Loq and I returned to the sheriff's office. We switched motorcycles and he rode off on my Triumph bound for the Warbler ranch to fetch his rig while I went inside. Everyone was already at their desks. They weren't the only ones. Gemma was sitting at mine.

"I thought I was the only one you took on moonlight rides," she said.

"It was work," I said.

"That's what all the dog-of-a-husbands say after a night out when they come home dragging their tails."

Her attempt at a withering glower turned into a teasing grin.

"You being here tells me you learned something at the veterinarian lab," I said.

"It was like I thought. The animals were poisoned, not infected. There's no epidemic," she said.

"The second part's good news, but the first part—it wasn't an accident, was it?"

Gemma's ponytail swished. "No. They were given lethal injections. I tested samples I took from a couple of the cows' rumens to be sure."

"Were you able to ID it?"

"Pentobarbital," she said. "It's a controlled substance. Livestock are typically euthanized with a shot to the forehead with a captive bolt pistol, but large animal vets will inject pento into a cow or horse that's become a family pet. Like putting down an old dog or cat."

"The sheep and hogs injected too?"

"They were. The question is why?"

"Whoever did it was taking quite a risk," I said. "Thing is, most people aren't willing to take one unless there's some kind of a reward in it for them. You know, getting an adrenaline rush from risking their life climbing a mountain or putting their life's savings on the line in Las Vegas to hit the jackpot."

Gemma gave an exasperated groan. "We're talking about killing animals here, not playing poker."

"What I mean is, there has to be something in it for whoever did it. Money's the most obvious."

"What?"

"Hear me out," I said. "Say someone snuck in and poisoned some of the Hardwards' stock in the middle of the night. Then that same person comes along and convinces the couple their animals died from an epidemic and the rest of their stock is at risk—if not already infected. He offers to take the live animals for pennies on the dollar to get rid of them. Since the Hardwards are going to go broke without any livestock to sell, he also offers to buy all their possessions for pennies on the dollar too."

"You mean the Hardwards were conned?"

"Call it what you want—swindled, rustled, robbed. They got taken."

"Do you have proof that's what happened, or is it only what you think?" Gemma said.

"Your pentobarbital moved it a lot closer to knowing," I said.

Gemma looked down at the top of my desk while she thought that over, then back at me.

"The Department of Ag doesn't have a police arm outside of a few brand inspectors whose main job is to make sure cows don't get mixed up while free grazing," she said. "There's no one there I can report these livestock deaths to who'd do anything about it. Likewise with the Oregon State Police. They're responsible for investigating animal cruelty crimes, but it's hardly high on their to-do list."

"Is that your way of saying you want my squad to catch who did this?"

"Now they're a squad?" she said.

"Whatever," I said.

"Then that makes me a squad member too. I want to bust whoever did this so they can never hurt another animal. Ever."

"Wouldn't think of doing it without you."

"Good, because while you were out roaring around on your motorcycle, I already started. I'm working with Jazz to input my notes and do a search for other ranches where this might have happened. We're also making formal requests to the Federal DEA. They're in charge of regulating and enforcing controlled substances like pentobarbital. By the way, Jazz is great."

"Input? Do a search?" I rolled my eyes. "Oh Lord, you've gone techno on me too."

Gemma smiled. "You know something, hotshot? You sound just like Pudge."

"I'll take that as a compliment."

She went to huddle with Jazz while I did the same with Orville and Trace to fill them in on last night's discovery.

"Loq's on his way to Fort McDermitt to gather intel," I said. "Was your FBI friend any help IDing the .38's serial number?"

"He left a message and asked me to call him back later this morning," Orville said.

"That going to interfere with your Mormon bishop meeting?"

"Negative. I am leaving for that shortly and will be back with time to spare."

I updated them on the pentobarbital.

"Trace, now that we got proof the stock was poisoned, there's no need for you to ride all the way up to the Triple Triangle's summer pastures to check the health of their herd," I said.

"We should still keep an eye on Simms and Dill Dillard," he said.

"What makes you say that?"

The young deputy took a few seconds to muster the words. "It's like late in the season. Some teams are sure to make the playoffs, but then a key player gets hurt and suddenly a team that was ruled out is back in contention."

"Good point."

I asked Orville if he had any luck on phone records from the Hardward ranch and a status report on fingerprints.

Before he could answer, Jazz burst in with her headset still on, the extension cable trailing behind.

"Got a call from a rancher Trace spoke to yesterday about Red Caldera," she said. "He says Caldera was just at his place. When the rancher asked him why the sheriff's department wanted to talk to him, Caldera jumped in his Caddy and drove away."

"Where's the ranch?" I said.

"Near Dunnean."

"On the Harney County side of the line or Malheur?"

"Harney," she said.

"That makes it our jurisdiction, but Caldera won't be in it for long. He's making a beeline for Idaho. Fastest route is up the gravel road to the Highway 20 junction in Juntura. Once he hits blacktop, it's a straight shot to the state line."

"Should I alert the Malheur County Sheriff and State Police to intercept him?" Jazz said.

"Not yet. Trace and I'll cut him off before he gets there."

As we raced out the door, I yelled, "Both rigs."

I stopped playing coy and hit the lights and sirens, drifting around the corners of the town's edge with Trace glued to my bumper. Once we hit the Highway 20 straightaway, I buried the speedometer's needle and ran the numbers.

We'd beat Caldera to the junction, even if he was flying— but hitting him there felt wrong. Juntura was a speck of a town, but it still had too many variables. People, houses, storefronts; too many ways for an innocent bystander to end up in the crossfire.

"Think, think, think." I said it out loud while drumming my fingers on the steering wheel, trying to recall all the roads I'd driven east of Burns during my years as a wildlife ranger.

I grabbed the mike. "We got to nail Caldera before he reaches Juntura. He has to cross over an irrigation canal about a mile south. We can cut off on a service road before town and box him in on the bridge."

"You want me blocking or tackling?" Trace said.

"Depends on what Caldera does. And Trace? He might have a pistol shoved in his right boot. He's right-handed. Holds his cigar with his left."

The irrigation canal's service road came up fast. I only slowed a bit to take it, knowing that if I misjudged the speed, I'd end up wet. I didn't. Neither did Trace. The road was little used and the ruts and bumps in it reminded me of the potholed one to the Hardward ranch. I pictured the dead couple and didn't let up on the gas.

"Here's the way we play it," I yelled into the mike as we neared the gravel road. "Kill the lights and siren. I'll be on the road north of the bridge so I'm aiming at Caldera. You hold back here. Once he realizes it's me coming straight at him, he'll try reversing. That's when you come in hot and heavy and block him between us."

"Sandwich play," he said.

"Yeah, and he's the meat."

We got into position and waited. It wasn't long before a tornado of dust came swirling up the gravel road. When the speeding red sedan reached the bridge, I hit the lights and siren and stomped the gas pedal. Caldera slammed on the brakes and threw it in reverse, only to smash right into the reinforced grill guard of Trace's oncoming rig. The Caddy bounced forward and stopped dead in its tracks.

The front door swung open and Caldera clambered out. The fat man started running, his summertime Stetson blowing off and sailing into the canal. Trace overtook him in four strides and dropped him with an open-field tackle worthy of a highlight reel.

I swung out of my rig. "Red Caldera, you're under arrest."

"What for?" he sputtered. "I didn't do nothing."

"Lying, cheating, and stealing, for starters," I said. "Also killing the Hardwards' livestock. The couple? We'll find out if you killed them too."

"I never touched 'em. They was dead when I got there. You saw yourself." He sputtered some more, gave a few coughs. "Honest, Sheriff. I swear. They was already dead."

Caldera started gasping for air. His jellyroll sides heaved. "Give me a sec, Sheriff. Lemme catch my breath. I got a serious heart condition."

Trace stood and waited. I didn't take my eyes off Caldera. He finally got to his knees and hands and started to push off the ground. Then his right hand suddenly darted backward.

I stomped on it, pinning his wrist to the gravel. "Touch that gun in your boot, it'll be the last thing you ever feel." I bent over so I was close to his ear. "You follow?"

14

———

Trace frog-marched Red Caldera up the stairs and shoved him into the cell next to the bruised and battered biker.

"You can't leave me up here," Caldera yelled at the young deputy. "I know my rights. I got the right to call my lawyer. That's the law."

"Sheriff and me are law too," Trace said. "Should've thought of that when you went for your gun."

Caldera looked over at the bruised and battered biker. "The deputy's lying," he said to him. "I did no such thing."

"Yeah, you did," Trace said.

"And you wrecked my Caddy too. Smashed the back bumper running into it and probably caused even more damage chaining it to the back of your rig and towing it here. I'm gonna sue." Caldera turned to the biker again. "I'm gonna. I know my rights."

"So do I," the biker said. "The right to peace and quiet so quit your bellyaching and shut up."

Trace spun on his heels without another word. Caldera's curses and the biker's laughter followed him down the stairs as

Orville barreled into my office as fast as he could twirl his wheels.

"We may have gotten a significant break in the case," he said, his words coming as fast as he'd sped down the hall. "I received a callback from my FBI friend about the .38 Special."

"What did he tell you?" I said.

"It has a very interesting history, which I will get to in a minute, but it was an aside he made that is the real news."

Orville took a deep breath. "The first conversation we had about the gun, I alluded that it was used in a marital double suicide or murder-suicide and the wife was a Vietnamese immigrant."

"And?"

"He began our conversation today by volunteering that an inner office memo has been making the rounds about an uptick in recent Vietnamese refugee homicides in the past few weeks."

"Did he give you any details?" I said.

"He certainly did," Orville said. "The first death was a man living in Orange County, California, who was shot dead inside his apartment. The local police wrote it up as a surprised-by-intruder. Next was a woman murdered in Richardson, Texas. That's in Dallas-Metro. It was the same MO. Killed in her residence."

"Let me guess, there's been one in Seattle too," I said.

Orville's head was going up and down faster than a mallard dabbling for river grass. "The week before the Hardwards were killed another Vietnamese woman was murdered. She was walking home, yanked into a dark alley, and shot to death. Her purse was missing. Seattle Police logged it as a mugging gone awry."

"Your FBI pal, did he try to connect those killings to the Hardwards?"

"Negative, but I do find it noteworthy that he mentioned those cases. I believe he was on a fishing expedition."

"Sounds like it," I said. "Do you think he'll add Mrs. Hardward to that memo?"

"Only if we were to conclude that their deaths were at the hands of a third party, but during all my conversations with him, I maintained it was a marital crime."

"But the fact there's a memo going around puts pressure on us timewise."

"I concur," Orville said.

"Did he give you anything on the paper trail of the .38?" I said.

"Indeed he did. He ran the serial number himself on the FBI's mainframe computer that was linked to the BATF's system via ARPANET."

"I'm not going to ask what all that is so don't bother explaining it."

"The weapon was manufactured by Smith & Wesson as part of a lot during World War II. The war ended before the gun was ever issued. The lot was moved to an armory in North Carolina and remained there for twenty years until it was eventually shipped to Vietnam in 1965."

"A lot of the weapons we used were World War II vintage," I said. "Grease guns, BARs, M1s. Grenades too. You'd pull the pin, toss it, and pray it wasn't a dud."

"This particular .38 was first assigned to an officer with the Army of the Republic of Vietnam. Later, he reported it as being lost and was issued a Colt .45 semiautomatic."

"No surprise there. ARVN officers wanted to mimic their American counterparts who strapped .45s. They thought they looked more stylish, like the Ray-Ban Aviator shades they all took to wearing. He likely sold the gun on the black market or traded it for something. Don't suppose that big old computer at

Quantico was able to trace where it went next and how it wound up on the Hardward ranch?"

"Negative," Orville said. "Many weapons went unaccounted for after the fall of Saigon. There was little if any way to track them, much less recover them. Computers can only provide accurate information when accurate information is first provided to them. As an IBM programmer once explained, 'Garbage in, garbage out.'"

"Guess there's still a role for us two-leggeds after all," I said.

"If I may speculate, using Bayes' theorem of likelihood again, regardless of how Mrs. Hardward obtained the gun in Vietnam, the probability of her bringing it with her to the US is highly likely."

"And if she came by boat and was carrying something valuable, she needed it in case of pirates," I said.

"While she may have dodged bad guys at sea, it appears increasingly likely that she was unable to do so here on dry land," he said.

"Why do you think your FBI pal didn't come right out and ask you point-blank about the Hardwards when he brought up the memo about the other three killings?"

"I asked myself that very question," Orville said. "My theory is it is because he lacks field experience. He interacts with machines, not humans, and is so data-focused, it blinds him to conjecture. Or as Sheriff Warbler would say, he doesn't know how to go with his gut."

"Turning to the Hardwards' marriage, what did you learn from the LDS bishop?" I said.

"He officiated the wedding ceremony himself. It was not a formal temple sealing, which is reserved for couples who must be deemed worthy by the church. It was a civil ceremony."

"What's the difference?"

"A sealing is considered for eternity while a civil ceremony is until death do us part," Orville said.

"Does that mean the church didn't consider Mrs. Hardward a true Mormon?"

"The bishop explained he'd never met Mrs. Hardward before and Mr. Hardward was not an active member of the ward."

I asked Orville if the church had orchestrated the couple meeting.

The chief deputy shook his head. "He said the local temple did not, but he was aware of arranged marriages between LDS men and foreign-born women elsewhere. This was a first for his ward and, to his knowledge, the stake. That is a region of wards much like a diocese is to Catholics."

"Does the church have an official role brokering marriages or supporting brokers?" I said.

"The bishop claimed it does not. He said marriage is a personal choice."

"Did you ask him how the couple met?"

"Mr. Hardward told him it was through his sister who lives in Utah," he said. "She knew a man at her temple who'd married a woman from Vietnam who had an unwed cousin. The two cousins connected, letters and pictures were exchanged between Mr. Hardward and the unwed cousin, and the couple agreed to marry."

I thought of the empty desk drawers, the heap of ashes in the incinerator, the only evidence of any letter a burnt scrap of one written in Vietnamese.

"We need to get hold of this cousin of Mrs. Hardward's and see what she knows," I said.

"It is on my to-do list. So far I have been unable to contact Mr. Hardward's sister to notify her of his death. Her phone goes unanswered and the local police have gotten no response when they knocked on the door to make the death notification in person. Once I do reach her, I will get the cousin's name and telephone number," Orville said.

"How long ago did the Hardwards marry?"

"The bishop said he performed the ceremony February before last."

"Did he know when Mrs. Hardward arrived in the States?" I said.

"He did not, nor did he ask her."

"The cousin must know. How did Mrs. Hardward get to Burns?"

Orville said the bishop told him she came by Greyhound. "The only people in attendance at the wedding were the couple, the bishop, and his secretary and a janitor who served as witnesses. There was no reception and Mr. and Mrs. Hardward left right after the ceremony."

"Sounds like a hurry-up wedding, but they would've needed to obtain a marriage license and sign it in front of the bishop," I said. "When Gemma and I got married, we had to go to the courthouse, provide ID to get the license, and then there was a mandatory three-day waiting period before we could wed. Longest three days of our lives, especially seeing Gemma was pregnant and about to give birth to Hattie."

"It was a beautiful ceremony, sir," Orville said quickly.

"Did the Hardwards show the bishop a license?" I said.

"He said they did. It was properly filled out, they signed it after the ceremony, and, as the officiant, it was his duty to submit it to the county clerk, which he says he did."

"Did you go by the clerk's office and ask to take a look at it?"

"Not yet," Orville said. "I had to rush back here for my call with my FBI contact."

"Have Jazz check it out. The more she gets to know the folks at the courthouse, the better. Also have her ask the clerk about the timing of the license. Was Mrs. Hardward there to sign it? Did she show any ID? That sort of thing."

"Jazz will appreciate having a more active role in the investigation. Her ambition is to—"

"Yeah, I know what Jazz wants. She doesn't make it a secret. I said it before, I'll say it again. She's not ready for active field duty."

"I concur," Orville said.

"Did the bishop remember Mrs. Hardward's maiden name? He had to have seen it on the license, say it while asking them their will-you-takes and hear it when they said their I-dos."

"The bishop scratched his head when I asked him since it was almost two years ago, and though he conceded he was not one hundred percent sure, he believed it was Kim Nguyen."

"Kim, huh?" I said. "And Nguyen? That's the most common Vietnamese last name there is."

"It definitely suggests an alias," Orville said.

"And one with forged paperwork to back it up for the marriage license." I rubbed my jaw. "You know, when Pudge complained about all the paperwork that goes with this job, I always thought he meant the piles on his desk. Now I realize he also meant all the paper trails you have to chase."

"Correct. I will track down who Kim Nguyen Hardward really was."

Orville then asked what the next steps were for dealing with Red Caldera.

"We got thirty-six hours before he has to be arraigned," I said.

"But you will have to inform District Attorney Sessions you arrested him," he said.

"I know, but the way I read the law, I don't have to immediately. Once I tell Sessions, he'll do everything he can to screw things up. Likewise Judge Manton. They don't want me solving this while the recall petition is still circulating."

"But you will have to tell him before the thirty-six hours are up since he will have to draw up the formal charges. The longer you wait, the more ammunition it gives him."

My reply was a yawn I couldn't stifle.

"Is that an editorial comment or ..." Orville squinted at me. "How long has it been since you last slept?"

I yawned again. "I dozed off for a few minutes after everyone left last night and before Loq showed up and we went to track the killer."

"That is an insufficient amount of time even for me. Because both of the cells upstairs are occupied, it is not feasible for you to take a nap in one of them like Sheriff Warbler often did. May I suggest you go home. The squad can certainly cover whatever might come up."

"Squad, huh? Now you're saying it too."

"It is more precise definition-wise," Orville said. "A squad is smaller in size than a team and more specialized."

"Like a squad to a platoon to a company to a battalion, yeah, I know."

I yawned again. "Look, I need to call Bonnie LaRue, and I'm still waiting to hear from Gemma what she found out from the DEA about pentobarbital and if we can link it to Caldera. Also, if his fingerprints have shown up inside the Hardward house or anywhere else. And then there are the phone records that need—"

Orville karate-chopped the air between us. "The squad is working on all of those things. As soon as we hear, we will let you know. Now, go get some sleep."

"Fair enough. I'll make my call and then head home."

"Excellent. I will hold down the fort in your absence."

I picked up the phone and listened to the dial tone while

thinking about what I was going to say. Finally, I dialed. The receptionist at the *Burns Herald* put me straight through to Bonnie LaRue.

"I thought we had a deal," she fumed. "You promised."

"It was always my intent to tell you and Sessions at the same time. I had nothing to do with his grandstanding," I said.

"So I learned when he called me five minutes before his performance and told me I'd better rush a reporter and photographer to the courthouse. He certainly made a convincing argument about your fitness being sheriff."

"I don't regret not telling him. Look how it turned out? Thanks to him, everyone knows the Hardwards were murdered."

"Are you saying the killer was a local?" she said.

"Nice try, but I'm not ready to divulge what I may or may not know about suspects or motives."

"You know you're not making this any easier on yourself," Bonnie said.

"Like I said before, my only concern is keeping people safe and solving the crime."

The newspaperwoman sighed. "Still going with the Gary Cooper lines. Well, they won't save your job, Nick. While I appreciate you trying to apologize, I certainly don't accept it."

"Not apologizing, only explaining."

"Then let me explain something to you." The newswoman huffed. "I have a cub reporter sitting outside the county clerk's office every minute of every day it's open for business. She'll know the very second the recall petition reaches the threshold number of signatures and is submitted. When that happens, I'll run a special edition that's already typeset. The front page has a screaming headline so big even the blind will be able to read it!"

The dial tone was even louder than before as she slammed the phone down. I'd no sooner cradled mine when it rang.

"What?" I said.

"Oh, sorry, Sheriff," Jazz said. "Am I interrupting something?"

"No, what is it?"

"I have Officer Mantioc on the line. Should I patch her through or tell her you'll call her back?"

"Put her on."

"I have some intel for you," was how Bina said hello.

"And I have some for you too," I said.

"What is it?"

"Not on the phone. There's a spot along the Silvies River south of town. Park in the pullout. Meet you there in ten."

I got to the river before Bina did. It felt good to be out of the office, out of my rig, to stand alongside a river I knew well, a river that began as snowmelt on the Aldrich Mountains a hundred miles north, meandered through valleys and across the Harney Basin, and split into two forks that both emptied into Malheur Lake.

I'd hiked and ridden Wovoka alongside its banks, paddled my canoe up and down it, and watched countless migratory birds follow it north to their breeding grounds in spring and south for the winter.

Flocks of violet-green swallows were now zooming low over the water, feeding on clouds of insects. I faced the sun and closed my eyes and let the call of the iridescent birds mix with the burbling of the river whose blue water reflected the sky. It slowly worked its magic and before long the tension and exhaustion from the past couple of days loosened and floated away with the current.

The *chee-chees* from the swallows and the murmurs from the river soon became words.

"You look at peace," a woman's voice said.

"I am," I said.

"How come?"

"Because I'm outdoors and surrounded by nature."

"Do you think murder can't happen here?"

"Not today it won't."

"Think again, *Trung si* Drake."

My eyes snapped open at the Vietnamese word for sergeant, my rank in 'Nam.

A car door shut. Bina Mantioc made her way down the path from the pullout.

"Are you okay?" she said. "You look like—"

"I've seen a ghost? I didn't, only spoke with one. A spirit, that is. Talking Woman."

Bina tilted her head. "Again? Loq told me about the booby-trapped sardine can."

"It was the same voice. She spoke in English and Vietnamese."

"What did she say?"

"Don't relax. There's going to be another murder." I told Bina what Orville had learned from his contact at the FBI.

"There already has been," Bina said.

"Another killing? Where?"

"A tribal alert was faxed to my office a little while ago. The murder wasn't here in Harney, but Douglas County. At a gas station off the interstate in Canyonville. It's run by the Cow Creek Band of the Umpqua Tribe."

Bina laid it out: Two cars pulled in, minutes apart. The attendant was pumping gas for the first when the shouting started—driver one screaming across the island at driver two. The second man threw a word back, and that was the fuse. The first driver got out and charged with a throat full of rage. The second man pointed a gun, fired once, and sped off.

"How does that link to the other killings?" I said.

"The gas jockey described both men as Chinese and speaking the same foreign language. However, the name on the dead man's driver's license is Vietnamese," she said. "State police confirmed it. He recently got his citizenship."

"Could the attendant recall any of the words?"

"The only one he recognized was 'comrade.' The victim called the shooter that a couple of times."

"Comrade?"

"That's what he said. He's pretty shaken up."

I asked her if the gas station was part of a reservation.

"Not an officially recognized one," she said. "The government terminated the Cow Creek Band's status back in 1954 like they did Loq's people. They've been fighting ever since to be reinstated. The tribal council gets the fax alerts and sent this one out."

"Was the shooter passing himself off as Cow Creek and staying there?"

She shook her head. "It sounds more like two people in the wrong place at the wrong time and they recognized each other. The pump jockey was able to give a description of the vehicle the shooter was driving."

"He'll have already dumped that by now and stolen another," I said. "You know Loq is at Fort McDermitt right now where we think the killer last stayed."

"Yes, he told me he was going," she said.

"Fort McDermitt to Canyonville is a long drive. Over four hundred miles at least. I believe the killer is heading back north. Probably to Portland because it has a sizable Vietnamese community."

"Okay, I'll alert my boss. Chief Tahamtaham will reach out to his tribal police counterparts at the reservations near Portland. That way they'll all be on the lookout in case someone shows up pretending to be an Indian and looking for a free place to stay."

"Thanks. I need all the help I can get. Along with the Hardward killings, I got my hands filled convincing the guy I just put in jail to tell me who else is part of the scheme to swindle the couple out of their livestock. It's a gang of some kind and I'm sure they've been doing it elsewhere."

"Kwalanawa," Bina said.

"What's that mean?" I said.

"It's Sahaptin for good luck."

"Back at you in English, Numu, and Vietnamese. We need all we can get."

15

———

By late afternoon the air had grown so hot it felt as if all of Harney County was a cast-iron Dutch oven with the lid clamped on tight. The only thing moving on the Hardward ranch was a plague of grasshoppers devouring whatever was left of the withered hayfields. The din of their snapping as they flew and rubbing their hind legs to scare off intruders made my fillings ache.

Not even nighttime would cool things down. Not even a wind blowing down from the high summits of the Cascades to the west or the Blue Mountains to the north. Harney was high desert, but it could also be a hot desert, a hard desert, and nothing was harder than the way the Hardwards had died in it.

When I first got there, I went inside the house to double-check the phone on the desk. It was still dead and the telephone cord leading to the terminal screwed into the wall hadn't been cut. I went outside and found the exterior terminal box. A cord led from it up the wall held in place by thick staples. I studied it closely and nearly missed it. Four feet up the wall the cord had been sliced clean through, the two cut ends moved back to be right in line. Maybe the phone company would know when the phone line went dead.

I started walking around the beleaguered ranch, but soon gave up trying to stick to the slender shadows created by the house and barn as I looked for something, anything, that could help me figure out why a man had ridden a motorcycle in the dead of night, knocked on the couple's door, sat at the kitchen table with them drinking yellow lotus tea and eating *banh pia*, and then shot them both in the head.

Questions swirled like the grasshoppers jumping around my boots. Who was he? Why was he killing Vietnamese refugees? Was it for something valuable they possessed or out of revenge? Or was he silencing people with secrets too dangerous to escape their lips?

Mrs. Hardward, or Kim Nguyen, or whatever her real name was, had left behind only a few clothes in the closet and the unfinished *Chim Lac* needlepoint. It wasn't much to show for having lived on the ranch for nearly two years. Where was anything personal, like letters or snapshots traded with the cousin who'd helped her find an American husband?

Were there none to begin with, or had everything been dumped in the fifty-five-gallon drum and turned to ash save for the one telltale scrap? Had she destroyed them after being warned someone was looking for her? Or did the killer do it to erase any way to trace her identity?

That begged more questions. If she knew a hunter was coming for her, then why didn't she use the .38 the moment he arrived? Why hadn't she shot him before he could shoot her?

The unknowns kept swirling. So did the grasshoppers. The sun was too bright. The air too hot. The answers too few. I knew all that, the same as I also knew the likelihood of Mrs. Hardward having a box filled with mementos to remind herself who she was, where she came from, and who she loved would rank extremely high on Chief Deputy Orville Nelson's favorite theorem.

My mother had such a treasure box. It was the one thing she never forgot, no matter how many times the Army moved us during my father's career. The box was an old tin Whitman's candy sampler. She kept it in the bottom dresser drawer beneath her sweaters.

I opened it once, hoping I'd find a chocolate peanut cluster. Instead I found a bundle of letters stuffed back in their envelopes and tied with a red string. I read the top one. My father had written it to her while stationed somewhere far away. I'd never heard him speak like the way he wrote. I only read the one and, stinging from shame, quickly put it back in its envelope and retied the red string.

The box also held an antique cameo brooch and a heart-shaped locket on a gold chain. I opened it. Photos of a man and woman stared back. I guessed they were my mother's parents, but I couldn't be sure. I'd never met them. My mother and father had eloped when they were teenagers and she was never welcomed back home.

In another envelope was a black-and-white snapshot of an infant. Written on the back in faded ink was the name Lizzie Drake and two sets of dates less than a year apart. Her birth was five months after my parents ran off. It was the first I ever knew I had an older sister. I closed the tin candy box and put it back in the drawer. I never told my mother I'd opened it, and if she discovered I had, she never mentioned it.

Mrs. Hardward's treasure box would be big enough to hold the .38 Special because she would've wanted to keep it hidden from her husband. But where? Not inside the house. He could've found it. Not in the barn. That was his domain. The hiding place had to be outside.

The heat was wearing me down and so was lack of sleep. I

was about to give up when I heard a neigh. The saddle horse was brown and so was the skin of its rider.

"Good afternoon, Manny," I said.

"You come back," the Big D's hired hand said.

"You speak English."

"A little."

"But not around Mr. Dillard."

"No."

"How come?"

"If he know I speak it, then he won't say things around me he don't want me to know." Manny Hernandez grinned. A couple of teeth were missing.

I asked him if he'd heard what happened to the Hardwards.

His head bowed. "Señor Dillard told me banditos kill them. *Muy triste*. Very sad."

"You used to do some work for them, right?"

"*Sí*. They need something, I do it."

"They pay you?"

"No, I do it for *la señora*. She very nice. Don' speak English so good like me. She give me *pan dulce*."

"What's that?"

"Little cake. Very sweet."

"*Banh pia*," I said.

"*Sí*. What *la señora* call it."

"Did she talk about where she came from, what it was like, what she did there, why she left?"

"A little. But then she grow very sad."

"*Muy triste*," I said.

"Now you speak Spanish." He grinned again.

"Why was she sad?"

"*La guerra*. The war. Many people killed. Her family also."

"She told you that? Husband and children?"

Manny nodded. "It make *la señora* be *una soldado*. A soldier. She very brave."

"When did she tell you she fought in the war?" I said.

"Last spring. I bring seeds and hear shooting. Bam! Bam! Bam! I think something bad happen. Maybe puma. Maybe banditos. I ride here fast."

Manny mimed whipping his horse. "It was *la señora*. She shooting *pistola* at can. Hit every time. Bam! Bam! Bam! Never miss."

"What did she say when you arrived?"

"Señor Hardward gone so she practice. You know, so when she need to shoot something she not miss. I tell her she good shot. She say she learned in Vietnam. How I find out she *una soldado*. She told me story. Then she said our secret. Thank me for bringing seeds."

"Seeds?" I said.

"*Sí.* For the garden. She plant flowers, vegetables. Rose, daisy. Tomato, squash. *La señora*, she have, how you say? Green thumb."

"The only plant I saw was the yellow lotus she was growing in a tub out front of the kitchen window. But all the water dried up and it died. I don't see a garden anywhere."

"Because now summer. Too hot. No *agua*. Vegetables all eaten. Flowers all inside for *el florero*. Vase, you say. *Girasol* only flower left. *La señora* like it very much."

"*Girasol*?"

"*Sí.* Flower like *el sol*." He pointed at the sun. "*La señora*, she like because yellow same as flag back home. Same as flower growing in tub. How you call it, lotus? She miss it, I think. Home."

"And you brought her sunflower seeds. *Girasol*."

"*Sí.* Señor Dillard, his wife also like flower. Many, many type.

She dead now, but he still grow them. I think to remember her. You know?"

"I do."

"Okay. I go. Back to work. *Adiós.*"

"Thanks, Manny. *Adiós.*"

I watched him ride off and then grabbed a shovel from my pickup and went looking for sunflowers.

A row had been planted along a sagging fence beyond the barn. Their stalks and leaves were brown and dried out. The big, round flower heads bowed as if mourning the death of the woman who'd given them life. Birds had pecked out the seeds and empty shells littered the ground.

There were nine sunflowers. Nine was a lucky number in Vietnam. It symbolized eternity. Six was a lucky number too. It represented good fortune. Four was an unlucky number. It was associated with death.

I didn't question where to start digging and jammed the shovel's blade into the ground in front of the fourth sunflower. Scoop, lift, dump, repeat. A bag came up. It was black and made of waterproofed canvas. Two snaps held down a flap. I unsnapped them and exposed a zipper. It sounded like a grasshopper rubbing its hind legs when I tugged it open.

Emptying the bag, I thought of my mother's Whitman sampler treasure box again. Out came a bundle of letters, papers, and photographs wrapped in oilcloth. I thumbed through the top ones. The letters were written in Vietnamese. An ID document was too. The name typed under a black-and-white headshot of a woman was Dao Pham. Although I'd only seen her when she was lying bloated on the floor and again on Doc's steel exam table with the gutters and drain, I recognized a younger Mrs. Hardward.

Another photograph was of her too. She had a shy smile and was holding an infant in her arms standing close to a man who was holding the hands of two young children. Another photo showed her standing at attention with other men and women dressed in dark uniforms and clutching Soviet-made Kalashnikov AK-47s. She was no longer smiling.

No brooch or locket with pictures was in the bag. No keepsakes passed down through the generations. No cheap souvenirs from a holiday. There was only a cardboard ammo box holding twenty-five rounds of .38 Special.

Putting everything back in the bag, I set it to the side and filled in the hole, tamping down the top layer with the flat side of the shovel. Instead of feeling like I was burying the past, I felt like I was freeing the present.

I carried the shovel and bag to my pickup and thought about who I could ask to translate the letters and the information on the ID document. The radio squawked.

"Nick, you there?" Gemma said. "Over."

"What's up?" I answered.

"Oh, good. I caught you. Where are you?"

"Hardward ranch. I was just leaving. Where are you?"

"At the Dulac ranch up past Williams Reservoir. Some of their cattle died unexpectedly during the night. I think they've been poisoned the same as the Hardward stock."

"Has Red Caldera been there recently?" I said.

"A couple of times in the past few weeks," she said. "The Dulacs say they kept trying to give him the brush-off. When their cows died, they called the Department of Ag who alerted me. I flew up, collected samples, and now I'm going to fly them to the lab in Corvallis. I'll have to spend the night waiting for the results."

"No problem," I said. "I'll head home now."

"You'll need to pick up Johnny at Blackpowder Smith's."

"But I won't be there for an hour."

"That's okay. Johnny said they're doing inventory. He doesn't mind working late."

"You mean, he doesn't mind the overtime Blackpowder will pay him."

"Our little entrepreneur. Already saving for college," Gemma said.

I left the dead and drooping sunflowers in the rearview mirror and navigated the potholed road, the waterproofed canvas bag of memories riding on the seat beside me. I briefly considered then rejected the notion of stopping off at the office. Logging the bag and its contents as evidence would take too long; I didn't want to keep Johnny waiting.

Once I hit the two-lane, I steered south to No Mountain. The sun was still baking the sea of sage scrub, triggering hot air to rise. A kettle of turkey vultures soon appeared, swirling in the updraft of hot air. The convection also created cumulus clouds, which cast shadows on the ground. That prompted a herd of pronghorn to race toward them seeking relief from the heat.

I passed the cutoff to the Warbler ranch and slowed when the two-lane became No Mountain's Main Street. Some of the false-fronted buildings that lined both sides of the one-blink stretch sported fresh paint and new windows. A couple had been completely rebuilt. The restoration was a reminder of a bombing and deadly shootout that occurred less than a year before and led me to becoming sheriff.

I pulled to a stop in front of Blackpowder Smith's combination dry goods store and saloon. Its front windows had also been replaced, but the blinds were uncharacteristically lowered and the "Open" sign unlit.

Figuring Blackpowder and Johnny didn't want any interruptions while taking inventory, I tried the front door. It was locked. I gave it a couple of raps.

"Hey, Johnny, it's Dad. Mom's working late. I'm your ride. Come on, open up."

Nothing.

I pictured my son back in the storeroom and the old codger snoozing in the bar. I knocked even louder.

"Wake up, Blackpowder! It's Nick."

The door finally opened. Johnny looked straight at me with a dazed expression. That's when I saw Blackpowder off to the side. He was slumped in a chair. By the time I realized not all the white on his face was his billy goat beard but a dishrag shoved in his mouth, the barrel of a pistol appeared over Johnny's shoulder.

A young woman was holding it, a woman with streaked dark hair. Only the streaks weren't from the sun or Lady Clairol. They were natural and golden blond, almost yellow. Yellow like sunflowers. Yellow like lotuses. The stories Johnny had told me about his time living on the streets of Saigon and being forced to join the VC as a child soldier started to roar.

"You're the girl with yellow hair," I said. "The *bui doi* who saved Johnny's life on the streets and again in the jungle. You're Sen Vang. Yellow Lotus."

"And you're the GI who killed so many of us," she said.

16

"Sorry, young fella," Blackpowder said when he finally spat out the gag. "The witch got the drop on me when I was behind the bar pouring my usual. Looked up and saw her fixing to plug me."

The crusty saloonkeeper snorted. "Either she rode in on a broom or has cat feet 'cause my floorboards made nary a creak."

I was sitting in a chair next to him with my wrists bound behind me too. Only mine weren't tied by a rope like his, but my own handcuffs locked tight by my own son. Johnny had also relieved me of my .45.

"For your own good," he said.

Sen Vang observed Blackpowder and me wordlessly. She hadn't lowered her pistol. It was a Makarov, but I wasn't ready to tell her everything I knew about such a gun.

As Blackpowder pattered on about how he didn't blame Johnny for doing what she'd forced him to, images of every story my son told me about his life in Vietnam began running like a Super 8 home movie.

It opened with his mother being stabbed to death in a whorehouse on Tu Do Street and a GI with a tiger tattoo bursting in from the cubicle next door and shooting the pimp who killed her. Then the other prostitutes began yelling at Johnny to run lest he be blamed. How an older *bui doi* girl with yellow hair and two boys found him crying in a doorway and adopted him into their ersatz family, teaching him how to survive on the streets.

Then there was a scene involving a crooked policeman and a street vendor selling *banh pia* who kidnapped the girl with yellow hair and locked her in a storeroom intent on raping her. A few nights later the crooked policeman caught Johnny and dragged him to a place called the field of dead dogs to silence him. Before the cop could fire his pistol, a guerrilla popped up out of nowhere and shot him. He took Johnny to a VC camp in the jungle where he was reunited with the girl with yellow hair.

The camp was commanded by a ruthless guerrilla called Comrade Minh. He thrust his pistol into Johnny's hands and ordered him to execute a prisoner tied to a stake to prove he wasn't a spy. When Johnny faltered, the girl with yellow hair put her hands around the boy's, placed her finger over his, and squeezed the trigger. The prisoner slumped. Johnny was accepted.

Harrowing scenes of gun battles and close calls followed, including one of the girl and Johnny being chased by a squad of GIs and hiding in a pond among yellow lotuses, how she earned her nom de guerre.

Another was the time they were discovered at an American air base while opening the gates for Comrade Minh and the other guerrillas who were armed with explosives. As sentries pursued the pair, the older and faster Sen Vang told Johnny to run up the ramp of a parked cargo plane and hide while she led the guards away. Johnny fell asleep, the cargo plane took off, and he woke up in the States.

The scenes switched to an Oregon orphanage and then to

the Warbler ranch and Johnny constantly struggling to adjust to life in America. Troubles at home. Troubles at school. Gemma and I trying everything to help him. It wasn't until I promised to take him back to Vietnam to search for the girl with yellow hair that he finally began to settle down.

That's when I learned the inherent problem with promises: Keeping them was always harder than making them. The war ended but the US refused to recognize Vietnam. Americans were forbidden from traveling there. But a promise was a promise and Johnny never forgot I'd made it. Nor did I. It was only a matter of biding time until I could fulfill it.

Now that time had come and in my own backyard.

I opened my eyes and locked them on Sen Vang's. "How did you find Johnny?"

She looked over the Makarov at me. "I never lost him."

The tribal alert from the Agua Caliente was right. She did speak English with a French accent.

"How did you know where he was?"

Her smile was thin. "The same way my country won the war. Our spies are everywhere."

"But you never reached out to Johnny to let him know you were alive," I said. "He worried about you."

"Don't play the sentimental card, *Trung si* Drake. It won't work."

There it was again. Sergeant. It was like Bina Mantioc had said: Nobody in law enforcement believed in coincidences, not even when they occurred in the spirit world.

"That's a 9x18mm Makarov," I said. "The same caliber used to shoot Mrs. Hardward and her husband at their ranch up the road." I gave it a couple of beats. "Or should I say, Dao Pham."

That spurred a blink, but not a word.

"I found her ID card. Letters and photos too. You're in one of them. Dressed in the same black outfit as her and clutching a Kalashnikov."

Sen Vang still had nothing to say.

"You know the FBI's going to match the slug from Dao Pham to the ones taken out of the other refugees your so-called crazy cousin killed while he passed himself off as an American Indian and hid out on reservations. Orange County. Dallas. Seattle. A man in Canyonville last night."

That got another blink. A big one.

"You didn't know about Canyonville, did you?" I said.

Though she didn't say a word, her expression did.

"You're not here to hurt Johnny," I said. "You're here to protect him from the man who's doing all the killing. The war between our countries has been over for five years. I've been home for ten. You and me, we're not enemies. We can work together to catch him and protect Johnny and anyone else on his hit list."

Her lips tightened to keep from saying yes or no.

Sen Vang was clearly of mixed race—her taller-than-average height for a Vietnamese woman, the blond streaks, the light olive complexion—but I knew from my own three tours that Vietnam was hardly homogeneous. The majority of the population were Kihn, aka Viet, but another fifty or so distinct ethnic groups were also native. I'd met a few during my time in the Central Highlands.

I looked at Sen Vang, took in her clothes, her hair, a copper bracelet on each wrist, and then closed my eyes. Another movie started to play.

The *thwap-thwap-thwap* of a helicopter filled my ears. The gunner manning the .50 caliber in the open bay yelling, "Clear!" The pilot's staticky voice in the speaker saying, "Thirty seconds to LZ. Twenty-nine, twenty-eight ..."

I twirled my finger. "Lock and load, Corporal."

"Roger that, Sarge," he yelled back. "Step lively, boys!"

The bird had barely set down when my squad hit the ground like we'd done a hundred times before and took up positions to provide it cover as it lifted off. We watched it go and then looked around for our local assets.

Two men suddenly appeared in front of me. They'd stepped out of the bush so quietly, not even a blade of grass whispered as it bent nor did a single cicada interrupt its trilling. The men were barefoot and wore black loincloths and red-and-blue checked headbands and indigo scarves with matching designs draped over their left shoulders. One held a spear, the other a machete. Both wore a copper bracelet etched with a design.

"Stand down," I ordered my squad who were pointing their weapons at the pair. "They're friendlies. Our pathfinders."

As my radioman DJ sized them up, he drawled, "Now I unnerstan' why Green Berets call this part of 'Nam Indian Country. Tonto got nothing on these dudes."

"Sergeant Drake," I said to them and tapped my chest.

The older one tapped his. "Y'Bin." He reached over and tapped the younger man's chest. "Y'Kha."

"Lead the way," I said.

We followed them all day. If there was a trail, it was next to impossible to see it; our pathfinders were that good. Two hours into the trek, Y'Bin signaled us to take cover and freeze. Minutes later a large North Vietnamese Army patrol passed us going in the opposite direction.

Once they were gone, I asked Y'Bin how he knew the NVA patrol was approaching. He pointed to a patch of sky showing above the tree canopy and mimicked a flying bird.

It was nearing sunset when we started up the crest of a hill. Y'Bin signaled us to freeze again. Y'Kha crept ahead. When he reappeared, he flashed teeth. Y'Bin returned the grin and waved us to proceed to the top. He stopped again and motioned at the valley below.

"My home," he said in broken English. "Your home."

It looked as if created by magic. The hillsides surrounding the valley were terraced. Each broad bench was lush and green. I made out rice paddies, rows of vegetables, and orchards ripe with fruit. Gossamer-like waterfalls sparkled. Flocks of colorful birds flew from one side to the other.

Plank-sided lodges built on poles and topped by thatched roofs twice as tall as the buildings dotted the valley floor. They surrounded a huge communal lodge with a massive thatch roof the shape of a giant axe blade that swooped into the sky.

More houses stood across the valley at the edge of the forest. They were encircled by elaborately carved wooden statues. Some depicted pregnant women, others couples in various sexual positions.

"Who lives in those houses?" I asked Y'Bin.

"The dead. They are tombs." He went on to explain in both words and gestures that the village would hold a big ceremony and play gongs and dance for days after a person died. Then they'd leave the tomb house to be reclaimed by the forest so the dead's spirit could be released.

Y'Bin led us down to the village. Women, men, and children came out to greet us. Like our two pathfinders, most of the adults wore copper bracelets. Y'Bin explained a Jarai woman would make a bracelet and present it to the man she wished to marry. If he accepted, they would both wear bracelets.

My memories of the Jarai village faded to black. I opened my eyes and locked them on Sen Vang's.

"If I tell you truths about you and your homeland, will you work with me to catch the killer?"

"We'll see," she said.

"Fair enough. You're not from Saigon or any city. You're from the Central Highlands. More specifically, Gia Lai Province."

Sen Vang blinked.

I nodded at her wrists. "Your copper bracelets are Jarai. You were wearing them in the photo with Dao Pham. Your mother's Jarai. Your father's French. Those are their marriage bracelets. Your people are matrilineal, like the Northern Paiute who live here, the Shoshone too."

Sparks flew from her eyes.

"Shall I go on?" I didn't wait for an answer. "Since the French ended combat in Vietnam in the early '50s, your father was a Legionnaire who decided not to return to France because he'd fallen in love with your mother."

"He was not a soldier," she said quickly. "My father was a professor at the Sorbonne. He came to our village after the French quit the war to research a book on the Jarai. He met my mother and stayed."

"Okay, one wrong for me to go along with all I got right. The other Indigenous groups who live in the Central Highlands call the Jarai 'mystics' because of two very powerful shamans, the King of Fire and King of Water."

"*Potaopui* and *Potaoia*," she said automatically.

"The Jarai's fierce protection of their homeland earned them a reputation among NVA and US forces alike as 'Mystic Warriors.' I saw it personally. I lived with the Jarai for a spell, served with them. They taught me about your culture, beliefs, history. Your people opposed the North and sided with the US because the communists threatened your traditional way of life and wanted to control the Central Highlands for war purposes."

Memories filled her eyes with tears.

"What happened to your village?" I said even though I could guess. "Why are you wearing both your parents' bracelets?"

"The NVA came to punish us," she said softly. "They burned

our village to the ground. My mother and father, they gave me these to remember them by."

"Because they were sending you away to safety."

"My aunt took me by the hand when the village was in flames and we ran into the forest. We ran for days, weeks. She was bitten by a krait."

I shuddered reflexively, remembering the name from my own time in country. The Malayan krait was the deadliest snake in Vietnam, even more poisonous than a king cobra. When cherries arrived, their platoon leaders would instruct them to avoid kraits at all costs, telling them not only was there no antivenom, but if bitten, self-administering a bullet to the head would be a less painful death.

"My aunt suffered terribly," Sen Vang said. "She begged me to leave her, but I stayed by her side until she died so I could sing for her spirit to be released. Then I started walking again. I didn't know where I was going, don't know how long I walked. One day a farmer pulling a wagon gave me a ride. When we reached the outskirts of Saigon, he told me to get off and I ..."

Her voice drifted like a dying echo.

"Learned how to survive," I said. "You taught Johnny and the two other *bui doi* boys how to as well. You kept on surviving even when you escaped the *banh pia* vendor's storeroom where he and the policeman did unspeakable things to you. Even after you fled Saigon and were conscripted by Comrade Minh and forced to fight for the VC, your village's mortal enemy."

Sen Vang grimaced and closed her eyes.

"You're a survivor," I said. "And you're still helping others survive. Let me help you. Let's save the people being targeted. Let's stop the killer from killing again. Together."

"Why do you care about me, about them?" she said. "Why would you help us? Is it because it's your job, *Trung si* Drake?"

"Partly, but mostly because of Johnny. I owe you. You saved him. In Saigon. In the jungle. Over and over again. Because of you, I have a son. A son I'll do anything for. Whatever it takes. No matter the cost. And I mean *any* cost."

17

———

I finally took off my boots, stood in the living room, and began stretching, trying to touch the beamed ceiling, trying to work out the crick in my back and the soreness in my shoulders. The aches were the good kind, the kind that comes from doing hard physical labor that clears the mind of runaway thoughts and makes focusing easier. But what had driven me to it was the worst kind of thought: Evil—merciless, soulless evil—had come to Harney County.

It had been three hours since I drove Johnny home from Blackpowder's. He'd gotten lost between two lives, the one he had in Vietnam with Sen Vang and the one he had in No Mountain with Gemma, Hattie, November, and me. He was so agitated on the drive, I thought he'd open the door of the pickup and jump out.

His confusion had spiked when I asked Sen Vang if she'd been whipped by a cat-o'-nine-tails. Her head dipped for a brief moment.

"I'll take that as a yes," I said. "Since my son's back doesn't bear whip scars, you must've gotten yours after the raid at the American air base went awry. Johnny escaped, but you didn't.

You got away from the sentries, but you didn't escape Comrade Minh's wrath, did you?"

She stuck out her chin. "You're guessing."

"No, I'm not. Dao Pham had cat-o'-nine-tails scars on her back."

While Sen Vang's lips didn't move, Talking Woman's voice rang in my ears: "If you think evil won't come to Harney County, *Trung si* Drake, think again. It already did and it'll keep coming back."

"It's Comrade Minh," I said. "Tell me I'm wrong, Sen Vang. Tell me he isn't the so-called cousin you're hunting. Did you know he knows you're here? He got to the Tulalip Tribes Reservation after you did. They told him you're looking for him."

The girl with yellow hair's grip on the Makarov tightened.

"Why's he here? Are the other victims like Dao Pham, they all served in his band of guerrillas? Did they wrong him or is he trying to keep them from talking or does one of them have something he wants? Something valuable."

Before Sen Vang could reply, Johnny started babbling in a mix of Vietnamese and American slang he'd learned earning tip money from running errands for GIs on leave in Saigon.

Jabbing his finger at Blackpowder and me, he started shouting, "*Durng tin ho, Sen Vang. Durng ti ho.* Don't trust them. They're the enemy."

"No, they're not," Sen Vang said and then switched to Vietnamese, speaking to him in a soft, soothing voice. Though I didn't know the meaning of her words, I could tell she was reassuring him more than I'd be able to.

Johnny sobbed and buried his face in her shoulder. As she patted his back, her eyes found mine. "Yes," they said. "It's Minh."

It took some more convincing, but Sen Vang finally released Blackpowder and me from our bonds.

"Tell me everything about him," I said. "Tell me why he's doing this."

"Not tonight," she said, nodding at Johnny. "It is too much to tell and too much to hear. The hour grows late. We all need sleep."

"Tomorrow then," I said.

When she agreed, I told her it would be a mistake for her to come home with Johnny and me.

"Why can't she?" Johnny said.

"It'd be dangerous for her," I said. "Too many people come and go at the ranch. Hattie's friends dropping by. Lyle Rides Alone bringing her home from work. Ranchers who need your mom's help. Even my deputies. We don't want someone seeing Sen Vang and telling others about her."

"Your father's right," she said.

"The lady's more than welcome to stay here in the bunk room," Blackpowder said. He meant the converted storeroom in the back used by customers too drunk to drive home. "I'll sit out here with my sawed-off and keep watch. Always sleep with one eye open anyway."

"Thanks," I said, "but Sen Vang needs a place where she can come and go without being noticed. Your saloon's the heart of town."

"Indeed it is, young fella. The ninety-proof lifeblood of it." He cackled and went to help himself to another whiskey.

I told Sen Vang about the old lineman's shack. "It's where I first lived when I came to Harney County and used it as my office before being elected sheriff. It's got a bunk, kitchen, and a bathroom. Best of all, it's at the edge of No Mountain and has no neighbors. What do you say?"

"Maybe," she said.

"Blackpowder can set you up with some food from his store

here. I didn't see a car parked out front, but I'm assuming you stashed wheels somewhere."

Sen Vang nodded.

I knew better than to ask her the make and model or even color. I scribbled down my home phone number.

"Take this. The shack's got a phone. Call me in the morning."

Johnny didn't want to let go of Sen Vang. "When will I see you again?" he said.

"Soon. Now go with your father and don't worry about Comrade Minh."

Once we were back home, Johnny began to shiver. It soon became shakes. I didn't have to explain anything to November as she watched him. Either she'd seen what had happened at Blackpowder's in dreamworld or she could read it in Johnny's face and mine.

"You need supper," she said in an uncharacteristically soft voice. "Go wash your hands and then come and sit. I will bring you a plate."

Johnny did as he was told.

"Where's Hattie?" I said to the old healer.

"She already ate and is in her room reading."

"I got to make a quick call. I'll be back in a sec."

I went to the office and closed the door behind me. In addition to a phone and fax machine, there was a CB and shortwave. I radioed Loq.

"Where are you?" I said.

"On my way to your ranch. I'm about thirty minutes out. We were right about Fort McDermitt. The killer stayed there. Same MO, masquerading as a Native. He was there for a few days and then left a week ago. No sign of the female looking for him."

"That's because she's here in No Mountain. The girl with yellow hair is Johnny's Sen Vang from Vietnam." I quickly filled him in about her and Comrade Minh. "If we're lucky, she took me up on my offer to stay at the old lineman's shack tonight."

"And you want me to babysit her," the Klamath said.

"From a distance. If you try to open the door, she'll fill you full of lead from the Makarov she's packing."

"Mm. You can take the Charlie out of the country, but you can't take the Charlie out of the person."

"That about sums it up," I said.

"It's a warm summer evening and the stars are out. They'll keep me company while I keep an eye on her," he said.

"She goes anywhere, let me know ASAP and tail her."

"And this Comrade Minh, what if he shows up?"

"Unlikely, seeing Canyonville was his last known whereabouts. My guess is he's headed to Portland, but if he does come to the lineman's shack, don't let him get the drop on you."

"I never took a bullet in 'Nam and I don't intend to start now."

Loq signed off and I joined Johnny at the dining table. November was standing behind him making sure he swallowed every bite.

Later, after Hattie came out for dessert and the kids went to bed, November tsked.

"You expect too much of Johnny. He may be on the path to manhood, but he is still a boy who saw his mother killed, fought in a war not of his own making, and is only here because Wolf wanted it so."

"The Numu Creator and Great Spirit is powerful and I trust he'll protect Johnny from the evil that's followed him here," I said.

"All the more reason you need to understand what Johnny is going through and protect him yourself."

"It's what I'm trying to do," I said.

"Then try harder." She harumphed and retreated to the kitchen.

I checked on Johnny. He was fast asleep. Something was different about his room and then I saw what. He'd retrieved the *Chim Lac* and hung it above his bed.

Despite my own exhaustion, I couldn't unwind. Dao Pham, Sen Vang, and a murderous guerrilla leader had air-dropped into my life when I finally thought I was free of Vietnam. Free of the horrors of war. Free of the blood that stained my hands, my conscience, and my soul.

I went out to the corral. Four horses immediately jockeyed for position along the rails for a pat, or even better, an apple. My buckskin stallion whinnied and pawed the ground. His mate—Gemma's sorrel mare Sarah—nickered as did their foal that had grown up to become Hattie's pony. The cutting horse Lyle Rides Alone had given Johnny stomped his front hoof.

"When this is over, we'll all go for a family ride," I said. "You four and us four. We'll take the trail up to the rise and see the view and then canter through the scrub. We'll ride fast and hard and leave all the evil behind. I promise."

Wovoka gave me the side-eye as if to say he'd heard it all before. The truth was, he had. Plenty of times.

I slid open the stable door and clicked on the lights. The stalls were clean and had fresh beds of hay. The floor was swept. Saddles were all placed on their stands, the tack neatly hung, the blankets folded and stored.

Johnny and Hattie had done too good a job with their morning chores; there was nothing for me to do.

I took another look around and spotted a pile of recently delivered one-hundred-pound sacks of feed that was next to a wall of hay four bales high.

"Finally," I said and set to work.

An hour later I'd hoisted and carried them all to the other

side of the stable. Standing back to admire my work, I still wasn't bushed enough to fall asleep. I started in again and moved the feed sacks and bales back to where they'd been. That did the trick. I clicked off the light and returned to the house.

I was doing my stretching when I noticed the creaking of a rocking chair keeping time with humming. November was sitting in the dark watching me.

"You're still awake," I said.

"I have been waiting for you," the old healer said.

"Why?"

"To tell you about Yellow Hair."

"You know she's here?"

"The girl from Johnny's and your green world? Yes, I have seen her."

"Here in No Mountain or up here?" I tapped the side of my head.

"Does it matter?"

"I suppose it doesn't. I think she's Talking Woman."

"Perhaps."

"Then what do you want to tell me about her?"

November harrumphed. "Not her, but Yellow Hair and his bluecoats at Greasy Grass. How he met his death and what happened to Shoots While Running's father and the Lakota girl called Walks on Clouds."

"No disrespect, Girl Born in Snow, but I'm exhausted. I haven't slept for—"

"Better to listen to the story now and learn from it or you might sleep forever."

I sat in Pudge's leather recliner and felt the weariness of the past couple of days lift with each word the old healer spoke as she continued to tell me the tale about Custer's Last Stand.

Same Knife—Walks on Clouds's uncle—eventually allowed her to untie the young Shoshone brave once known as Buffalo

Dreamer and now called Snakehead to tend his wounds to repay her debt to him. But, Same Knife warned, as long as the Lakota were at war with the US Cavalry and their Crow, Arikara, and Eastern Shoshone allies, Snakehead can never be freed.

Walks on Clouds cut his ropes and helped him into the tipi she shared with her newly widowed mother. She made a place for him near the fire and applied bear grease to his burnt scalp, the cuts on the sides of his head where his ears once were, and to the deep slits from the corners of his lips to the center of his cheeks.

The bear grease's healing power worked and the blisters on his scalp hardened into scales and the other wounds turned to scars that made his earless skull and newly widened mouth resemble a spitting serpent's.

One day, Snakehead accompanied Walks on Clouds to the river to fetch water. When he looked down, he jumped as if bitten. He didn't recognize his own hideous reflection. It made him remember the looking glass Summer Moon had given him. He slipped it out of the leather pouch, closed his eyes, and held it up to his face. He thought of her. Then he opened his eyes and saw not the serpent's face, but the Shoshone maiden's who'd been born on the same day as him. He could also see his village alongside the great Snake River and his mother and father.

A couple of days later, people started taking down their tipis and fitting their horses and dogs with travois. He asked Walks on Clouds what was happening. The camp is moving again, she said. The bluecoats are coming. The time for Sitting Bull's vision of the great battle with Yellow Hair is growing closer.

Snakehead helped her strike the tipi, load a travois, and move to a new camp alongside Rosebud Creek. One morning he woke to the din of gunfire, war cries, and the pounding of hoofs. The bluecoats are attacking the camp, Walks on Clouds told him. Crazy Horse and Gall are leading our warriors to defend us.

The battle raged for six hours. Finally, both sides withdrew. The bluecoats retreated to a supply camp fifty miles to the south, which left the Lakota and Cheyenne warriors a chance to regroup.

Everyone in the big camp made ready to move again. Where to now? Snakehead asked Walks on Clouds. To the Greasy Grass River, she replied and explained it was named for the lush, dewy grass lining its banks that made horses' legs and bellies look greasy when they walked through it.

When the pair had raised their tipi at the new encampment, Snakehead went down to the Greasy Grass to collect water. This time when he stared into the river, he saw his reflection as he once looked, his long hair flowing, his eyes shiny, his jaw set. He was on his pony riding into battle beside Lakota and Cheyenne warriors. He could see bluecoats fall from their bullets, arrows, and lances. But then he saw something else.

That night, Snakehead asked Walks on Clouds to take him to Same Knife's tipi so he could tell him what he'd seen. My uncle will never agree to it because he doesn't trust you, she said. Snakehead insisted. I can show him something he needs to see about Sitting Bull's vision and all the tomorrows to come, he said.

Walks on Clouds took him to her uncle's tipi where he was seated in a circle with other war chiefs. Snakehead held the looking glass in front of Same Knife's eyes. Look into it, he said. See the great battle as Sitting Bull himself has seen. See you and your warriors charging the bluecoats, your bullets striking your enemies, your arrows flying fast and true. See the bluecoats fall. See Yellow Hair die. See Crazy Horse and Gall and all the warriors dancing in victory.

Same Knife looked into the looking glass. I can see it, he

said. It is as you describe. It is a great victory for us. Yes, Snakehead, said, but now look into the looking glass again. See that the bluecoats are not finished. They are strong in number and their greed for land and buffalo even stronger. They will keep coming back and there will be more battles.

Then we will fight them again, Same Knife said. We will fight them and we will win until they are no more forever.

Snakehead shook his reptilian-looking head. That will only happen if Lakota are joined by more tribes than Cheyenne and Arapaho, he said. Look into the looking glass and see how much stronger Lakota can be when they fight the bluecoats alongside Paiute, Shoshone, Crow, Arikara, Ojibwe, Oneida, and Apache warriors. See Lakota fighting the bluecoats alongside warriors from all the tribes that share the land between the Great Waters. When we fight as one, we will win, he said. When we fight against our Indian brothers, we will lose.

Same Knife grew angry. You're trying to trick me, he shouted. I knew it. You're a spy. You want me to join with Crow, Arikara, and Shoshone warriors? Never! They are our enemies since time began.

It's not a trick, Snakehead said. We all share the same enemy now, and it's the bluecoats. They are mighty but so are we if we fight as one.

Same Knife threw the looking glass at the rocks encircling the fire, but Snakehead snatched it before it hit and slid it back into the leather pouch. I will show you it's no trick and I'm not a spy, he said. When we go into battle, I will ride in front. If the bullets from my Shoshone father's rifle don't kill bluecoats, then you can kill me. The other war chiefs sitting around the fire started to murmur and then grunted their approval. Finally, Same Knife agreed.

Over the next few days, the encampment grew even bigger as more and more Lakota, Cheyenne, and Arapaho warriors and their families arrived. A Sun Dance ceremony was held and Sitting Bull envisioned the defeat of Yellow Hair and his bluecoats again.

One morning, scouts rode in with news. Yellow Hair and two hundred bluecoats were riding toward them from the north. As the warriors prepared for battle, Walks on Clouds gave Snakehead her father's blanket. Take this with you, she said. It will protect you from the bluecoats' bullets and let Lakota and Cheyenne warriors know you are with them. I will see you after the fighting is over when we women come to tend our wounded and strip our enemies of their weapons so they cannot use them against us in the spirit world.

Crazy Horse and Gall led the charge. Same Knife and his warriors, including Snakehead, rode close behind. As they neared the bluecoats, Snakehead suddenly galloped out in front. See, Same Knife said. He goes to warn them. No, another war chief said. He goes to frighten them.

It was true. When the bluecoats got a look at his reptilian face, they cried out that he was the devil and began firing wildly, some even turning tail and running away. Crazy Horse signaled for all to attack. Bluecoats fell from Lakota and Cheyenne bullets and arrows. Snakehead chased after the soldiers, firing his father's rifle over and over, his aim true, his bullets deadly. When his ammo ran low, he jumped off his pony, swinging the rifle as a club and slashing with his knife.

The remaining bluecoats ran up a hill. Snakehead ran after them as bullets rained down. Lakota and Cheyenne warriors were charging up it too. Some fell, but Snakehead kept climbing.

Suddenly, a woman's voice called out.

Only it wasn't November's or Walks on Clouds's or Sen Vang's or Talking Woman's. It was coming from the office. It was coming from the radio.

"Sheriff Drake, Sheriff Drake. Emergency! Can you hear me? Are you there? Over."

I jumped out of the recliner, fast-stepped to the office, and grabbed the mike.

"I'm here, Jazz. What is it? Over."

"We're under attack," she said.

"By who?"

"District Attorney Sessions. He showed up with a court order demanding the immediate release of Red Caldera. Chief Deputy Nelson refused to comply and forced him out of the building. The DA came back with some Burns city cops."

I glanced at my field watch. It was nine o'clock. "Who else is there besides you and Orville?"

"Only Trace," she said. "Everyone else went home for the night. He's outside with Orville blocking the front door. I locked it from the inside. Sessions and the cops are threatening to break it down. It's getting ugly."

"Hang tight. I'm on my way," I shouted.

Running for the door, I called to November, "Sorry. You'll have to tell me the rest of the story later."

"Unless it is too late for you," she replied, her tsk louder than the echo of the last gunshot fired at Greasy Grass.

"I'm working hard to make sure that doesn't happen. Now, go wake Bina. Ask her to come down here and stand guard. I want another pair of eyes and ears in the house. A good shot too. I'll be back as soon as I can."

18

If a cow had wandered onto the unlit two-lane to Burns, we both would've wound up ground meat. Lucky for me and any free-ranging critter, the road was clear and I made the drive in record time.

The squat pink building was awash in flashing red from the spinning gumballs on three city cop cars. Deputies Nelson and Wakefield were blocking the front door. Their weapons were holstered but their body language said something entirely different.

I hopped out of my rig and pushed past the *Burns Herald* reporter and photographer who'd been in front of the courthouse when DA Sessions and Judge Manton made their public declaration of war.

The judge was nowhere to be seen, but Sessions was strutting back and forth in front of my two deputies like a bantam rooster, puffing out his chest and crowing he was going to have them arrested.

When he caught sight of me, Sessions jabbed a pudgy finger. "Your lawlessness ends tonight, Drake! I'm taking you and your men down right here and now. You're finished, you hear? Kaput.

Gone. Either open the door immediately or the chief and his men will break it down!"

He hooked a thumb at a policeman who wore a graying brush mustache and a seen-it-all, done-it-all expression. A pair of beefy patrolmen flanked him. One was slapping his palm with a billy club; the other wielded a bosher to smash open the door.

I closed in on the police chief. "I don't know what kind of story the DA told you to get you to come out here this late at night, Chief, but I'm here now and I'll handle it."

"Well, it's a humdinger of a story, I'll *hand* you that," he said.

"What did he tell you?"

"That you got a man locked in a cell upstairs without having charged him. Says you denied him due process."

"Sessions should spend more time studying up on civil legal codes than campaign laws," I said. "We had Red Caldera under surveillance for cattle rustling. When he got wind of it, he made a run for Idaho. My deputy and I interceded and red-lighted him. He pulled a gun on us. That's a felony and we arrested him."

"Judge and jury decide guilt, not you. And due process is still due process," the police chief said.

"That it is, but while I may be new to sheriffing, I do know how to count. There're still twenty-four hours before Caldera has to be charged."

"The DA does the charging. He says you didn't tell him about the arrest."

"He didn't," Sessions shouted. "And it's not the first time either."

The chief trained his brush mustache at me. His two beefy bookends squared their shoulders.

"Sounds like you got a bad habit of not informing him," he

said. "Didn't tell him when you found the two murder victims the other day and now again with the fellow upstairs."

"Cigarettes are a bad habit, Chief. Keeping information close to the vest to avoid tipping off a ruthless killer or a band of cattle rustlers is smart policing."

I chinned at Sessions and the reporter–photographer team he'd brought with him. "Staging what he's doing late at night is all about getting himself on the front page because he knows busting down my door in the dark will make for a more dramatic photo."

"Appears to me you've been keeping the DA in the dark yourself," the chief said.

I leaned in close and lowered my voice to all but a whisper. "I'm going to tell you something about the dead couple that no one outside my department knows. There've been similar killings in other states."

"You tell Sessions that?" he said in a low voice.

I shook my head.

"Why not?" he said.

"Because he'd broadcast it from here to eternity to ensure the recall election and give his nephew another shot at my job. I don't give a shit about that, but I do if it gives the killer a heads-up the law's onto him."

Sessions started flapping his arms. "Whatever Drake's whispering to you, don't believe him, Chief. He's making stuff up to try and cover his ass for wrongful imprisonment."

Neither of us blinked as the police chief mulled it over. Finally, the mustache twitched. "Doesn't change a thing. He's got a court order signed by Judge Manton authorizing the immediate release of your prisoner. I'm only here to make sure it gets carried out."

"You've been chief, what, twenty years or more?" I said. "In all that time did a DA ever bring Sheriff Warbler over to check on the way you keep house? Did Pudge ever demand you release someone you had reason to keep locked up?"

The mustache twitched again.

"Exactly," I said.

The chief looked at Sessions and then at my deputies blocking the door and then back at me.

"The Hardward killings, they were committed in the county, right?" he said loud enough for all to hear.

"They were."

"And the fellow upstairs? You arrested him in the county, not inside the city limits, and jailed him right here, which, in effect, is county, right?"

"I did and it sure is. Same as the City of Burns is your jurisdiction and its jail too."

"Then what we got here is a matter of jurisdictional boundaries. There're laws about crossing them and I for one don't aim to," he said.

Sessions's crowing turned into squealing. "Hold on, Chief. I'm ordering you to bust down that door and escort me inside so I can exercise this court order."

The chief slapped his badge. "I don't answer to you; I answer to this. You want someone to hold your hand going inside the sheriff's office and release a man he says drew a gun on him and his deputy? Then best you ask the man whose office it is."

"Whatever Drake whispered to you, I can assure you it's a lie," Sessions said. "Lest you forget, Burns City Police and Harney County Sheriff's Department have a mutual aid agreement. It takes precedence over jurisdictional boundaries. You yourself put it into practice last week."

"You mean when the call went out to bust up that brawl at the Pine Room and spare any more bystanders from getting hurt. Simple fact is, Deputy Wakefield was faster off the line of scrimmage than my boys here and took down that biker all on his own."

The chief whistled. "If you'd ever seen him play ball like I have, it wouldn't've surprised you. Saw him catch a pass and run it into the end-zone with three defenders hanging off him. Led the Seahawks to their first-ever winning season."

Sessions stamped his foot. "What I'm saying is, the sheriff's department didn't have to ask you permission to make an arrest inside your jurisdiction. Just as you don't have to ask Drake's permission to intervene in his jurisdiction when a crime's being committed."

"Maybe not formally, but it's the neighborly thing to do. Always has been. Always will be." He turned to me. "Right, Sheriff?"

"Right, Chief. Always will."

"Then we got an understanding. Come on, boys. We're done here."

Before starting toward his car, the police chief said, "DA's right about one thing, Sheriff. That arrest your boy made, I could've insisted it be turned over to my department. Would've bolstered my numbers. City council members keeps track of them. They appointed me and they're my boss. See, I'm a hired gun, not elected like you and the DA. Elections? I don't give *two* shits about them."

"Then why didn't you claim the arrest?" I said.

"Because I believe fairness is a measure of a man. Your boy? He earned that arrest fair and square. He ever wants to switch teams, I'll take him in a heartbeat."

"I'll tell him."

"No you won't," the police chief said. "He's too damn good to lose and you know it."

As the cops took off, I brushed past a red-in-the-face DA Sessions and told Orville and Trace to step aside. I gave a few knocks on the glass front door and Jazz appeared on the other side. She was holding something behind her back.

"Go ahead and unlock it. We're coming in," I said.

"Are you sure?" she said.

"I'm sure."

"I mean, if you were being coerced and really didn't want me to, you'd give me a sign of some sort, wouldn't you?" She double-winked, the long black eyelashes taking flight like a pair of ravens.

"It's okay, Jazz. Cops left. DA's coming in for a little sit-down in my office. If there's coffee in the pot, I sure could use some."

Still keeping her hand behind her back, she unlocked the door.

"If what you're holding is what I think it is and it's not licensed, then we got a problem," I said.

"It's licensed," she said. "I have two hundred registered hours on the range."

"Twice what the average police academy graduate has," I said.

"Their fathers aren't my father."

"Torch give it to you?"

"Heck no," Jazz said. "He said if I wanted a gun bad enough, I had to buy it myself. Used the money I earned babysitting."

I walked into my office and sat behind the desk. DA Sessions was close behind. He slapped a document down and said, "Consider yourself officially notified that you've been ordered to release Red Caldera immediately."

I gave the papers a quick read. "Unconditional release? He's part of a ring that's been poisoning cattle to scare ranchers like the Hardwards into believing their entire stock has been exposed to an epidemic. He takes the cows off their hands for pennies on the dollar."

"Do you have any hard evidence he's doing it?"

"We're gathering it."

"Until you have something more than conjecture, you have nothing to hold him on," he said.

"He pulled a gun on Deputy Wakefield and me when we stopped him from fleeing to Idaho. That's more than nothing. It's something."

"Who says he did?"

"Me. Trace."

Sessions leaned forward. "Any other witnesses?"

"Only the two of us."

He crowed. "Even a green public defender would have that quashed. You'll be lucky if Caldera doesn't sue Harney County for false arrest. If he does, then it won't only be your job you lose; it'll be everything you own to pay the county restitution."

"You're making a big mistake," I said. "Caldera's guilty. Right after he left the Dulac ranch earlier this week, their livestock began dropping dead from being injected with pentobarbital, the same substance found in the Hardwards' stock."

"How do you know that?"

"My wife's a vet and does work for the Department of Ag. She took samples at the Hardward ranch and flew them to the lab in Corvallis. They came back positive for pento. She's doing the same with samples from the Dulacs' cows right now."

"Did anybody see Caldera injecting them? Catch him with penti, penta, pento—well, whatever-you-call it—in his possession? Witness him selling livestock from the Hardwards or any other ranch that had stock dying?"

When I didn't say anything, the DA pursed his lips. "My, my. You don't have a thing. Release him now. That's an order!"

I crossed my arms and leaned back in my chair.

"You're a bigger fool than I thought," Sessions said. "You ignore this order, you're defying the court. Judge Manton can have you arrested."

"That's why you're doing this, isn't it?" I said. "Another way to get me out."

"Maybe you aren't so dumb. But don't think this is the only court order you're going to get. You're in for a very rough ride if you don't admit you made a mistake taking this job and resign."

"What do you really want?" I said.

Sessions sneered. "I already told you. You gone. You're incompetent. You should never have been elected. Harney County deserves better and we're correcting that."

"You and the judge. Yeah, I get that part. You want me out and your nephew in so he can do your bidding. But what's in it for you? What do you really want?"

The DA licked his lips and then took out his snow globe-patterned hanky and dabbed at them.

"Oh, I see," I said.

"See what?" he said.

"Something bigger. That's what you want."

"I didn't say that."

"Your actions do. All the press you're working so hard to get? You want to be known outside of Harney County. You want to be known all over Oregon. What, you want to run for state attorney general?"

Sessions's face twitched.

"And Judge Manton, he wants bigger too. Oregon Supreme Court justices are elected, aren't they?"

He dabbed his lips again.

I exhaled loudly and then called to Orville who was hovering right outside the door. "Bring Red Caldera down. He's free to go."

"And give him his car keys too," Sessions said.

"I was wondering how you knew I had a new jailbird," I said. "Ran the plates and came up with this cockamamie plan to accuse me of breaking the rules."

"Underestimating me is another mistake you've made," he said. "I have eyes everywhere."

Trace escorted Red Caldera down the stairs and handed him over to Sessions. As the pair started to leave, I could hear Pudge Warbler's gruff voice in my ear.

"Hey, Sidney," I said. "A wise man once told me a stumbling block is a stepping stone to success. But sometimes it's just a rock you trip over and break your damn neck."

I clicked my cheek. "See you on down the road. You too, Caldera."

19

———

Orville led the blitz into my office with Trace and Jazz tailing close behind.

"This is a clear abuse of power and District Attorney Sessions cannot be allowed to get away with it," my red-faced chief deputy said.

"Agreed, but he's not our main concern right now," I said. "Red Caldera is. He's our best shot at catching the others doing the rustling."

"But Sessions is letting him get away. Once he reaches Idaho, we cannot touch him."

"Caldera only thinks he's getting away."

"Call the play," Trace said. "You want me to nail him or tail him?"

"Tail, but not in your rig," I said. "He'd spot you a mile away plus you can't cross into Idaho in it. You need to be driving an unmarked."

"But we do not have such a vehicle," Orville said. "We never had a budget for one and Sheriff Warbler always believed that arriving in a marked vehicle gave a law officer the upper hand."

"I can't take my own rig," Trace said. "It's in the shop and they're waiting on parts."

"Then you can drive my wife's station wagon," Orville said. "I will take you to the house to get it."

"That'll put me ten, fifteen minutes behind Caldera."

Jazz rolled her eyes. "Guys, my car's parked right here. Come on, Trace. You drive and I'll take a radio and keep the sheriff and chief deputy updated."

When I hesitated, Orville said to me, "No active field duty, remember. She has not been trained nor had sufficient supervision."

"True, but we got two cases going on at once here," I said. "Something big just happened with the Hardward murders."

"What?"

"I know who did it."

The trio sounded like owls all at once.

"The killer was VC during the war," I said. "The girl with yellow hair hunting him confirmed it. She came to No Mountain. Johnny knew her over there. I ..." A memory screamed. It was my old redfaced DI. *While you're busy talking, your enemy's gun is cocking.*

"More on that later. Jazz, do you know what a ride-along is?"

"Of course. I did it all the time with beat cops in San Francisco," she said. "Also with plainclothes detectives, but never ever with my father. No way."

"Yours is the VW bug with all the bumper stickers, right? You stay in it the whole time handling directions, the radio, and nothing else. Orville will cover dispatch while you're out. You report into him regularly. You got that?"

"I'll get my keys," she said and ran off.

Trace started after her.

"Hold it, Trace," I said. "Jazz is your responsibility now. You guard her closer than any quarterback."

"Of course, Sheriff, but the Q was never my only duty. The whole team was. Same here."

After the pair left, I gave Orville a rundown on Sen Vang and Comrade Minh.

"Loq's got eyes on the girl," I said. "She's spending the night at the old lineman's shack. Last known on Minh was Canyonville, but he's on the move. My guess his next target is in Portland. If he sticks to his pattern, he'll try and talk his way into staying on a reservation near there. Bina's boss is alerting his counterparts at all the ones in the area."

"What do you want me to do?" Orville said.

"Any luck tracking down Mr. Hardward's sister and the Vietnamese woman at her temple who played matchmaker? She could either be another target of Minh's or have a direct line to him."

"Negative. I am still trying."

"Keep at it, don't let up. The matchmaker's key."

"Affirmative. When do you expect to learn if the samples Gemma took at the Dulac ranch prove positive for pentobarbital?" he said.

I looked at my field watch. It'd be midnight soon. "Gemma will call me as soon as she finds out. It'll be late morning at the earliest."

"Tomorrow is shaping up to be a very busy day. If you need to take a rest, I can alert you if Jazz calls in with any pertinent information."

My instincts said no, but my mind and body said yes. "Good idea. Since Caldera left a bunk empty upstairs, I'll go stretch out."

The biker watched intently as I opened the cell next to his, stripped the sheets and blanket off the bunk, and lay down on the bare mattress without taking off my boots or holster.

"What about me?" he said. "You let the fat dude go, why not me? I got rights too."

"It's been a long day," I said. "Two days actually. You stay quiet, then maybe when I wake up I'll be in a mood to listen."

The biker didn't answer, only mimed zipping his lips.

I closed my eyes, crossed my arms like a corpse in a coffin, and fell fast asleep. While my body let go of the tension, my mind couldn't. Fractured flickers of scenes in Vietnam raced by. Tracking the enemy in the Central Highlands with Jarai pathfinders. Riding on a mad carousel of firefights at Khe Sanh and Hue, in the mangrove swamps south of Saigon. Leading my squad into an ambush that left all of them dead.

Coming face-to-face with Talking Woman, her hair a writhing tangle of Malay kraits, her bright red lips the color of dragon fruit. A herd of dead cows stampeding straight at me. Dao Pham planting rice in a paddy that suddenly sprouted with sunflowers, their seeds full metal jacket bullets. A VC guerrilla smoking a Marlboro while wielding a cat-o'-nine-tails on a child soldier's bare back. The child turning to me and asking why wouldn't I stop him. The child becoming Johnny and then Sen Vang and then finally Hattie who cried "Daddy, Daddy, save me!"

I woke in a sweat and sat up. The biker was staring at me.

"What are you looking at?" I said.

"Is it okay if I talk now?" he said.

"You can start by telling me why you're staring at me."

"'Cause how you sleep. I seen speed freaks less jittery than you. Man, whatever you was dreamin' about, I don't even wanna picture."

"You sure that's all you want to talk about?" I started to get up.

"No offense, Sheriff. Just sayin'. But whatever's eatin' you, maybe I can help you out."

"How's that?"

"Info, man," he said. "Info."

"What kind of information could you possibly have for me that I don't already know?"

"The fat dude who was where you are? He told me somethin'."

"What?"

"It's good. I promise. I'll tell you, I will, but I need somethin' for it."

"Like what?"

"A get out of jail free card, what else?"

I stood up and stretched. The crick in my back had been made worse from lying on the sagging mattress.

"No way," I said.

"It's good what he told me. I swear. All I'm askin' for is a skate on what I done. I couldn't help myself. See, I got D and D."

"No, you got the entire alphabet. It was my deputy who arrested you. Drunk and disorderly for brawling and smashing up the Pine Room. Busting pool cues over a couple of heads? That earned you an A and B. Assault and battery. Throwing the eight ball at the bartender? You're lucky he ducked. All you smashed was the mirror behind him and not his skull. If you'd hit him, you'd be looking at ADW. Assault with a deadly weapon."

His scraggly hair shook. "You got it all wrong. D and D? For me, that means 'damned and doomed.' Have been ever since I were borned. My daddy was a mean-ass drunk. Beat the snot out of me every day all day until he got hisself killed holdin' up a liquor store. My momma was even meaner. Never nursed me. Poured stale beer in a baby bottle and said, 'Have at it.' Made me change my own diapers too."

"Did you ever go to school?" I said.

"I went. I went in the front door and right out the back." He cackled. "Only school I ever stuck with was reform school. Six years. Weren't half bad. Three squares a day. Better than I ever got back home."

"Big deal. So you had a hard life. Lots of people have and they rise above it."

"Some do, sure. But me? My wirin's all messed up." The biker slapped the side of his head. "It's always roarin' upstairs louder than my Harley. Drives me plumb loco."

"If you're looking for a ticket out of here to the state hospital instead of prison, you'll have to convince someone other than me," I said.

He pressed his face against the bars. "But you could put a word in for me. Judges passin' sentences dig that kind of stuff. A sheriff goin' to bat, so to speak."

"Okay, I'll play along. Why would Red Caldera tell you anything that you think's worth my while?"

"'Cause I threatened to kickstart him like I do my bike. He believed me. Weren't no lie neither. I was gonna. Seein' I'm D and D, you know."

"Damned and doomed. Yeah, I get it. Okay, tell me what he told you."

"If I do, you gotta promise me that get out of jail card."

"Doesn't work that way. You got to tell me first."

"You mean I gotta trust you?"

"I'm the sheriff. Who else can you trust?"

The biker howled. "Man, you need to get out in the world. Stories I could tell you about bein' shaken down every time Johnny Law pulled me over for speedin'. Always travel with a sawbuck folded around my driver's license. Guess what? It's always gone when they hand back my ID."

"I got work to do," I said. "You change your mind and have something worth my time, rattle the bars."

"Now, hold on. I know when I been dealt a hand two cards

shy of a pair. Here it is. The fat cattle dude, he said he'd let me in on a deal he's doin' if I didn't kick the shit out of him."

"Which is what?"

"Gettin' cows on the cheap. And when he said cheap, he meant like free. Said he'd give me five hundred bucks from the next shipment he's doin'.'"

"When's that supposed to happen?" I said.

"As soon as he got out. Guess what? He just did. How, I don't know, but when that jock deputy came to haul his fat ass back downstairs, fat cattle dude gave me the wink."

"He tell you what he does with the stock?"

The biker nodded. "He butchers 'em and wholesales the meat."

"Where?"

"A place right up near the Grant County line. The forested part. There's a lumber mill there gone tits up. Has one of them old metal wigwam burners. You know, what they used to burn up wood scraps and such. They do the butcherin' inside it. Anybody happens to pass by, they think the stink is coming from old ashes stirrin' up."

"What town is it in?" I said.

The biker rubbed his beard. "He didn't tell me. Only that it was up near the county line and abandoned. Can't be that many of them, can it?"

"I'll need to check it out first," I said.

"And if it is what I say it is?"

"I'll write the letter to the judge myself."

"Fair enough," the biker said. "Think you could do one more favor for me, seein' I gave you all that and havin' to trust you on the backend?"

"What is it?"

"The chick who brings up my grub? The one with the eye makeup and nails? Man, she's a fox and a half. Could you put in a good word for me? Tell her I'd dig takin' her for a spin on my Harley. She looks the kind who likes wind blowin' through her hair."

"I'll let her know and I'm sure she'll give you the answer herself," I said, picturing Jazz's reply.

"Thanks, man. Waitin' on that'll help pass the time. You know what I'm sayin'?"

20

L oud voices and the smell of coffee were filling the first floor of the office when I came downstairs. The dayshift of deputies had arrived with the dawn.

Orville spotted me and wheeled over. "I must say, you look rested. There is coffee as well as a box of donuts from Bella's. Powdered. Glazed. Jelly. Would you like one?"

"I sense something's up. What is it?" I said.

"The men are upset we did not call them in for reinforcement last night. They saw the front page of this morning's *Burns Herald*. It has a photograph of DA Sessions with the chief of police and his officers bunched right behind him standing toe to toe with Deputy Wakefield and me."

"What'd you tell them?"

"That the Burns city cops backed off and went home when you got here."

"Is that the end of it?"

"I may have mentioned there is absolutely no reason the incident should affect the way they play softball at their game with them this Saturday," he said.

Both departments fielded summer teams. So did the fire department and Bureau of Land Management.

"Sounds like you gave a green light to pitch inside and slide hard," I said.

"Better they work out their differences on the diamond than on the street out front."

"What else is in the article?"

Orville hesitated. "It has a quote from District Attorney Sessions about your qualifications as sheriff."

"Leave the sugarcoating for the donuts. What did he say?"

"That once again your blatant disregard for the rules of law proves not only are you incompetent, but can never be trusted to safeguard the citizens of Harney County as well as people throughout Oregon."

"He's definitely running for state AG."

"So it would appear," Orville said.

"What's Trace and Jazz's status?" I said.

"They were able to catch up to Red Caldera. He was fairly easy to spot and follow since one of the taillights on his Cadillac was broken."

"Did he drive straight to Idaho?"

"Affirmative. They saw him turn into a driveway in a wealthy neighborhood in Nampa. The address comports with his home address. Jazz said the house is set back from the road and very large. It appears Caldera is doing quite well for himself."

"Is he still there?"

"He was when Jazz last checked in. They are parked nearby with a sightline on the driveway. If he leaves, they will know about it and resume the tail."

I told Orville about my conversation with the biker.

"Do you think it is accurate?" he said.

"Part of what Caldera told him must be. You know the rule of lying. There're always some facts in it so the liar only has to remember the things he made up. The location of where they're doing the butchering has a ring of truth to it because of the details he gave. Especially the part about an abandoned lumber mill with an old wigwam burner."

"That is a good detail. They were also called beehive burners because of their conical shape. The last were phased out after the Clean Air Act banned them. A lot of older mills shut down rather than retrofit. I can do a search to identify any in that area and have a deputy conduct a drive-by."

"Good idea, but only a drive-by," I said. "We don't want to tip off anybody there serving as a lookout."

"Those will be my precise instructions."

I told Orville to keep me posted, grabbed a cup of coffee and donut, and went to my desk. I was reaching for the telephone when it rang.

"November said you left last night in a hurry," Gemma said.

"I was just about to call home to check on Johnny and Hattie. You beat me to it. What else did November tell you?"

The silence on the phone lasted a few seconds and I knew it wasn't because we'd been disconnected. Finally, a loud sigh came across.

"I'm trying to remind myself that it isn't always possible for a sheriff not to bring his work home," she said. "Pudge did a pretty good job at that, but he couldn't always."

"That's why I had Sen Vang spend the night at the old lineman's shack and not our place. Loq's babysitting her. If she tried coming to our house, he would've stopped her."

"But who was there to stop Comrade Minh?"

"You know about that?" I said.

"Of course I do, hotshot. November put Johnny on the phone. He told me."

Now it was my turn to burn up a few seconds trying to figure out what to say. "He was spotted way over in Canyonville and is on the run. Even so, I asked November to get Bina to stand guard in the main house."

"So she said."

"Look, I realize the situation wasn't ideal, babe, but ... well, it was what it was. How did Johnny sound to you?"

"I'm a large animal veterinarian, not a child psychiatrist, but I am a mother and I'd say he's in shock. His two worlds—"

"Collided," I said. "I witnessed it. It'll be up to us to set things right again the same as we did when he first came to live with us, but it's going to take time."

"That's an understatement." Gemma sighed again. "I called home expecting you to be there to give you some news myself. The Dulac cattle that died? It was pentobarbital. Same as the Hardward stock."

"That's as good as a smoking gun." I gave her the down and dirty on Red Caldera. "Trace and Jazz are tailing him. We got a line on where the healthy stock he swindled are being butchered."

"And you have the wherewithal to focus on that and not on the killer who's likely to be coming after our son?" she said.

"As sheriff, I'm sworn to do both, but sometimes hard choices got to be made. I know what my priority is. That's why I'm leaving for No Mountain right now to talk with Sen Vang and put another layer of protection around Johnny. What's your ETA home?"

"As fast as my little plane can fly."

"See you there."

I told Orville I was returning to No Mountain. "Anything changes with Trace and Jazz's situation, radio me. I want to know the moment it goes down."

I hadn't been on the road ten minutes when the radio chirped.

"Sen Vang's on the move," Loq said.

"Where to?"

"Your place."

"Radio Bina and give her a heads-up."

"Already did."

"And you're tailing Sen Vang?" I said.

"You got it."

"Not much traffic out there. She's sure to spot you if you get too close."

"She already did," he said.

"How do you know?"

"Because she waved to me when she was leaving the shack. She knew I was hiding out there the whole time."

"Sen Vang's clever. She's managed to stay alive ever since her village was attacked, as a *bui doi* on the streets, a guerrilla, and now as, well, whatever she's doing," I said.

"We both know what she is, brother. Don't lose sight of that," he said.

When I arrived home, everyone was sitting around the table except for my wife and daughter.

"Where's Hattie?" I said.

"I asked Lyle Rides Alone to come get her," November said. "What is to be spoken here is not for her ears. Perhaps our own ears will not want to hear it also."

Sen Vang was watching November closely. I wondered if she could see her own grandmother in her. Then she turned to look at Bina.

"I like your earrings," she said. "They remind me of birds that used to fly over my village."

"And I like your bracelets," the Umatilla tribal cop said. "The engravings tell your people's story the same as weavings do my people's and totem poles do for our brothers and sisters who live in the north."

Johnny was silent. He sat between November and Sen Vang, but had a hard time meeting my gaze.

"Everything is going to be okay, son," I said. "We're going to sort it out right now."

As I sat down, I took a deep breath and let it out slowly, wishing it would blow away the evil that was threatening my family and all the people who lived in Harney County, knowing it was up to me to figure out a way to make that come true, and wondering if ordering Jazz and Trace to tail Red Caldera would haunt me the rest of my days.

21

———

Dawn came to Nampa an hour earlier than No Mountain, not because of the 150 miles that separated them, but due to a meridian, an imaginary line that demarcated two time zones. Spending all night crammed behind the wheel of the Volkswagen Bug surveilling Red Caldera's house had left Trace Wakefield's knees feeling like he'd played both offense and defense against the Oakland Raiders.

The deputy decided he'd better get out and stretch before the sun lifted the blanket of graying sky that was keeping the VW shrouded from view. He eased the tinny door open so as not to wake Jazz Flambeaux. She hadn't uttered a word for the past two hours. Trace was grateful for that after having listened to her tell graphic stories about her life without sparing any details.

He unfolded himself from the seat and imagined his boots were filled with angry bees because his feet stung from staying still so long. As he started for a thicket of shrubs to take a leak, he heard the VW's passenger door open.

"What do you think you're doing?" he whispered. "You're supposed to stay in the car at all times. Those were the orders."

"I can't," Jazz whispered back. "I got to go, same as you."

"Okay, but we better take turns."

"Why?"

"Well, you know."

She put her hands on her hips. "No, I don't know."

"Uh, in case Caldera leaves the house and drives off," Trace said.

Jazz groaned. "Don't you have a sister?"

"No, a brother. Why?"

"Ever had a girlfriend?"

"What's that got to do with anything?"

"In other words, you've never gone to the bathroom in the presence of a girl before." She issued another groan. "Here's how it's done, big man. You take one side of the shrub and face west and I'll take the other and face east. And Trace?"

"What?" he said.

"You're not in a locker room anymore so no snapping towels and grabbing ass."

As he turned to stare toward Oregon, she started laughing.

Trace was just finishing when her laughter turned into a hiss. "Don't move. Vehicle coming down Caldera's drive. It's turning our way."

The deputy's back was to it, but he kept from spinning around. The thrum of an engine grew closer and the shine from headlights grew brighter. Soon they were replaced by red glows from a pair of taillights. It wasn't the Caddy, but a pickup truck. A white Ford. He immediately thought of the Hardwards' missing rig.

"Could you make out the driver?" Trace said.

Jazz had already stood and pulled up her black jeans. "It was

Red Caldera. I saw his face from the glow of a stogie clamped between his teeth."

"See the license plate? Was it Oregon?"

"I couldn't make it out."

"Let's get a move on and resume the tail," he said.

"As soon as you're finished." Jazz winked at him.

Trace glanced down. His fly was unzipped.

She laughed and ran to the Bug. By the time he got there, she'd already fired the ignition from the passenger seat. He slipped behind the wheel, shoved it into gear, and hit the gas.

Traffic was light and they kept their distance following the white pickup.

"It sure looks like he's going back to Oregon," Jazz said.

"Radio the station and let the chief deputy know," Trace said. "He might have new info for us."

She made the call on the handheld and Orville Nelson picked up saying, "Location and situation?"

"We're about to cross back over the Snake River," Jazz said and told him why they left the stakeout.

"That being the case, Caldera's two most likely destinations are the Dulac ranch out by Williams Reservoir or an abandoned lumber mill near Foster's Creek. It's up by the Grant County line."

"What's with both locations?" she asked.

"Sheriff Drake's wife confirmed the Dulac cattle were killed by a lethal injection the same as the Hardward stock. Caldera could be going back there to make his pitch about taking the rest of the herd off their hands."

"And the lumber mill?"

"The sheriff received information it is being used as an illegal slaughterhouse."

"How did Sheriff Drake learn that?"

"Red Caldera told the biker with a promise of a payoff in

exchange for the biker not inflicting great bodily harm on him. The biker traded the information to the sheriff in hopes of receiving favorable treatment. I pinpointed the location."

"You mean Caldera gave it up when the biker said he was going to beat the shit out of him?" Jazz hooted.

"There's something else," Trace said. "Caldera swapped his Caddy for a white Ford pickup. We didn't get a read on the plates, but it could be the Hardward rig."

"If that is the case, then Caldera is either simple-minded or reckless," Orville said. "That pickup is a valuable piece of evidence."

"What's our play, Chief?" Trace said.

"Follow Caldera to wherever he goes and report in regularly. Be aware that I previously assigned a marked unit to do a drive-by of the lumber mill. He left about ten minutes ago and is en route. The drive will take him approximately two hours."

"And if Caldera's going to the Dulac ranch, we still follow him?" Trace said.

"Affirmative," the chief deputy said. "Inform me immediately so that I can alert the Dulacs. If Caldera attempts to convince them their cattle are diseased and he can help by taking them off their hands, we will have the ranchers as eyewitnesses. That and the fact their cows were poisoned the same as the Hardwards' stock will be irrefutable evidence. District Attorney Sessions will not be able to thwart justice this time."

"Cool," Jazz said. "And we'll swoop in and slap the cuffs on Caldera."

"Not 'we!' Only Deputy Wakefield. Remember the sheriff's orders. You are to stay in the vehicle at all times."

"Aw, come on," Jazz said.

"You heard me," Orville said. "And Trace?"

"Yes, Chief?"

"You are not to engage with the suspect if he goes to the

lumber mill. Your assignment is surveillance only. We do not know how many accomplices he may have. If Caldera makes you during the tail, break off and return here immediately."

Radio static joined the buzzy chugging of the Bug's tiny rear engine.

"Do you read me, Deputy?" Orville said. "Are we clear on that?"

"10-4. I stick with the play as drawn," Trace said.

Jazz swore under her breath as she clicked the radio off.

"What's wrong?" he said.

"You stay in the car, honey, this is man's work," she said. "Don't worry your pretty little head about killers and rapists. We'll take care of them."

Trace let a big rig stay between them and Caldera even though it blocked his view of the white pickup.

"My class at the academy, there were only a couple of girls, er, women in it," he said. "They worked harder than the rest of us to prove themselves."

"You mean all the men, including yourself."

"I'm not saying it was fair, but, well ... You want something bad enough, you do whatever it takes."

"What you did to make the pros," Jazz said.

"Uh-huh. I wanted it bad."

"Any girls on a pro football team?"

"Well, no."

"My point," she said. "No matter how hard they tried, how good they were, how much they wanted to play football, they couldn't. Ever. Men made the rules."

Trace started to say something, but dropped it. He couldn't argue with facts.

After several minutes, Jazz broke the silence. "There! The turnoff up ahead. Caldera took it."

She picked up the map and traced a route with her finger.

"He's taking the county road north. Guess what? There're a few turns he'll have to take, but it leads to a loop road near Foster's Creek. According to the map, the old lumber mill is the only thing on it."

Trace slowed the VW and then made the turnoff. He pulled to the side.

"What are you doing? Aren't we going after him?" Jazz said.

"If the mill is the only thing up there, we don't want Caldera to spot us in his rearview," he said. "We know the route he's running. We know where the end zone is. We'll intercept him there."

"But what if I'm wrong?" Jazz said.

"You called the play. I trust you."

"You do?"

"What I said."

Jazz smiled to herself.

"Radio the chief deputy," Trace said. "Tell him the play."

Jazz did and Orville reiterated that they were to proceed with caution and not confront Caldera. They waited a few minutes until the white Ford pickup was a dot and then resumed driving.

The county road cut across a tabletop dotted with sagebrush and juniper as it ran toward a line of foothills stubbled with ponderosa pines and creased by gullies. Black-capped buttes stood at either end. The blue shadow of a forested mountain range rose in the background.

"It's gorgeous," Jazz said. "Don't you think?"

"I see tough and rugged," Trace said. "Hard terrain to chase someone down in."

"But why would we be chasing him? We're only surveilling."

"A play falls apart, conditions on the field change; might have to call an audible."

"Is that what you think will happen, we'll be chasing him?" she said.

"If he and his gang aren't chasing us," he said.

"So you know, I have a gun in my purse," Jazz said. "It's licensed and I have lots of hours on the range."

"A Beretta 9mm semi. I know. I saw it," Trace said.

"When?"

"While you were asleep. Butt was sticking out. I reached for it."

"Mine or the gun's?"

"What?"

Jazz laughed. "That was too easy. You're so serious."

Trace hunched over the wheel. "Rustlers are no joke. Chief deputy's in a chair because of them."

"I didn't know that. I mean, I wondered, but ... Argh, what my dad always told me. Think first, talk second."

After a few minutes of silence, Jazz said, "What do you do when you're not working?"

"What do you mean?" Trace said.

"You know, do you play sports, watch TV, polish your car. I don't know, whatever guys do when they're not working."

"Read, mostly."

"Read?" she said. "You don't have a TV?"

Trace shook his head.

"I would've thought you'd be glued to it on weekends during football season. College ball on Saturday. Pros on Sunday. That's what my dad does," Jazz said.

"Don't care to watch it since I don't play it anymore," Trace said.

"Reading, huh? Like books?"

"Uh-huh."

Jazz smiled. "Okay, let me guess what kind. Mysteries. Westerns. James Bond stuff. All the sexy femme fatales. Am I right?"

"I like history. Ancient history. Roman. Greek. The Trojan

War. Also exploration books. Especially to the South Pole. Shackleton's journal. Robert Falcon Scott's."

"You don't like novels?" she said.

"I read them. *Moby Dick. Don Quixote*," he said.

"Wow. The heavy stuff. I never would've guessed that in a million years. How did you get into reading?"

"My mom was a school teacher," Trace said. "Books were better than an airplane ticket and a lot cheaper is what she always said, especially if you have a library card."

"You know something? You're full of surprises," Jazz said.

"Intersection coming up," he said. "Left or right?"

"Take the left and go ten miles. Then there's a right that leads to the top of the hill and a turnoff to the loop road where the old mill is."

Trace's eyes were focused straight ahead, but he was seeing the terrain on both sides of the road looking for linebackers rushing in.

Jazz said, "You know I want to be more than a dispatcher. I want to be a deputy in the worst way."

"I know," he said.

"You've got the experience. I can learn from you. I'll do whatever you say."

Trace downshifted as the road curved and started climbing. Ponderosa pines began crowding the shoulders. The temperature was rising with the sun and the scent of sap wafted into the Bug. It smelled like a cross between vanilla and butterscotch and made the deputy think of ice cream.

"Did you hear me?" Jazz said.

"The old sheriff, Pudge Warbler? He hired me right out of the academy," Trace said. "Taught me the first rule of being a deputy."

"What is it?" she asked.

"Stay alive."

"Really? I would've thought it'd be always have your partner's back."

"What I thought too, but Pudge—Sheriff Warbler—he set me straight. Said you can't do that if you're dead. Sheriff Drake? He'd tell you the same thing."

The road reached a saddle in the hills and led to the left. Between breaks in the trees, they could look down and see across Harney Basin.

"Look, there's Steens Mountain way off in the distance," Jazz said. "Is that Malheur Lake shimmering down there?"

"Uh-huh," Trace said.

"I haven't had the time to go there yet. Have you?"

He nodded.

"I've heard Sheriff Drake going on and on about the Malheur Refuge," she said. "All the wildlife living there. The birds. The deer and elk and even bears. How there's a cave where the Paiute Indians came out of. You know, a myth."

"Have you met November, the old Paiute woman who lives with the sheriff and his family?" Trace said.

"Not yet," she said.

"Well, she's a medicine woman. A healer. A dancer too. She'll tell you it's no myth, the cave you're talking about. November sees stuff."

"What kind of stuff?"

"Everything in this world and the next. Spirit world, her people call it. Then there's dreamworld too. I'm not sure how all that works, but, well, it's what the sheriff told me," he said.

They drove a bit longer. "Slow down," Jazz said. "There's the loop road that leads to the mill."

"You sure it's a loop and not a dead end?"

"It's a loop on the map. It leads to the mill and then comes back down to join this road."

"Mill being closed, it doesn't get much traffic, if any," Trace said.

"We're only a couple of tourists sightseeing in our cute little VW if anybody sees us. We smile and drive on by."

They made the turn.

"Buildings up ahead on the right," Trace said. "Got to be the mill."

Instead of braking, he downshifted to reduce their speed so the brake lights wouldn't flash.

"That big rusty thing, it's a wigwam," Jazz said. "There were a bunch of them in Klamath Falls where I went to college. The lumber companies were supposed to tear them down, but they didn't."

"You see the white pickup anywhere?" Trace said.

"No. Maybe Caldera parked it around the back of the wigwam or in that old run-down warehouse-looking building. Go slow so I can look for it when we pass."

A haul road ran between the rusty wigwam and dilapidated building. They were crossing in front of it when exhaust pipes rumbled and rubber squealed. A tractor-size forklift shot toward them. Trace stomped on the gas to get out of the way, but the big machine broadsided them.

Metal screeched as the forks skewered the Bug's body on either side of the passenger door. The little car's tires smoked as the forklift shoved it across the asphalt and onto the dirt shoulder. Then the VW lost contact with the ground as the forks began to rise on the lift's mast.

Trace made a grab for his sidearm, but the impact had pinned his holster between his seat and the handbrake in the center well.

"Your gun!" he shouted as the forklift kept raising the little car while moving closer to the edge of the shoulder. "Shoot him before he drops us over the side."

Jazz reached for her bag, felt the butt of the Beretta, and yanked it out.

The window was up, but she didn't waste time lowering it. The driver was obscured behind the forklift's mast, but Jazz pointed and pulled the trigger anyway. The laminated safety glass fractured. She pulled it again and again, the bullets punching a hole through the window. Shells ejected. Cubes of glass flew. She didn't duck, didn't blink, but kept on firing.

Rounds were pinging off metal. More metal was screeching from the pierced VW sliding on the forks as the driver began jockeying the lift back and forth to shake the little car loose.

Then he tilted the mast forward.

Metal screamed as the Bug slid off the forks. Jazz screamed too as they plunged. The wheels hit the side of the hill and the car began to roll over. Trace cranked the steering wheel hard to the left, the same as he would turning into a skid on black ice instead of trying to fight it.

"Too soft. Too slow," someone yelled.

He'd heard the words before. It was what his high school football coach always shouted during practice. And then air whistling through the broken passenger window and rocks pinging against the wheel wells and something smacking the windshield drowned out all the noise including the voice and everything swirled down a black hole with no bottom.

22

Sen Vang started describing her life as a guerrilla. As we listened, I could see the jungle paths she walked, feel the rain as it fell, hear the splash of puddles and the squish of mud. I could see the flash of automatic weapons fire, sense the concussion of mortars, and smell the acrid stink of gunfire. I could hear the cries of the frightened, the gurgling of the wounded, the rasping of the dying, and the deafening silence of the dead.

"No one in our unit set out to become a guerrilla with the National Liberation Front," she said. "Certainly not me as a Jarai whose entire family and village were wiped out by North Vietnam's regular army. Not even Comrade Minh. He was a young farmer who lived in a tiny village with his wife and two small children."

His sole concern, Sen Vang said, was growing rice and feeding his family. He was neither aware of when Vietnamese revolutionary forces led by Ho Chi Minh won a decisive victory against the French after nearly a century of colonization nor did he know that a resulting treaty partitioned the country and his village lay south of the dividing line.

One morning when the young farmer awoke, Sen Vang went on to explain, his wife told him their children were burning up with fever and he and their water buffalo would have to work the fields without their help.

The water buffalo was the family's prized possession. He helped them build paddies, turn the waterwheel for irrigation, and haul rice after the stalks had been harvested, laid along the dikes to dry, and threshed and bagged. They named him *Be Trau*, which meant Little Buffalo, a sign of respect. He was so valuable and beloved, that he slept inside their hooch so they could guard him from tigers.

The young farmer and water buffalo labored all day and long into the night. By the time they finished, the moon was high overhead and guided them home. As they neared the village, flames were leaping from a hooch, the sparks mingling with stardust. Be Trau bellowed with fear. The farmer was frightened for his family and grabbed the water buffalo by the rope tied to his nose ring and ran.

When they entered the village, two men dressed in black jumped out from behind a hooch and pointed rifles at the farmer's chest.

"Please let me go," he said. "I live here. I must see about my wife and children. They're sick and need me."

"The only thing you need to do is obey," one said.

The other grabbed the rope tied to the water buffalo's nose ring.

"Please, don't hurt Be Trau," the young farmer begged. "Please!"

A third man approached. He wore all black too and pinched a lit cigarette between his left thumb and forefinger that he held close to his lips.

"What do we have here?" he said to the two men.

"This man says he lives here," one said.

"And he says this is his water buffalo," said the other.

"Do you know who we are?" Pinching Cigarette asked the young farmer.

"No," he said, bowing.

"We are soldiers in the People's Army."

"I don't know about such things. I'm only a simple farmer."

"No, you are more than that," Pinching Cigarette said. "You are a man. A man who can fight. Fight the oppressors. Fight to liberate the South so we can all be one nation again and never bend a knee to anyone."

The young farmer bowed even lower. "I know nothing about fighting. Nothing about war. I only know how to grow rice, care for my family, care for my water buffalo, and help feed my village."

Pinching Cigarette drew a pistol and placed the tip against the farmer's bowed head.

"You will not fight to liberate your nation? You will allow yourself to be shot like a dog?"

"Please, my family needs me," he begged. "My children are sick. They will starve without me."

"Your fellow countrymen will starve without you! Do you put your children above them? Are you not a patriot?"

"No. Yes. I mean, I don't know. Please, my family."

Pinching Cigarette gestured to one of the black-clad men. "Bring his wife and children to me. We shall see how patriotic he is."

The men dragged out the young farmer's wife whose arms were wrapped around two sobbing children. Pinching Cigarette walked up to the boy and pressed the barrel of his pistol against the side of his head.

He turned to the young farmer. "Tell me again. Are you or are you not a patriot who will fight for liberation?"

"I am!" the farmer cried. "Please let them go. I will do

anything you want, give you anything you need. Rice? I have two sacks in our hooch. Take them. They're yours."

"Not mine. Ours!" Pinching Cigarette screamed. "Not me. We! We the people. We the people of the Democratic Republic of Vietnam who are here to liberate our oppressed brothers and sisters like you and your wife."

He raised his pistol and fired a shot in the air. Other black-clad guerrillas came running.

"Round up all the men in the village. We'll make liberators of them yet," Pinching Cigarette said. "Take all the rice you can find. Take this water buffalo too."

The man holding the rope to Be Trau's nose ring gave it a yank. The beast bellowed and shook his massive head.

"If he won't go, then shoot him," Pinching Cigarette said. "We can't leave him for the enemy to use."

"Don't kill him," the young farmer begged. "Be Trau will listen to me."

"Then he is your responsibility. He will help us transport weapons."

The young farmer hugged his wife and children goodbye. "Don't worry," he said. "I'll return. You'll see. Be Trau too."

Days turned into weeks and weeks into months. The young farmer stopped counting. He stopped counting all the miles he and Be Trau walked, all the loads they carried, all the times they ferried ammunition to Pinching Cigarette and his soldiers during firefights, all the black-clad bodies that he and the water buffalo dragged into shallow graves after the shooting stopped.

One day, Pinching Cigarette ordered the young farmer to fetch water. The nearest pond was half a mile away. He and Be Trau set out. When they reached the pond, he pictured home. He could see the rice paddies he'd built, the orderly squares made by earthen dikes, the flooded fields, and the beautiful green stalks poking above the silty water. He could see the joy in his wife's eyes when he returned home, hear the laughter of his children, and the contented mooing and burping of Be Trau settling down beside the family for the night.

Shouts pulled him from his reverie. Three soldiers dressed in the tan uniforms of the Army of the Republic of Vietnam confronted him.

"Who are you?" the sergeant demanded. He wore a holstered pistol and carried a whip made from a short stalk of bamboo.

"A farmer, nothing more," he said.

"What are you doing here?"

"Collecting water for my village."

The sergeant demanded he tell him where his village was.

The farmer pointed in the direction where Pinching Cigarette and the guerrillas were camped.

"You don't have water there?" the sergeant said.

"Our spring dried up," he said. "Now I get it here and take it back."

"You're lying."

"Why would I lie? Come see for yourself? We are poor, but we have a little rice to share. Are you hungry?"

The sergeant scowled. "We don't need your moldy rice. We need your water buffalo. Men, secure the animal."

One of them grabbed the nose ring rope.

"No!" the young farmer cried. "Please, don't take him. He's all I have."

The sergeant answered by clubbing him with the butt of his whip, knocking him to the ground.

Dazed, the farmer watched as the sergeant approached Be Trau and started ordering his men to lead the water buffalo away. When the animal balked, the sergeant began whipping his backside. Be Trau bellowed in pain, which prompted the man pulling the rope to yank harder and the other to club the beast with the butt of his rifle.

The young farmer picked himself up, charged the sergeant, and tried to wrestle the whip away. As they grappled, the sergeant let go of it and drew his pistol. The young farmer grabbed the gun's barrel and shoved it upward as it fired. The bullet struck the sergeant in the throat. The two privates started firing their rifles. One tried to shoot the young farmer without hitting his sergeant. The other shot Be Trau again and again.

The young farmer picked up the sergeant's pistol and shot back. Both soldiers fell. He dropped the gun and ran to Be Trau. The water buffalo had sunk to his knees, his bellows turning to cries and then gasps and then silence as he toppled over.

"Be Trau!" the young farmer cried. "Be Trau!"

He ran back to the sergeant and picked up his whip. It had nine braided strands of hemp tipped with fishhooks. He began lashing him.

Pinching Cigarette and his men came running at the sound of gunfire. By the time they got to the pond, the sergeant was cut to ribbons and the young farmer was streaked with his blood.

"Be Trau!" he cried with every crack of the cat-o'-nine-tails. "Be Trau!"

"You can stop now, comrade. He's dead," Pinching Cigarette said. "The others are dead too. It appears you are a soldier, after all."

The young farmer glared at him. "He was hurting Be Trau. I had to stop him. Stop all of them. But look what they did to my little buffalo. Look what they did!"

"Yes, but now you must use your anger for the cause. The look in your eyes, I've seen it before in the most fearless warrior of all. I name you in his honor. Come, Comrade Minh. Let us go and kill our enemies, for now they have grown fat with American GIs."

Sen Vang told us that Comrade Minh wouldn't let go of the cat-o'-nine-tails when he followed Pinching Cigarette back to camp. Nor did he let go of it that day nor the next or ever. His reputation as both fearless and heartless grew. It earned him his own *Dia phuong quan*, a regional force of guerrilla fighters.

"The missions he led were always highly dangerous," she said. "The casualty rate among his own fighters was also very high. It forced him to abduct women and children to replenish his unit's ranks."

While Comrade Minh never admitted it, Sen Vang said, the reason he picked women and children was in hopes of finding his family. A year after he killed the three soldiers at the pond, he returned to his village. There was nothing left. All the hooches had been burned down. All the people had vanished.

"Comrade Minh grew even more ruthless after that," she said.

The failed mission at the US airfield where Johnny got away was another tipping point.

"He whipped all of us and threatened to execute us if we tried to flee," she said. "Comrade Minh punished himself too by whipping his own back."

"But the war finally ended," I said. "What happened then?"

"Our unit disbanded," Sen Vang said. "We had been fighting for so long, we knew nothing else. Everything was upended, especially for those living in the South. Saigon became Ho Chi Minh City but it was no longer the capital. Everything was run from Hanoi."

She described horrible reprisals. ARVN soldiers who weren't executed were sent to reeducation camps. South Vietnam's security forces and government workers disappeared.

"What did you do after the war ended?" I said.

"I made my way back to Saigon to look for the two other *bui doi* boys who lived on the streets with Johnny and me." Her blond-streaked hair dipped. "I never found them. I got a job translating letters and reports because I could read and write Vietnamese, French, and Jarai. Eventually, English too."

"And Comrade Minh?" I said.

"I did my best to try and forget him and the war, although that was nearly impossible. The memories. The nightmares. The faces. The voices. The guilt." Sen Vang shuddered.

"It was the same for me when I came home," I said. "They treated me for combat fatigue, but I read psychiatrists gave it a new name this year. Now they call it post-traumatic stress disorder."

"Many Vietnamese soldiers suffered emotional trauma too, both North and South," she said. "But the government would never acknowledge it because Hanoi had won. How could their victorious soldiers be sick? All were heroes."

I asked what Comrade Minh did when the war ended.

"I'd always hoped he returned to his old life. You know, being a farmer, growing rice, living in a peaceful village. But then I learned he didn't."

"When?" I said.

"A few weeks ago," she said. "A man and woman came to question me. They were government officials and knew what I did during the war. They asked me about Comrade Minh. When was the last time I saw him? Had he ever contacted me? I told them the truth. I never saw him again after I left the camp."

"But they knew what he'd been up to," I said.

"Yes, they told me he'd joined the Ministry of Public Security."

"Hanoi's secret police," I explained to the others. "What was his assignment?"

"Tracking down traitors," she said.

"To arrest or assassinate them?"

"The government would never admit to anything like that," Sen Vang said. "After I told the two officials I hadn't any contact with him, they wanted to know about former members of the unit. Again, I couldn't answer because I didn't know. Then they started questioning me if I'd been in contact with members of the unit who left Vietnam for the US."

"Boat people?"

"Yes, many did leave by boat, but others by different ways," she said.

"You mean through arranged marriages like your friend Dao Pham?" I said.

Sen Vang nodded. "Decades of war had left three million Vietnamese dead, the majority young men. The population was overwhelmingly female and brokering marriages became a business. Most of the brides were sent to China and South Korea, but some went to America."

I asked how since there were no diplomatic ties between the US and Vietnam. "Still aren't," I said.

"Vietnam's always had ways to smuggle goods, even the human kind. Trails up and down the country and paths through the jungles and over the mountains to Cambodia and Thailand with no border guards to worry about. Boats too. Papers, passports, tickets? All came with a price that men looking for a wife were willing to pay for."

She added that brokers created fronts to work with churches and charities in America and Europe and used them as pipelines for brides.

"Is that when the two officials told you people from your unit who'd emigrated to the States had been murdered?" I said.

Sen Vang nodded.

"Did they also tell you they suspected Comrade Minh was the killer?"

"Yes, although they made it clear he was no longer with the Ministry of Public Security. The government will never publicly admit they ever knew him."

I asked her if the officials told her why he was doing it.

"They didn't," she said.

"Did you ask?" I said.

"You don't question government officials," she said. "Ever."

"But you must have some idea."

Sen Vang didn't answer nor did her expression give any clue.

"So let me get this straight," I said. "These officials contacted you because they knew you could identify Minh and you also knew folks from your unit who'd moved to the States. Dao Pham, for one. It was you who wrote her a warning letter that uncle was looking for her. You didn't mean Uncle Ho; you meant the other Minh, the one who's never stopped grieving for his little buffalo, Be Trau."

Her eyes widened. "You found my letter?"

"What was left of it. I think Dao burned it so Minh wouldn't find it and track it back to you. It looked like she'd tried to erase everything about her that could be traced to her old life. The few mementos she kept, she buried among sunflowers, including a .38 Special she must've picked up during a battle or in Saigon. She took that out in case Comrade Minh found her, but he shot her and her husband before she could shoot him."

Sen Vang grimaced. "Dao was like an older sister to me. Always looking out for me. Always so brave."

"And these government folks who talked to you. They sent you here to find Minh."

She nodded.

"What are you supposed to do when you find him? You can't arrest him," I said. "Our two countries don't have an extradition policy. No policy of any kind. You have no authority here. You're not even supposed to be here, at least not officially, and certainly not legally."

She raised her chin. "My orders are to help US authorities arrest Minh for his crimes here. They can either imprison him for life or, preferably, execute him. What they can't do is ever allow him to return to Vietnam."

"And when you say US authorities, you mean the FBI," I said.

"No! Hanoi neither trusts nor forgives them. It never will. Not after how the FBI helped the CIA do what it did in Vietnam."

Sen Vang recited a list that included political assassinations, Operation Phoenix, which killed civilians helping the VC, funding and training paramilitary activities, and running the secret war in Laos.

"Then what kind of authority are you talking about?" I said.

Her eyes held mine. "A local law enforcement authority such as a county sheriff. One who I have a personal connection to."

23

———

The roar from a single-engine plane buzzing the ranch rattled the windows. Everyone glanced at the ceiling even though it blocked a view of the sky.

"Come on, Johnny," I said. "Mom's home. Let's go meet her."

Gemma's plane was beginning its descent as we walked to the airstrip.

"I know how tough this is for you," I said, "but the main thing you need to know is your mom and I love you and will keep you safe. We're not going to let Comrade Minh hurt you. Okay?"

He was staring at the ground as we passed the corral. His horse, Kosse Bbo, neighed. The name meant Dusty Road in Numu, what the Paiute called the Milky Way. Lyle Rides Alone had chosen him for Johnny because the stallion's dark coloring matched the boy's. The two bonded and the horse helped him adjust to his new life in America.

"I know," Johnny said. "But you have to keep Sen Vang safe from Comrade Minh too. Promise me you will, no matter what Mom says. Promise."

"I promise," I said. "And your mom will want to do the same for Sen Vang. Trust her."

The plane landed, turned around at the end of the strip, and taxied back. Johnny grabbed the chocks and blocked both sides of the wheels. When Gemma stepped down from the cockpit, he threw his arms around her.

She looked over at me. I touched the corner of my eye and walked back to the house without saying a word. November and Sen Vang were in the kitchen as a pot of water boiled. The Paiute healer was explaining the different plants she gathered to make tea and their medicinal properties. Sen Vang told her how Jarai did the same in the Central Highlands.

"Artichoke tea is good for digestion," she said. "My favorite is made from chrysanthemums. It's very calming."

"Yellow lotus tea is also good for that, is it not?" November said.

"You know what my name means in English," Sen Vang said. "You know many things. You are wise, Aunt November."

"My mother named me Girl Born in Snow. What did yours name you?"

Sen Vang looked into the pot of boiling water. "H'Linh. It means girl with spirit in Jarai, but it has been a very long time since anyone has called me by that name."

"Your mother still does," the old healer said. "Her words are in the wind, the song of birds, in the flow of rivers. You only need listen with your heart to hear her speak to you, and through your heart you can always speak to her."

Johnny and Gemma came in. Before he could introduce Sen Vang, Gemma rushed forward.

"I've always wanted to meet you so I could tell you how grateful I am for everything you did for Johnny," she said. "I know you love him like we do. You'll always have a home here with us."

"I also thank you for everything you have done for him," Sen Vang said.

"On the walk from my plane, Johnny told me what you need," Gemma said. "You can count on Nick and his deputies to catch Comrade Minh. Loq and Bina will help too. And November and me, of course."

As they finished making tea, Loq nodded at the door. We went outside.

"What is it?" I said.

"Why?" he said.

"Why did Gemma say all that? Because she knows I have to catch Minh to keep Johnny safe."

"No, why is Minh killing the people he fought alongside? Do you think it's because he has what our Lakota brothers call Chante Ishta, Soul Wound?"

"November's been telling me about the Battle at Greasy Grass. Did the Lakota suffer combat fatigue?" I said.

"Native warriors have never been immune to it," he said. "It's called by many different names. Ghost Sickness. Spirit Loss. The Long Night. It's what happens to a warrior when he feels he can't come home mentally or spiritually."

"That new article I read that named it PTSD? It listed cases of what soldiers who suffer from it do. They don't go around killing other soldiers. They kill themselves. I saw that myself when I was at Walter Reed. A fellow GI hanging from a bedsheet."

"Sorry you went through that, brother," Loq said. "But my question remains. Why's Minh doing it? If it's something valuable he's after like stolen loot from Hue that we were talking about, then why track these folks down and kill them?"

"He must do it after he questions them," I said. "You know, do you have the treasure or whatever it is he's after. If you don't have it, do you know who does. No matter how they answer, it's bang! Doesn't let them tip off the next person on his list."

"I don't buy that Minh's been able to do all this on his own," the Klamath said. "How did he figure out how to enter the US, smuggle in a Soviet-made gun, come up with a scheme to pass himself off as Native American? How does he know where all these people who were once in his unit live?"

"Like Sen Vang says, he worked for the secret police after the war. He's bound to have picked up some special skills besides putting bullets in people's brains."

"But the war's been over for five years. Why's he doing it now? What took him so long to get here?"

"Except for the initial wave of war refugees that got airlifted out of Saigon, most took years to get here," I said. "That whole time they were off the radar. Traveling by boat or on foot. Living in other countries trying to make money for passage. Hiding out. No documents."

I scuffed the ground with the toe of my boot. "Take Dao Pham, Mrs. Hardward. She'd been here less than two years and the name on the marriage license isn't even her own. Probably same thing with the others. It made it harder for Minh to find them."

"Minh's not the only one who got himself smuggled into the States packing a Makarov. Sen Vang did too. He may be stealing cars, but she's renting them, paying for lodging, maybe even flying from state to state. Someone's bankrolling her."

"The officials who sent her," I said.

"About that. She didn't come out and say what kind of office she works at," Loq said. "Her war record? I bet it's security-related."

"Roger that," I said. "When I first met her, she said she'd always known where Johnny was living. Her words? Through spies, how the North won the war. And when I called the

Ministry of Public Security Hanoi's secret police, she didn't blink, but she was trying hard not to. My gut tells me she's been working for them ever since the shooting war ended."

The long mohawk shook back and forth. "A *bui doi* from a Native village whose people are known as mystics who survives on the streets of Saigon and then in the jungle as a child guerrilla and now as a spy agency's international asset. No wonder I can't make sense of what Talking Woman is telling me."

"Likewise," I said.

"What's your next move?" Loq said.

The sun was arcing higher and the temperature climbed with it. The change led to an updraft that triggered a dust devil near the corral. That spooked the horses. They began snorting and trotting in circles.

"Ask you to take Sen Vang aside and convince her she's got to trust you so she won't hold anything back about Comrade Minh's motivation, her role, and how she plans to catch him," I said.

"Why me, because I'm Maklak and she's Jarai? We're supposed to trust each other because we both have Native blood?" He looked down his high cheekbones. "Aren't you forgetting something? I spent a lot of time fighting VCs."

"I thought you could charm her with your wit," I said.

"Funny," he said. "And what are you going to be doing?"

"Keep chasing down leads. First up is the cousin in Utah who arranged for Dao Pham to come over and marry Ol' Daniel Hardward."

"You think she was VC too?"

"Definitely. And with Minh's unit too. She might know what he's really trying to find here. Treasure or someone or secrets. She might even have it herself."

"If so, that puts a bull's-eye on her back."

"That's why we got to get to her first. Orville is working to get her particulars through Daniel Hardward's sister," I said.

Loq's eyes narrowed. "You want to talk to her or use her as bait?"

I didn't answer because I didn't want to admit I'd been considering it. Putting the woman at risk to save Johnny would mean crossing a line that separated lawmen from bad men.

Loq kept studying me and then nodded. "Mm."

"Yeah. Mm," I said.

"Sounds to me like you got a decision to make that'll determine if you're really cut out for sheriffing or not," he said.

The door to the kitchen swung open. Gemma poked her head out. "Orville's on the phone. You better come quick. He says it's urgent."

"DA Sessions must've cooked up another dirty trick to spring on me," I muttered and headed inside to find out what.

24

An old enemy slapped him awake. Pain. Deep pain. Burning pain. The kind that makes you puke or makes you mad. The kind of anger that makes you rant and rave or grind your teeth and keep on running.

Running. Running for the final white line, four inches wide. Never stopping no matter how many men are trying to bring you down. Hanging from your hips, hanging from your shoulders. Ripping your arm out of the socket. Tearing the ligaments, the tendons, the muscles. Snapping the collarbone. Driving the sharp broken pieces through your flesh, through your veins.

The final white line, four inches wide. You don't stop when you reach it. You keep on running, running to make sure. Even when the men hanging on you let go. Even after the cheering stops. Even when the real pain begins. You keep on going to make sure. Make sure you won and pain lost.

Trace Wakefield's eyes snapped open. All he could see was green. The green of a ponderosa pine. And then his memory snapped back. The VW. Careening down the hillside. Fighting the wheel to keep it from rolling. The windshield fractured by a branch that caught the car. Had he flown? Was he up in a tree?

His shoulder hurt like hell when he turned to look out his window. It wasn't sky below him but ground. Right next to him. Covered with dirt and weeds and a fallen limb lying there. A limb with branches, the biggest holding the Bug in place. Holding them.

Them?

Then he remembered that too. He glanced over. The woman was moaning. That meant she was breathing. That meant she was alive.

"Jazz? Jazz, you with me?" he called. "Can you hear me?"

"Au, au, ow," she groaned.

"Can you move?"

"Move? Move where? Where are we? What ... Au, ow. Augh."

"We're in your car. On a hillside. The forklift. Red Caldera tried to kill us," he said.

"Asshole." Jazz Flambeaux spat as she said the word.

"We got to get out of here. Can you open your door? Mine's jammed."

"I'll try. Au, ow. No, it's stuck."

Trace didn't know how long he'd been knocked out, floating in the black hole like he had when they rolled him into surgery to fix his shoulder. Fix it, but not enough so the team would re-sign him. Nor would any other. Except for one. The Harney County Sheriff's Department.

"We got to move fast," he said. "Caldera made us when we were tailing him. Waited at the mill to push us off the road. He'll climb down here to make sure we're dead if that branch doesn't break first."

"How are we getting out of here?" Jazz said.

The deputy didn't answer. He was gritting his teeth while trying to shoulder open the VW's door, the pain making him angry, the four-inch-wide white line keeping him shoving. Shoving harder.

The latch snapped. Hinges creaked. The door swung open. The tree branch broke. Trace stabbed with his right hand. Felt a wrist. Grabbed it. Rolled out. Slammed into the ground pulling Jazz with him. The VW lurched. The tires rolled. Faster and faster. Rooster tails of dust rose. Metal crunched. The gas tank exploded. Flames crackled.

"Got to go. Got to keep running," Trace said, sitting up. "Caldera, he'll ... Can you move?"

"I ... Uh, yeah," Jazz said.

He didn't let go of her wrist as he got to his feet, pulled her up, and started charging, not down the hill, but across it.

"Make for the forest," he said. "Don't stop. I go down, you keep going."

They ran in a crouch, but no one shot at them.

Reaching the cover of trees, Trace finally let go of Jazz's wrist and halted. His chest heaved as he sucked in air, blew it out.

"Your left arm. It's hanging funny," Jazz said.

"Shoulder's dislocated," he said. "Not the first time. Not even the second."

He looked back to where they'd run from and then up the hill to the road. Nobody was standing at the edge looking down. No one was climbing down either. Caldera must've thought they were goners when they went over the side.

"You need a doctor," she said.

"No, I need your help is all. Stand behind me, put your arms around me, grab your wrists, and hold tight."

When she'd done that, he crossed his hands in front of him with the left on top, and slowly raised his arms straight up as if trying to touch the top of the nearest tree. He held the position for a few seconds as sweat beaded on his forehead and his old enemy screamed in his head to give up, to let go, to stop running.

"I heard that!" Jazz said. "The pop."

"Yeah," he said. "It does that when the humerus slides back into the socket."

He slowly lowered his arms and said, "You can let go now."

"Are you sure?" Jazz said.

"Yeah, it's fixed for now."

"But are you really sure you want me to let go?" she said, her tone teasing.

Trace patted her locked wrists and said, "Did you keep hold of the radio?"

"Ah, shit. It must've slipped off my lap when we hit. But I didn't let go of this."

Jazz pulled the Beretta from the back of her waistband and brandished it.

"No way I was going to lose it. I spent a lot of Saturday nights in high school babysitting snot-nosed kids to save up to buy it."

That prompted Trace to pat his right hip. "What do you know?"

His holster had popped loose from the center well where it'd been stuck. He drew his service weapon.

"Not even a scratch on it," he said.

"Now what?" Jazz said.

"We hoof it," he said.

"Where to?"

"Stay below the loop road and follow it. Get to where it meets the main road and flag someone down. Get to a CB or phone. Make the call."

"Is that what you really want to do?" she said.

"What do you mean?" Trace said.

"We've never seen another car since we left the county road. We could be waiting for hours. And even then, there's a good chance the driver could be coming up here. You know, part of Caldera's gang."

Trace's hand went to the butt of his pistol. "Have to take that chance. Got to call it in."

"Do we?" Jazz said. "Caldera thinks he killed us. Now he has to move everything up there to another wigwam somewhere so he can keep rustling herds from hardworking people. He'll get away with it."

"Sheriff Drake's orders were loud and clear. He told you to stay in the car the whole time and me to make sure nothing happens to you."

Jazz made a point of staring at where her VW crashed and burned. Then she looked at Trace, her black eyebrows arching.

"Too late for that, big man. We're already oh for two on following orders. I know I can live with the sheriff firing me as long as I take Red Caldera down with me. What about you?"

Trace rotated his shoulder to ease the pain and keep his arm from stiffening up. He thought of the books he'd read. Leonidas and the Spartans refusing to surrender. Julius Caesar defying the Senate and crossing the Rubicon. The South Pole explorers always pushing on no matter how cold it got, how thick the ice grew. Captain Ahab and his white whale. Don Quixote and his windmills.

Flexing his bicep and making a fist to show his old enemy what he thought, Trace said, "No pain, no gain. Game's on the line."

The deputy led the way as they angled up to the loop road and dashed across the asphalt and into the trees.

"You hear that?" Trace said.

"What is it, the wind? It sounds so sad," Jazz said.

"It's cows. They're lowing. They moo like that when they're upset."

"How do you know that?"

"I grew up on a ranch. Our cattle lowed, especially when we separated the calves from their mothers," he said.

"Caldera must have a bunch of cows penned up near the wigwam and the poor animals can sense they're about to be butchered," she said.

"We're getting close to the warehouse. Let's check that out first. Try to get eyes on how many men Caldera's fielding."

They stayed in the trees and resumed walking. Both were carrying their weapons. Trace held up his hand and stopped.

"What is it?" Jazz whispered.

"There's a footpath ahead. Leads down to the warehouse. I'll go have a look. You stay here. If I'm not back in five, then head for the main road as fast as you can."

She started to protest, but Trace waved her off. "Stay put."

He followed the path, stopping every so often to listen. The area around the dilapidated building had been cleared at one time, but now was overgrown with weeds and crowded with junk. Old fifty-gallon drums like the one the Hardwards had used as an incinerator. Stacks of rusty pipes. The body of a pickup that was new thirty years ago.

Trace didn't hear any voices coming from inside the building. No noise of any kind. No big saws sawing, edgers edging, stackers stacking. Sighting a doorless opening, he slipped inside, revolver first.

The area was little different than outside. Stacks of old lumber towered among piles of junk. The wood was gray and warped and shot with holes from woodboring insects. The deputy walked past them and into another cavernous room.

It couldn't have been more different.

Pickups and horse trailers were parked in one area; tractors, combines, plows, and harrows in another. There were boxes filled with hand tools, pallets stacked with bags of feed, and a heap of tack—saddles, cinches, bridles, reins, and bits.

Trace shook his head as he realized he was looking at loot

taken from the Hardwards and other ranchers who'd fallen victim to Caldera's swindle.

Moving to the vehicles, he checked the first couple of pickups for keys. None were in the ignition. Nor was a key in the third, but something else was. A CB radio. He reached through the open window, uncradled the mike, and flipped the on switch. A faint yellow glow greeted him.

Trace twisted the knob to channel 9, which was reserved for traveler assistance and emergency service.

"Breaker, breaker," he said into the mike. "Need a 10-5 to Harney County Sheriff's ASAP. Seahawk 11-99. Repeat, Seahawk 11-99. Breaker, breaker. Appreciate you sending the 10-5, good neighbor."

He repeated it a couple of times, hoping for a response from a trucker or someone who would know that 10-5 meant relay the message and Orville would certainly know the officer needs assistance code.

Before he could send it again, voices and footsteps were coming his way. Trace turned off the radio and ducked.

"Red needs to swap out the white Ford he drove up for another ride," a man said.

"What the hell was all that about, you shovin' that car off the road?" said a second man.

"Red said they was busybodies followed him up here looking to make trouble," the first man said. "Wanted to teach them a lesson, I guess."

"Pretty harsh lesson," the second man said.

"I'm not gonna lose any sleep over it. Not when I'm counting up all the money I'm making thanks to him."

"You're right about that. Easy work, easy money. You say Red needs 'nother ride? The blue Chevy three-quarter ton been here the longest so it'll be the coldest on Smokey's GTA list."

"Drive it on over to him and then bring the Ford back here. Swap out its plates and lose the old ones like always."

"Will do."

"Alrighty then. I got to get back to loading. You want me to set aside a box of fresh steaks for you?"

"Nah. I still got half a beef in my freezer as it is."

The first man laughed and left. The second man started walking toward a blue pickup, pulling the cord on a heavy-duty retractable key chain attached to his belt. Trace charged from behind, threw his forearm around his neck and locked his elbow.

The man started gasping and then choking, his knees buckling, his fingers trying to pull Trace's arm away.

The deputy knocked the man's sweat-stained brown cowboy hat off and hissed in his ear. "How many up here including you? Don't lie."

The man gasped, kept clawing at the forearm. Finally, he sputtered, "Ff ..., ff ..., four."

"Including Caldera?"

"Uh-huh."

"You're lying." Trace squeezed harder.

The man started kicking.

"How many total?" he said.

"Ff ..., ff ..., forgot Red," the man sputtered. "Ff ..., ff ..., five."

Trace squeezed again. When the man went limp and blacked out, he dragged him to a horse trailer, shoved him inside, and cuffed his wrists to the bars of the stall. Then he relieved him of the retractable key ring and went back out the way he came.

When he reached the top of the footpath, Jazz wasn't there.

25

———

Trace Wakefield stared straight ahead, not seeing, but visualizing a play. A path leading through the trees to a clearing. Two dozen cattle lowing inside a pen on one side, a rusty wigwam standing on the other. Skinned and gutted carcasses hanging on meat hooks inside it. Red Caldera twisting Jazz Flambeaux's arm while two men wearing blood-drenched aprons sharpened butcher knives. Another man standing next to the open door of a huge rendering oven glowing blue from rows of gas burners while heatwaves billowed from it.

The deputy blinked and a chalkboard with circles and x's appeared in front of the scene. Some of the circles sprouted lines with arrows. Some of the arrows aimed straight at the x's. Others curled around them. Trace shook his head to erase the board and revisualized the circles and x's, making adjustments to the lines with arrows until two were running straight downfield.

Satisfied, he murmured, "Ready. Set."

He squared his shoulders, raised up on the balls of his feet, and twisted his hips a couple of times to loosen them.

"Go," he said.

Trace kept his center of gravity low as his legs pumped, his boots churned, and his eyes swept the field for defenders. When he reached the clearing, he slammed on the brakes.

The field of play was not at all how he'd envisioned.

The cattle pen was fenced with barbed wire and had heavy metal stock gates. It was crammed with fifty or sixty head, at least.

A boxy refrigerator truck was another variant. The twenty-five-foot-long reefer was parked next to the wigwam. The engine was running to keep the cooling system on. A man was standing beside the cab smoking a cigarette. He wore a green and yellow John Deere ball cap and a shoulder holster.

The forklift that had pushed the VW over the side was moving a pallet stacked with cardboard boxes toward the back of the reefer. A big man with tattooed biceps the size of ham hocks was at the controls. He wore a gun too.

Red Caldera was standing near the doorway to the wigwam. The opening was the width of a pickup. The fat man was wearing a new summertime Stetson. His jowls flapped as he yelled at someone inside the old, rusty beehive. Although his words were lost to the forklift's engines, Trace could tell he was pissed off.

Jazz was nowhere to be seen. An image of her hanging from a meat hook inside the wigwam flashed. Before Trace charged into the clearing firing his weapon at the three men, Sheriff Warbler's voice growled the second rule for being a deputy: "The biggest mistake in saving someone is thinking you might already be too late. Being too quick on the draw guarantees you'll violate a deputy's first rule too."

Trace backed into the cover of trees and returned to the dilapidated warehouse. He picked up the brown cowboy hat and found the blue Chevy three-quarter-ton pickup. He got behind the wheel and yanked the cord on the retractable key chain. It held a dozen or more keys.

He looked for one with a Chevy logo. No such luck. He eliminated a few more because they were padlock keys. He picked a silver key and tried it. No go. He tried another. Didn't fit. Neither did the third or fourth.

Running out of keys, Trace held his breath and slid in the fifth. It went in all the way up to the head. He gave it a turn. The ignition fired. He put on the brown cowboy hat and pulled the brim down low. Then he slouched behind the wheel and put the Chevy into gear.

When he pulled out of the warehouse, he drove straight to the wigwam's open doorway as the forklift continued to load the reefer. Red Caldera gave the blue pickup a quick glance and went back to yelling at whoever was inside.

Trace slowed down as he neared, the different play options running through his mind. Park, get out, keep head down, rush Caldera, shoot anyone inside the wigwam who wasn't Jazz. Park, get out, shoot the reefer and forklift drivers and Caldera, and then rush inside.

The one play he didn't see was gunfire suddenly erupting at the cattle pen. Jazz was there. She'd opened the gates and was shooting her Beretta in the air. Lowing turned into bellowing as cows surged forward and stampeded into the clearing.

Trace looked back at Red Caldera. Angry recognition flashed in the fat man's eyes and his jowls turned crimson as he cursed. Trace stomped on the gas and aimed right at him. Caldera moved fast despite his size and dove inside the wigwam.

The deputy drove straight into the open doorway, wedging the Chevy's front end in it up to the windshield. He jumped out and ran toward the forklift. The driver tried to duck behind the mast like he had when pushing the VW over the side and went for his weapon. Trace was ready for it. He aimed and fired, putting a slug right in the tattoo on the driver's bicep. He put another in the man's hip to make sure he'd stay down.

Then he wheeled and chased after the reefer truck. The driver had scrambled into the cab and was pulling away, pounding the horn to get the surging cattle to move. Trace juked around cows and bulled others aside. The reefer truck was gaining speed. The deputy ran faster.

He caught up, grabbed the side mirror, and jumped on the running board. As he raised his gun toward the cab window, the driver slammed on the brakes while yanking a pistol from his shoulder holster. Trace pitched forward. He lost his grip, somersaulted through the air, and crashed to the ground.

A gun fired. And then again. Then three more times in fast succession. Trace never felt the bullets strike. His old enemy had won. As he felt himself sliding into a bottomless black void, he forced his head up to see how short he'd come of the finish line —that final white line, four inches wide.

Only he couldn't see it.

Instead he saw Jazz standing ten yards in front of the stalled reefer, her black combat boots planted shoulder-width apart, her knees slightly bent, her arms extended, holding the Beretta in a two-handed grip. Three bullet holes speckled the truck's windshield. They also dotted the driver's face.

Trace got to his feet and went to her. "It's okay," he said. "It's okay."

"He shot at you and it was ... I felt like ... I felt like I was on the range ... and he ... he was paper ... like the targets ... but he isn't ... paper," Jazz said. "Is he?"

"It's okay," Trace said. "You saved my life. Saved your own. Caldera, he's in the wigwam. Another man too. I got to go get them."

"No!" she said.

"I got to," he said. "Can't let them get away."

"No," she said again. "We got to."

Trace knew better than to ask if she was sure. Do that during a game and it'd cut a teammate's legs off before the snap.

"Let's go," he said.

He didn't have to say any more than that. It was like Jazz already knew the play. While she circled the wigwam to check for exits, he made sure the forklift driver wasn't going anywhere. The burly man was still alive. Trace relieved him of his gun and then went to stand behind the blue pickup.

"Harney County Sheriff's," the deputy yelled. "Two ways to play this, Caldera. We back up the Chevy and you two come out with your hands on top of your heads."

"Screw you," Caldera yelled back. "I got an army on the way. They'll be here any minute."

"Then we do it the second way."

"Yeah, and what's that?"

Trace hesitated when Jazz joined him. He looked at her and she winked.

"We stuff a rag in the Chevy's gas tank and strike a match," she called out. "We'll see how much smoke and heat that old wigwam can take."

"Who the hell you think you are, you crazy bitch," Caldera yelled back.

"Jazz Flambeaux," she said. "Maybe you heard of my father, Detective Torch Flambeaux. Lighting crooks on fire runs in the family. I'm counting to three. One."

"You're bullshitting," Caldera said. "That'd be murder."

"Who's going to know?" she said. "Your men out here? They won't talk. They can't. Two."

Another man started yelling from inside the wigwam. "Let me outta here. I don't want to die. I'm only a meat cutter. Red, he made me do it."

"Shut up," Caldera yelled. "She's bluffing."

"So's he," the other man yelled back. "There's no one coming. It's only us. Let me out. Come on. I don't want to die!"

The man's cry turned into a yelp and then the rusty wall of the wigwam clanged as Caldera threw him against it.

"I'm unscrewing the gas cap," Jazz said, banging on the pickup's side. "I'm sticking in the rag. The match is in my hand."

"Time's up," Trace said. "What's it going to be, Caldera?"

"Okay, okay. You win," the fat man said. "Let me out. I got something to trade."

"What?" the deputy said.

"You got to promise the sheriff will go easy on me I tell you what I know. You follow?"

"You're still bluffing."

"No, I'm not. Honest. I'm only the broker. The middleman. The one behind all this? He's the one you want."

"What's his name?"

"You got to let me out first. That's my deal."

"I don't make deals. I'm only a deputy."

Caldera didn't respond.

"Ouch!" Jazz cried out. "Match is burning my finger. I'm going to drop it. Don't want to ruin my nails."

"Okay, okay," Caldera said. "Move the pickup. I'm coming out."

"Hands on your head when you do," Trace said. "You try going for a gun in your boot again, Jazz will douse you with gas and I'll light you up myself."

26

———

The handset in my home office felt like it weighed ten pounds and was burning my ear as Orville Nelson reported what happened at the old lumber mill.

"Deputy Wakefield placed Red Caldera under arrest as well as three other men, one of whom sustained two GSWs," the chief deputy said. "A fifth man is deceased."

"I take it you've sent additional units," I said.

"Affirmative. The deputy who was conducting a drive-by on my orders arrived shortly after the shootout. Two more are en route."

"What's Trace and Jazz's status now?"

"They repurposed a pickup and horse trailer and are bringing down the four prisoners, including the wounded one," he said.

"They locked them in a horse trailer?"

"As Plato said, necessity is the mother of invention."

"You're taking an awfully long time to tell me how the fifth man died, Orville," I said.

"Apparently he was dispatched in the gunfight," he said.

"Dispatched? Meaning what I think you mean?"

"Yes, sir."

"Ah, shit. That's a problem I don't need right now. I told Jazz to stay in the car and Trace to—"

"It may not necessarily be problematic," Orville said.

"How's that?" I said.

"By all accounts, it was a clean shoot that resulted in the saving of a deputy's life by a licensed gun owner who demonstrated not only considerable accuracy and resolve, but coolness and courage while under grave threat to their own person."

"You know, Orville, only you can come up with more words than a dictionary to say 'Ah, shit.'"

The chief deputy didn't contradict me.

"I'll have to deal with that and the fallout that comes with it later," I said. "Right now getting Caldera and the others safely behind bars is priority one."

"Yes, about that," Orville said. "Trace reports that Red Caldera swears he was only a middleman and there is a mastermind behind the operation whose name he is willing to divulge in exchange for leniency."

"Sounds like BS. What he's really hoping is he can get down here in one piece and DA Sessions will spring him like he did before."

"I concur with your theory."

"Can't let that happen again," I said. "I also can't spare you to go up there and conduct the crime scene investigation with Doc. A lot's happening with the Hardward case right here and now."

I gave him the topline on Sen Vang and Comrade Minh. "I still need help finding Dao Pham's cousin in Utah who set up her marriage. I need to talk to her and get her out here."

Orville gave an uncharacteristic groan. "My apologies. I have been so focused on the immediacy of the shootout and arrests at the old mill, I nearly forgot. Earlier today I received a return phone call from Mr. Hardward's sister. She is in Mexico doing missionary work and only heard about her brother's death last night."

"Is she coming home?"

"Negative. She said her brother is already with the Lord and she will honor his passing by completing her missionary service."

"But you asked her about the cousin," I said.

"Affirmative. She gave me her name and phone number. I have not had a chance to call her."

"Give it to me. I'll do it."

I jotted the name and number down on a scratch pad. Then asked him what time Trace and Jazz were due back.

"I'll be there when they get in and I won't be alone," I said. "It's time to fight fire with fire. We'll see how Sessions and Judge Manton like them apples."

"Spoken like Sheriff Warbler himself," he said.

Loq and Sen Vang were still out by the corral.

"Good news or bad?" the Klamath said.

"Good on the rustling case," I said. "We've made arrests."

"Will they stick this time?"

"I'm working on it to make sure they do." I turned to Sen Vang. "Did Dao Pham ever talk about a female cousin who she was especially close to?"

"Why do you ask?" she said.

"When she married Daniel Hardward, he told the preacher the couple met through her cousin living in Utah who was married to an American too. They exchanged letters and so on."

"What's her name?"

I glanced at the piece of scratch paper. "She took her husband's last name. Snow. Ann Snow."

Sen Vang startled. "Is it Ann or Anh?"

"My deputy gave it to me. Maybe he heard it from Daniel

Hardward's sister wrong or the woman Americanized it. Why? Does Anh ring a bell?"

"Anh Tran was in our unit. Dao and Anh were very close. They were from the same village."

"And both left after the war ended and the unit disbanded?" I said.

"Yes, but not at the same time. Anh left first. I left a week later. Dao was leaving the next day."

"Why did Dao wait and not go with Anh Tran?" I said.

"I don't know," she said. "It was a very hectic time with much uncertainty. Many of us slipped away in the dark to return to our old lives without saying anything. That's what Anh did, I did, and I assume Dao did too."

I asked Sen Vang if Comrade Minh was still there when she left.

"He was. He seemed lost, unsure of what to do next, where to go. His family was gone. His village too. He'd been fighting a lot longer than all of us. It was his life."

"Did he get angry when people slipped away?"

"Very. He felt betrayed."

"Something doesn't fit," I said.

"What do you mean?" she said.

"The killings here. Minh going after his own soldiers, folks in his unit."

"War trauma," she said quickly. "What you were saying about, what is it, PTSD? Comrade Minh certainly suffers from it."

"I don't doubt he does, but soldiers with it typically hurt themselves, not other soldiers," I said. "He's hunting and killing them for another reason."

She glanced at the horses. "I don't know what you mean."

"I think you do. I think it's why you're here."

Sen Vang shook her head, making the yellow streaks in her

hair appear like sun rays shining through partially drawn window blinds.

"If we're going to catch him and stop him from killing anyone else—Anh, Johnny, yourself—you got to be straight with me."

Her thin lips all but disappeared as they pursed.

"I think Minh's doing it for money," I said. "Some kind of treasure. Something that was taken during the war. Something valuable. An icon or jewelry or artifact like the kind that was looted from the Citadel. Somebody in the unit took it. He knows it and wants it for himself. The Ministry of Public Security sent you to get it and bring it back. You work for them."

"You're wrong," she said and started to leave.

Loq had been watching her. "Wait," he said. "Listen to the voices of your ancient ones."

"What?" she said.

"It's what I do. My people, the Klamath, tell stories about Gekas. That's our word for Coyote, the trickster."

He looked up at the sky and then back at Sen Vang.

"Coyote was always jealous of the stars because they were higher than him and much admired by all people. He told the birds that the Great Creator wanted him to lead a council in the sky and tricked a hawk into carrying him up to the stars. Once there, he began lying to them about all the powers he had on earth. The stars saw through his lies and stopped holding him and he fell all the way back down and was a scavenger forevermore."

"What does that have to do with stopping Comrade Minh?" Sen Vang said.

"Mm," Loq said. "The ancients tell another story. Five sisters —water monsters—guarded a dam on the great river to keep all the salmon for themselves leaving the Klamath people to starve. One day Coyote disguised himself as a baby and convinced the sisters he was lost. While they were distracted by his innocence, he broke the dam, releasing all the salmon into the river for the people to eat."

He looked down his high cheekbones at her. "A liar for one's own gain or a liar to outwit an enemy to better the tribe, which Coyote are you?"

Sen Vang started to bolt. I grabbed her wrists, encircling the marriage bracelets handed down by her mother and father.

"*To-mo* and *Bak*," I said. "Hare and Tiger. When I was with the Jarai, they told me stories passed down by their ancients. I'm sure your parents told them to you too because they're more than legends; they're life lessons. How Hare tricked Tiger by lying about a delicious hive full of sweet honey that turned out to be a wasp nest. How the King of Fire safeguarded the Sacred Sword of Power through cleverness rather than violence."

Sen Vang glared at my hands covering her wrists. I let go. The copper bracelets gleamed in the high desert sun and seemed to mesmerize her.

"Be Trau," she said in nearly a whisper. "Comrade Minh is after Be Trau."

"Little Buffalo?" I said. "The water buffalo the ARVN soldiers killed? I don't understand."

She held up a palm. "No, the Be Trau that would fit in here. It's a figurine, a touchstone to Vietnam's past a thousand years old. Maybe more. It's a water buffalo carved from jade. The horns are made of ivory, the hooves of gold. The eyes are rubies."

Sen Vang dropped her hands. "There were always stories about priceless treasures being transported along the Ho Chi Minh Trail. Artifacts looted from Hue. Gold and jewelry handed over by rich merchants in exchange for sparing their lives. Opium to trade for weapons. But it was the story of the water buffalo that drove Comrade Minh to do what he did.

"Somehow he learned the figurine was being smuggled

down the trail," she said. "Had it been traded for Soviet guns or Chinese rockets or a rich family's passage to a boat that would take them to freedom? Who knows? Comrade Minh didn't care. Nor did he care who had it or what he had to do to get it. He grew obsessed with the idea of owning it."

She took a deep breath, shook herself as if covered with dust.

"He ordered us to march north to intercept a convoy. The journey was very dangerous. ARVN soldiers were patrolling the trail. GIs too. Helicopter gunships flew overhead, shooting at anything that moved.

"None of us dared question the mission. Comrade Minh would've executed us on the spot if we had. After days of dodging the enemy, we finally reached a place on the trail and lay in wait. First came the convoy's guides and then the porters carrying the cargo. Old men and women on foot staggering beneath the weight of towers of heavy crates strapped to their backs. Children pushing bicycles laden with boxes and bags. A man pushing a wooden wheelbarrow piled high with bamboo cages filled with live chickens. I can still hear them cluck and crow."

Sen Vang shuddered and took another breath. "When the entire convoy was passing in front of our ranks, Comrade Minh jumped up and opened fire with his Kalashnikov. He ordered us to do the same. It was shoot or be shot." She choked back tears. "It was over in minutes. Guides, old men, old women, children too. All lay dead or dying, including the chickens."

"And he found the figurine, the water buffalo?" I said.

"An old woman was carrying it in a silk pouch strapped around her waist secreted beneath her blouse. Comrade Minh took it and ordered us to gather up all the weapons we could carry and march south."

"When was that?" Loq asked.

"It was after Johnny got away," Sen Vang said. "A year later.

Maybe two. Time, it was so hard to keep track of in the jungle, in the war. You know?"

Loq and I both knew it too well. Sometimes a day felt like a week and sometimes a week would be over in a flash.

"What then?" I said.

"Comrade Minh always kept the figurine with him. No matter if we were in camp or on the march or in a fight. We could hear him talking to it at night. That's how we learned he called it Be Trau, how we learned the story of why he became a solider."

"Did he lose the figurine or did someone steal it from him?"

Sen Vang frowned. "I don't know for sure, but he thinks someone took it."

"And he must think it was someone who came to the States. They took it in case they needed to trade it for passage. Why he's been hunting them down and killing them if they don't either produce it or tell him who has it."

When she didn't answer, I said, "And the Ministry of Public Security sent you to collect it and bring it back. That is, if it's still here and wasn't already sold or traded."

"If it had been, the ministry would know. It's part of Vietnam's three-thousand-year-old history."

"It's more than that," I said.

"What do you mean?" she said.

"It's how we catch Minh. We make him believe we have it."

"How are we going to do that?"

"We tell him we do."

27

I brushed past the receptionist's desk while hooking a thumb at the seven-point star on my chest and strode to Bonnie LaRue's office, but it was empty.

"Where is she?" I yelled to a copyboy carrying a stack of newspapers so high he could barely see out from behind it.

His eyes opened wide. "Uh, she's in the back, Sheriff, where the—"

I skirted past him and crossed the newsroom as editors and reporters looked up from their typewriters. When I pushed open a door, their muttering was lost to the whirring of motors, clacking of rollers, and *thump-thump* of plate cylinders. The smell of ink and fresh-cut paper hung heavy.

Bonnie LaRue was holding a front page hot off the press. She peered over it and tilted her head at me. Her hair appeared redder than ever.

"Fight fire with fire," I muttered.

"If you've come to talk me out of running the extra I told you I was going to run, you're wasting your time," she said and turned the front page around.

The headline screamed that the recall petition had gathered

enough signatures and been submitted to the county clerk for recording.

"I'm not here for that," I said. "I got a story for you that's a lot more important than me."

"And I'm supposed to believe you?" The publisher scoffed. "Nick, I'm a newspaper woman. Have been ever since I met my husband, God rest his soul. Suspicion and skepticism flow through my veins, not gullibility and certainly not sympathy."

"I said I'd always do my level best to tell you when something that affects public safety happens. It's why I'm here."

"Fine, I'll play along," she said. "What is it?"

"We busted the gang that's been rustling cattle. My deputies are bringing them in right now. We also got a break on the Hardward murders. Yes, murders plural, not murder-suicide. I'll be making a statement about both cases."

"And I suppose you've already informed District Attorney Sessions." Bonnie's tone was as biting as the sound the press's paper cutters were making.

"He'll learn about them, all right, but not from me. I'll leave that up to you when you ask him why he let the rustler's ringleader go yesterday."

Her brows arched above the periwinkle cheaters. "And when are you going to make this so-called big statement of yours?"

I checked my field watch. "In five minutes."

She let go of the front page. It fluttered to the floor like an overgrown snowflake streaked with soot. "You're telling the truth, aren't you?"

"You knew Pudge better than most. What did he used to say? He didn't even shade it."

"You're right, it's what he always said. But what I need to know is what you say about the truth?"

I didn't answer. I was already legging through the *Burns Herald's* office to my rig that I'd left double-parked out front. No sooner had I sped around the corner and pulled into my parking spot than a white 1972 Ford pickup towing a horse trailer rattled to a stop right out front of the squat pink building. Trace Wakefield was behind the wheel. Jazz Flambeaux was riding shotgun. Both looked dead serious.

Chief Deputy Orville Nelson came rolling out the office's front door, a short-barreled riot gun cradled on his lap. The deputy accompanying him was holding a 12-gauge pump at port arms. The three of us triangulated the pickup.

In its chrome front bumper I recognized the fast-approaching reflections of the reporter and photographer from the other night. Bonnie LaRue was hurrying close behind, her high heels mimicking a typewriter as they click-clacked on the sidewalk. The *wee-ooh* of an ambulance's siren grew louder. All the commotion was starting to draw an audience.

"Deputy Wakefield," I said loud enough to wake the dead. "Sit report, now."

"We got four suspects we apprehended while they were butchering rustled cattle," he said. "They were also in possession of stolen automobiles, farm equipment, and horse tack."

"What makes you think it was all stolen?"

"Ear tags on the cows have the same numbering system as the Hardwards' poisoned stock did. This pickup is registered to Daniel Hardward. The trailer here was reported missing from a ranch in Catlow Valley."

"Did you read the suspects their Miranda rights?" I said.

Trace patted his breast pocket. "Right off the card. The injured suspect too."

"I called the ER," Orville piped up before the reporter could shout a question about how the suspect had been hurt. "Ambulance will be here in seconds."

"You transported your suspects in a rather unorthodox manner, Deputy," I said.

"Yes, sir," Trace said. "Had to make do after one of the suspects pushed our vehicle off the road with a forklift."

"Were you in the vehicle at the time?"

"Yes, sir. Took quite a fall, but got lucky."

The ambulance screeched to a stop without turning off its siren. The din drowned out the reporter's questions about the attempt on Trace and Jazz's lives. The attendants placed a big man whose bicep and hip were wrapped with blood-stained rags onto a stretcher. That drew a chorus of oohs and ahs from the growing crowd of onlookers. The ambulance sped off.

The reporter started firing questions again as the photographer snapped away, stopping only to change rolls of film.

"What led you to the crime scene, Deputy Wakefield?" the reporter asked.

"I'll answer that," I said. "I'd ordered surveillance on Red Caldera who was our primary suspect in a cattle rustling scheme. I'd arrested him two days ago but the DA released him yesterday. My deputy tailed him to an abandoned lumber mill near Foster's Creek where we received a tip an illegal slaughterhouse was being operated."

The reporter started firing off more questions, but I held up my hand. "Hold on a second while my deputies move the suspects inside and complete the booking process."

The photographer snapped away as Red Caldera and the others were led away.

Bonnie LaRue said, "I have a question for you, Sheriff Drake. Why did District Attorney Sessions want to release your suspect and Judge Manton agreed to it by issuing a court order?"

"Since I don't know what they were thinking, you'll have to ask them," I said. "What I can tell you is what the facts show. Letting Caldera go put my deputy and a civilian office worker in grave danger. You heard him; one of the suspects pushed their vehicle off the road while they were in it. That man will face charges for attempted murder in addition to rustling. If we find out he was ordered to do it, that person will likewise be charged."

That elicited more oohs and ahs from the lookie-loos.

"Why did you send a civilian out to tail a suspect?" the reporter asked.

"In law enforcement circles, that's called a ride-along as part of training," I said. "Deputy Wakefield was tailing the suspect with direct orders not to engage with him and the civilian was there to observe. That all changed when they were pushed off the road. Realizing the suspect and his accomplices wanted to kill them, my deputy took direct action to stop it."

"You mean, he did it to save himself," the reporter said.

"No, to save others. If the bad guys were willing to kill a law officer, that means no one in this county was safe." I made eye contact with the crowd. "My team put their lives on the line for all of you. I wouldn't have it any other way."

Heads nodded.

The reporter chewed his lip as he scribbled. "That makes sense for Deputy Wakefield—he's trained and it's what he signed up for—but the young woman—"

"Is new to my department and currently serves as our dispatcher while she actively pursues a career as a sworn law enforcement officer," I said. "She's already earned a college degree in computer sciences, logged two hundred hours of firearms training, and is studying to take the police academy exam. I have no doubt she'll pass it with flying colors."

The reporter kept writing notes and was about to say some more when Bonnie said, "I have a question, Sheriff."

"Go ahead," I said.

"Deputy Wakefield stated both the cattle and the vehicle belonged to the late Mr. and Mrs. Daniel Hardward. Do you believe the men arrested today are responsible for their deaths?"

"The Hardward investigation is still active. Given what we learned today, we're going to be taking a lot closer look at the timeline. We already know Red Caldera was the one who discovered the Hardwards' bodies. We also have an eyewitness's testimony that contradicts Caldera's admission of how many times he's visited the Hardward ranch."

"What can you tell us about the progress you've already made on the case or explain the lack of it?" she said.

"I can't go into specifics, but we have identified the make, model, and caliber of the weapon that was used. The coroner has also discovered forensic evidence that points to it being a double murder, not a murder-suicide as was originally assumed. I can't say anything about suspects we may or may not have identified because I don't want to tip my hand."

"When will we know more?" Bonnie said.

"Soon. We're working on getting Mr. and Mrs. Hardwards' bodies released to their family so they can proceed with a funeral and burial. There's been a delay because of an absence of official identification."

"What do you mean?"

"While Mr. Hardward has been formally identified—he had a driver's license and birth certificate—Mrs. Hardward lacked those sorts of things being a refugee from a war-torn country, namely Vietnam. That's not uncommon for people who arrive in the States like she did."

"You mean boat people," the reporter said.

"I mean war refugees because they're people who can't return to their homeland even if they wanted to since they'd likely be killed. It's people who see America as a safe harbor because that's what it's always been and what we've always stood for."

That got a few uh-huhs and a couple of handclaps. Someone

said, "The sheriff knows what he's talking about. He served in 'Nam. Earned a Purple Heart too."

I turned my gaze on Bonnie LaRue. "Fortunately, we've been able to locate and contact a close relative of Mrs. Hardward who also came to the States around the same time she did. This relative has agreed to come to Burns, view the body, and make a formal identification."

"What's the relative's name?" she said. "Where do they live?"

"Her name is Anh Tran Snow. That's spelled A-n-h. T-r-a-n. Snow's her husband's last name. Like Mrs. Hardward, she's also a war refugee and married an American. I can't give you her address for privacy's sake."

"When's she coming?" the reporter piped up.

"Tomorrow. Mrs. Snow will make the identification at the coroner's and then proceed directly to the Hardward ranch to collect some of her cousin's personal effects. She told me she wants to say goodbye to her there because her religious beliefs say that's where her spirit still is."

"We'll want to speak with her," Bonnie said.

"It's something I can certainly ask her if she's willing to and let you know. Now, I better get inside and begin the paperwork on processing these arrests."

I waited as the onlookers began to disperse. When the last had gone, Bonnie turned to the reporter and photographer.

"Go camp outside the DA's office. I'll be along shortly to break this news to him and when I ask why he released Caldera, I want photographs of his expression. Lots of them. Close-ups. Then we'll call on Judge Manton across the hall and do the same."

As the pair rushed off, the newswoman said, "If you're expecting me to thank you, you're going to have a long, long wait. Cops and press? It doesn't work that way."

"Never thought it did," I said.

"As long as we're clear on that."

"As rain."

"I must say for a man who professes to hate politics, you delivered a pretty powerful stump speech,." Bonnie said.

"Only told your reporter and the folks listening what happened."

Her eyes rolled behind the periwinkle cheaters. "As your father-in-law would say, horse pucky."

"Can I ask you something though?" I said.

"What?"

"When you run this story, will it also go out on the wire. You know, Associated Press, UPI?"

"Why do you care?" she said.

"When I was in Vietnam, the wire reporters' stories and photos went everywhere, from small-town papers to big-city ones. Everyone saw them. Made quite an impact on public attitude about the war."

Bonnie held her gaze on me a full five seconds. "You want me to put this on the wire to make sure someone sees it. Who?"

When I didn't respond, she said, "Fine, I'll do it. But I better be the first person you call when whoever you want to read it reads it and whatever happens you want to happen happens."

"I got to get back inside," I said.

She grabbed my forearm. "You know something, Nick? I'm beginning to understand why Pudge talked you into running for sheriff."

"How's that?"

"You have the same quality that always drove him. A big, old conscience," she said. "But one that isn't so big and so old that it gets in the way of doing whatever it takes for justice's sake."

28

———————

Two of the three suspects had already been booked and taken to the cells upstairs. Red Caldera was hand-cuffed to a chair seated across from Chief Deputy Orville Nelson. Trace Wakefield stood nearby.

"Nearly finished here, Sheriff," Orville said.

"Take your time to get it right," I said. "The only place Caldera's got to be is the cell waiting for him upstairs." I gave it a couple of beats. "And then the one at the State Pen where he's going to be spending the rest of his life for trying to kill Deputy Wakefield and my dispatcher."

"I did no such thing," Caldera shouted, his jowls turning red. "I never laid a hand on 'em. You follow?"

"Follow? What I heard is your man followed your orders to push them over the side using a forklift. Isn't that what you over-heard, Deputy Wakefield?"

"That's right, Sheriff."

"He's lying," Caldera shouted. "I never said anything like that."

"Are you calling me a liar?" Trace said.

"No, no, not you. Benson. The one you shot. He's lying."

"What Benson's doing is singing," I said. "He sang all the way to the hospital and the whole time they were taking slugs out of his arm and hip. Singing to the doctors and nurses how you ordered him to kill my deputy and dispatcher. Using the forklift? That's a deadly weapon, same as a gun."

"Benson did it on his own. That's the truth," Caldera whined, his shoulders slumping.

"I suppose it's also a lie that you're only a middleman. What you told Deputy Wakefield. There's someone else who's been orchestrating this whole swindle."

Caldera sat up straighter. "That really is the truth, Sheriff. I can prove it."

"How?"

"I can and I will, but it's worth something and I need something for it. I can't give it away."

"From where I stand and you sit, it doesn't look like you're in much of a position to horse trade," I said.

"Well, it's all I got and I'm gonna use it," Caldera said.

"Fair enough."

I turned to Orville. "When I checked on the condition of the cells, it appears we're getting pretty crowded and going to have to double up. When you're finished booking Mr. Caldera here, put him in the cell with the biker. Apparently, they're buddies."

"You can't do that!" Caldera shouted. "He'll kill me. He already tried once."

"We inspect the cells regularly," I said. "There're no weapons in any of them."

"His boots! They're lethal. He was kicking at me through the bars. He'll stomp me, for sure. He's batshit crazy."

"I don't doubt he is. Sure acts it. Talks like it too. Told me he's damned and doomed. I suppose I could see about putting you in your own cell."

"Thank you, Sheriff. I sure would appreciate it."

"But that's worth something and I'd need something for it." I slapped a pen and sheet of paper in front of him. "Write down the ringleader's name and everything you know about him including a way we can prove he's done what you say he did. If it pans out, you won't be bunking with the biker."

"But what about letting me walk?" Caldera said.

"Never. You tried to kill my people. I won't tolerate that."

As he began to scribble, I hooked a finger at Trace. "My office. Now."

Walking down the hall, I said the same to Jazz. I took a seat behind my desk and leaned back as the pair stood at attention. I didn't make them sweat as long as my old DI used to when he'd leave us broiling in the sun.

"I don't want to hear any excuses of why you chose to do what you did," I said. "You can read what I said about it in the *Burns Herald* and my explanation of why a civilian was in the vehicle in the first place."

I leaned forward. "Don't make a liar out of me, Jazz. You will take that deputy's exam and you will ace it. You'll also get counseling for killing that man, no matter how justified it was. Taking a life changes you. Forever. It's up to you with the help of a shrink to make sure it changes in the right way. Trust me, I know from experience."

"Can I say something, sir?" Trace said.

"No, you may not," I said.

"May I?" Jazz said.

"What?"

"I already took the exam. Plenty of times."

"You keep flunking it?" I said.

"No, I always get a hundred percent. I memorized all the possible questions and answers. Some people watch TV at night. Others read dusty old history books." She winked at Trace. "Me? I test myself and ask and answer the questions before falling asleep. Go ahead, ask me one. Ask me ten. A hundred."

"Don't need to. I believe you. Trust you too. I trust you'll get the phone number for the head doctor from Orville and make an appointment today. Trust you'll take the test for real. And I also trust you won't complain when I put you on probation for twelve months, starting right now."

"Does that mean you're making me a—"

"Get back to work," I said. "And close the door behind you."

I stared at the stack of paperwork, shook my head at it, and picked up the phone. Gemma answered on the third ring. I told her what went down and what I hoped was going to happen tomorrow.

"Babe, I need you to load up the kids and November in your plane and take off," I said. "The Shakespeare Festival's going on in Ashland. Fly over there and watch some plays. Stay in a nice motel. Eat in a fancy restaurant. I'll let you know when it's safe to come home."

November had taught Gemma a lot of things in all the years they'd lived under the same roof. How to speak Numu. How to make fry bread. How to weave. Which plants were good for healing and which ones for killing pests. But the one thing the old healer didn't teach her was how to tsk and harrumph.

"The hell I will!" Gemma shouted. "Damn you for even thinking I'd light out. And double damn you for thinking I'd teach our kids to turn tail and run instead of standing and fighting. This is my family, my home, my ranch. I'm not going anywhere and neither are they."

When the horse doctor blew air, I could see the wisps of blond hair that had escaped from her ponytail whisking across her face. I also knew she wasn't through.

"If I even hinted to November you said that, she'd turn you into a restless wind that spends eternity bashing itself against

Steens Mountain. And I'd take the kids out to fly kites in it every single day and tell them that's what happened to you because you believed we lacked courage."

"I knew you'd feel that way and say all that too—well, maybe not the wind and kites part—but I had to try, you understand? Things go sideways, it won't only be me who could get hurt."

"I know," she said. "And that's why we're all going to make damn sure it doesn't."

"Hold tight," I said. "I'll be home in a bit."

I took it as a good sign no wind was blowing when I rattled across the cattle guard and parked in front of the ranch house. Sen Vang's car was there, but both Loq's and Bina's rigs were gone.

Gemma was in the corral taking a curry comb to her sorrel mare. Hattie was practicing twirling a lariat and trying to lasso a wooden sawhorse with horns nailed to it. Everything looked normal, peaceful, like it should be. But I knew it could all change in a blink.

If November had overheard my call with Gemma, she didn't let on when we assembled at the table and ate supper. Hattie asked Sen Vang if she'd ever ridden a horse and clapped when our guest said yes, that when she was a little girl she had a pony.

"She was a pretty little Mongolian," she said. "The Central Highlands where I lived is about the only place in Vietnam that does have horses."

"What was her name?" Hattie said.

"*Chim Ruoi.* It means hummingbird. I named her that because she was little and could fly."

"My pony's Shell Flower, but I call her Shelly. She can fly too. We're learning how to barrel race and we're going to win blue ribbons like Momma used to."

Sen Vang smiled, but I could see the glisten in her eyes.

After supper and all the dishes were cleared and the kids were readying for bed, Sen Vang found me in my office.

"I'm going to go say goodnight to Johnny, but it's really goodbye," she said. "No matter what happens tomorrow, I won't see him again."

"Are you sure about that?" I said.

"Yes. His life is here now and I'm too much of a reminder of the past. I want him to hold on to what was best about Vietnam and not memories of the worst."

"We're going to make tomorrow work," I said. "You have my word on it."

"We'll see," she said.

After she left, I was setting out a couple of extra magazines to take with me in the morning when the phone rang.

"I got a call from my boss," Bina Mantioc said. She was still at her office, working late. "Chief Tahamtaham has been checking in regularly with his counterparts near Portland. All of them have been on alert in case Comrade Minh showed up."

"And?" I said.

"Minh was spotted southwest of Portland in a grocery store in the Grand Ronde community. He said he was a tribal member and was asking who he should talk to about free lodging when he spotted the *Portland Oregonian's* evening edition. They'd run the *Burns Herald* story on the front page, including the sidebar on the Hardward murders complete with their photographs and news about Anh Tran Snow coming to Burns."

"Is he still there?" I said.

"No, he left in a hurry and took the paper with him. Do you think he reads English?"

"Enough to recognize Anh Tran's name and Burns."

I hung up and turned around. November was standing in the doorway.

"I need to tell you the rest of the story about Snakehead and the Battle of Greasy Grass so you will know what to do when the time comes to do it," she said.

I gestured at the leather couch that Pudge used to nap on when the office was his. "Make yourself comfortable."

"You remember where we left off?" the old healer said as she pulled her shawl tighter around her shoulders. "Snakehead had ridden ahead of the others and was fighting with no fear that he could be wounded or killed."

The battle was over in less than an hour, November continued. Yellow Hair and his bluecoats and their Crow and Arikara scouts lay dead or dying. Lakota and Cheyenne warriors whooped and began to take scalps.

Snakehead saw a wounded Crow scout sitting by himself. The Crow said, Go ahead and kill me, for I am not afraid to die. No, said Snakehead, you must live. Why? said the Crow. Look into my looking glass, Snakehead said. See this battle. See the next and the next. The bluecoats aren't your friends. They will kill every Crow the same as they are trying to kill Lakota, Cheyenne, Shoshone, and all the tribes that share the land between the Great Waters.

The Crow looked and saw all that. But what can I do about it? he said. Go home and tell your chief what you have seen, Snakehead said. Tell him we must fight as one to beat the bluecoats. Then he took the blanket Walks on Clouds had given him and put it over the wounded Crow's shoulders. Go, he said. Leave this place. If anyone sees you, they will recognize the blanket as Lakota and think you are one.

Snakehead went back to the hill littered with dead bluecoats, including Yellow Hair. He saw Walks on Clouds and other women from the camp going from body to body collecting weapons and uniforms. He watched as Walks on Clouds approached the body of a bluecoat. As she tugged on his gun belt, he suddenly rolled over. It is you, she cried, the man who killed my father. Before she could draw her knife, he shot her with his pistol. Snakehead ran toward them, firing his rifle as he did, his aim straight and true, the bullets finding their mark in the bluecoat.

But it was too late. Walks on Clouds was dead. Snakehead picked her up, his cry renting the sky over the battlefield. He carried her body to his pony and took her back to the tipi beside the Greasy Grass River so her mother could tend to her.

That night there was a victory dance, but Snakehead was too sad to join. Same Knife told him to dance to honor Walks on Clouds. Dance to honor our fallen warriors, he said. Dance to celebrate the strength of Lakota, Cheyenne, and Arapaho warriors for today we beat the bluecoats without needing any help from Crow or Arikara.

Snakehead took out his looking glass to show him the battles that would follow so he could see how wrong he was, but Same Knife would have none of it. If Lakota won't listen, Snakehead said, then perhaps my own people will. And so he mounted his pony and rode for thirty days, across the great plain of tall grass, along the river that took him up the mountain, and down the other side where he reached the Snake River and followed it home.

When Snakehead rode into his village, children hid behind their mothers at the sight of him. Young braves threw rocks at him. Even when he dismounted in front of his family's wikiup, his parents recoiled in horror, thinking him an evil spirit. No one recognized him. No one except for Summer Moon.

Buffalo Dreamer, you finally came home, the young woman cried, and ran up to him, unflinching at the sight of his scaly and earless head, his mouth widened like a serpent's. How did you know it was me? he said. Because I've been watching you in my looking glass, she said. I saw you at the Battle of Greasy Grass and what you did. I saw what you saw, that Lakota and

Cheyenne aren't our enemies. No other tribe is. I saw who our real enemy is.

His father said, Is all this true? Yes, Snakehead said. Then you come home with much honor, my son, for it is not always easy to choose between friend and enemy, right and wrong. And for that you deserve a new name. You will be Buffalo Dreamer no longer. Nor Snakehead. From this day on, you will be known as True Eyes.

It is a good name, Summer Moon said, a strong name, a beautiful name, as beautiful as the warrior who bears it. The couple walked down to the edge of the great Snake River and listened to the song the river had been singing since the beginning of time. Summer Moon asked True Eyes to marry her and he said yes. Their firstborn was a son who became known as Shoots While Running, because he, like his father, was a great warrior and fought for his people's right to live free.

"True Eyes," November said, "spent the rest of his life trying to convince all the tribes to unite. Although he had some success, it was never enough to drive the invaders out."

The old healer's eyes were free of their usual rheum as she stared into mine. "So you see, my son, while the looking glass is able to reveal what could be, it is up to those who look into it to make it so that it will be. Remember that tomorrow when it is time for you to look."

29

---

orning came fast and bright, the sun blazing so hot it burned away the dawn before gray had time to turn pink. I sat on the edge of my desk at the sheriff's department and waited.

The front door finally opened and a woman entered. Her hair was tucked up in a black beret with a veil. It matched the color of a long dress that reached her wrists and ankles. She clutched a purse with both hands.

"Mrs. Snow?" I said. "Mrs. Anh Tran Snow?"

"Yes," she said.

"I'm Sheriff Nick Drake. I'm sorry for your loss."

Jazz came from behind her desk. "Condolences, Mrs. Snow. I hope your journey wasn't too difficult."

When the woman in black shook her head, the veil made a noise akin to a whisper. "Not physically. Emotionally? Very."

Trace walked down the hall and I introduced him. He offered his sympathies.

"Mrs. Snow and I are going to walk over to Doc's," I said. "After we're finished there, we'll come back and she'll follow me to the Hardward ranch."

"Yes, sir," they said in tandem and left.

I waited a couple of minutes so the pair who I'd tasked with walking point and sweep could vanish into the shadows—discreet and deadly. Then I escorted Mrs. Snow outside. Despite the heat and her black clothes, she didn't falter on the way to Doc's. I kept my gun hand loose, eyes searching.

When we reached the morgue, Doc and Orville greeted us. The old sawbones looked haggard from lack of sleep after spending long hours at the abandoned lumber mill processing the crime scene there. Orville displayed his usual energy as he recited a set of instructions.

"I apologize for the formalities," he said, "but we must ensure the identification is completed in accordance with the guidelines so that it will withstand any challenges in a court of law."

The black beret nodded.

We followed Orville and Doc into the morgue cooler and stopped in front of a refrigerated drawer.

"Ready?" Doc said.

"Wait," Anh Tran Snow said.

"Do you need a moment?" I said.

"I would like to be certain it really is Dao Pham before I have to look." She took a breath. "Dao has scars on her calves and back. She has a birthmark here." The woman touched her chest above her left breast. "It is the shape of an apple."

"Right on all accounts," the old sawbones said. "Those are all in my notes."

"But we still need you to make a visual identification," Orville said.

Mrs. Snow took another deep breath. This time the veil shuddered. "I am ready," she said.

The drawer squeaked on its rollers as Doc pulled on the handle. A sheet had been draped over the body and arranged around the head so only the face was visible. The eyes were closed and the skin was marbled.

The woman in black reached out and touched the body. "Dao. Honorable friend. Beloved cousin. You are finally safe. You are with your family and friends now and one day I will join you."

When she withdrew her hand, I nodded at Doc and he closed the drawer.

Mrs. Snow seemed frozen in place. I put my arm around her and guided her out of the cold room and into the glare of a summer day. We walked back to the office with Trace and Jazz repeating their discreet escort. A few passersby stared at the woman in black, but no one tried to approach us. I helped her into her car and got into my rig. I drove slowly out of town, checking the rearview—not just to make sure she was close behind, but to confirm Trace and Jazz had stayed put as ordered.

The road to the Hardward ranch felt like it had more potholes than the first time I'd driven it. I thought about how little time had passed since then, yet how much had happened. It brought back what Sen Vang had said about the difficulty of keeping track of time in war—and I finally realized why the case felt so familiar.

I came to a stop before crossing the final hundred yards. I picked up my binoculars and scanned. No other vehicles were present. No sun reflections glinted off a rifle scope. I continued on and parked in front of the weather-beaten house.

Mrs. Snow got out of her car. She hadn't taken off her beret or veil.

I said, "Do you want to go inside or—"

"I would like to walk around first and let Dao's spirit know I am here," she said.

My senses were on high alert as I gritted my teeth and trailed behind her, knowing I was the target. If Comrade Minh had acted on the story in the newspaper, he'd want her alive and me in a refrigerated drawer next to Dao Pham.

Despite the sun and heat, she took her time. She paused at the tub where yellow lotuses had once bloomed, pinched a dried stalk, and held it up to her veiled nose. I followed her through the barn and along the gully that had been turned into a graveyard for poisoned livestock. Then she reached the back fence and studied the row of sunflowers with their bowing heads and carpet of shells.

"It is quite hot and dry and I grow thirsty," she said.

"There's water in the house," I said.

As I went to the kitchen and poured two glasses, she walked through the house. If she was hoping to find anything, she was in for a disappointment.

I found her sitting on the brown sofa with the crocheted Afghan draped over the back. She clutched her purse on her lap and was staring at the magazine picture of the green field dotted with blooms of purple lupine, orange mallow, and pink mariposa lilies pasted on cardboard and tacked to the wall. I sat beside her.

"The colors remind me of home," she said. "My village was so beautiful, so peaceful until ..."

She took a sip of water and put the glass down. I did the same.

"Dao must have been very homesick living here," she said, "but now she can go anywhere she wants."

"You mean, in the spirit world?" I said.

Before she could reply, the front door swung open and a short, powerfully built man stormed in. He aimed his Makarov at me, but I already had my .45 out and pressed against Mrs. Snow's temple.

"Shoot me and she dies and you'll never find Be Trau," I said.

Comrade Minh's sneer turned into a frown and his eyes

shifted between the woman and me and back again. He squinted as if it would help him see through her veil. "It you Anh Tran?"

She nodded.

"You will no kill her," he said to me.

"I fought in 'Nam for three years. Are you certain about that?"

Minh barked something to her in Vietnamese. I pulled her closer. "What did he say?"

"He asked if it is true I took Be Trau from him."

"And you said, *Da*. I know that word. It means yes."

Minh spoke rapidly, but I got the gist. If Anh Tran gave him the figurine, he'd let both of us live and vanish.

"Drop the gun," I said before she could answer. "You killed Dao Pham and her husband. I'm not letting you walk."

"Then you die," he said.

I ground the muzzle into her temple, making her wince. "And so will Be Trau. All over again. You'll never see him. Not even in *dia nguc*. Hell."

Minh's eyes shifted back and forth. He chewed his lower lip.

"I no alone," he finally said. "Quang Do here. I bring from Portland."

"Quang Do was our sharpshooter," the woman said. "He was very good."

"Is still," Minh said and gave a crooked smile.

"And you two got here last night, hid your vehicle, and lay in wait," I said.

"Here like Vietnam," he said. "Many place to hide."

"I know," I said. "I've lived here ten years. My brother? His people for ten thousand years."

"What that mean?"

"Means I didn't come alone either."

"You lie," Minh said.

"Sometimes I have to," I said, "but not now."

"I make sign, Quang Do shoot."

"If you do, you sign his death warrant."

He sneered again and started to raise his hand. A rifle shot cracked like a thunderclap. The echo found the open door and rolled into the room like an ill wind.

Minh's smile didn't fade. "Quang Do good. Your man dead."

I shook my head. "I know that sound. It's my brother's Winchester .30-30. I have one just like it."

An owl hooted from the direction of the shot.

"And that's him telling me now he's got a bead on you," I said. "Drop the gun, Comrade."

The old VC hesitated. "You lie."

"No, Quang Do lies in the dirt. You're about to join him."

Minh glared at Anh as he finally lowered the Makarov and let it fall to the floor. "You! You do this. Take Be Trau. Make me kill them."

"You killed them all on your own," she shouted and jumped up. "You killed all those innocent people on the Trail. You whipped us. Beat us. And when the war ended, you hunted your own soldiers and killed them. Back home and now here."

Sweat shone on Minh's forehead. "For Be Trau! My Be Trau."

The black beret cocked. "Yours? No! The people's Be Trau. Do you want to see him?"

"You have Be Trau?" he said. "Show me."

"First I'll show you this."

She swept off her beret and its veil. Yellow-streaked hair fell to her shoulders.

"Sen Vang!" he cried. "It you."

"Yes," she said and yanked her Makarov out of her purse. She shot him in the heart, and then shot him again as he fell backward.

A shadow filled the doorway. It wasn't Minh's spirit leaving; it was Loq. The Winchester was clamped to his shoulder.

"Minh's down," I said. "All clear."

He kept his rifle trained on Sen Vang. "Drop your weapon," he said. "Do it. Now."

She shuddered and let the gun fall. "I can't ... can't believe he's finally dead."

The Klamath gave me a hard look.

"That wasn't part of the plan," I said. "You know it wasn't. Sen Vang was only supposed to pretend to be Anh Tran so I could get the drop on him."

"I'm sorry, but I had my orders," she said. "Hanoi couldn't risk Washington using him for propaganda leverage when the day comes and we start negotiating for recognition and trade."

Loq's long mohawk rippled. "I knew it. Talking Woman turns out to be a mystic and a Charlie playing both sides all along."

Sen Vang glared at him, but all I could see was a little girl whose parents were killed and her childhood snatched away—a girl who'd learned how to survive in the harshest of conditions, now living under a system that had yet to learn how to forgive and forget.

She turned to me and held out her wrists. "Go ahead. Put on the handcuffs."

Streaming sunlight made her mother and father's copper bracelets gleam. I shook my head, picked up Minh's Makarov, stepped outside, and fired two shots into the air. I came back in.

"My department was closing in on this man for killing the Hardwards," I said. "He ambushed me here after Mrs. Snow left. I wrestled him for his gun and turned it on him."

"You sure you want to start walking that trail now?" Loq said. "It's bound to get steep and rocky."

"I'm learning not everything's so black and white with this job."

Loq nodded. "True that. But what about the man out there with my round in him? I'm not your deputy, and if those politicians gunning for you find out what happened here, they'll use it to bury you once and for all."

"That's why I'm going to get my shovel and bury him."

"Aho, brother. Maybe you are cut out for this job, after all."

I turned to Sen Vang, and as I looked at her, I didn't think of all the firefights I'd fought in Vietnam against people like Comrade Minh and her, but the Battle of Greasy Grass and the looking glass.

"You, Loq, and me," I said. "We know the true cost of war. Go home. Tell your government the US is no longer the enemy. Work to make it so I can bring Johnny there to pay his respects to his mother and ancestors."

Sen Vang hesitated, then steepled her hands and bowed. "I'll try," she said.

Then the girl with yellow hair stepped over Comrade Minh's body and drove away.

30

———

Dawn came bright and fast the following morning. I'd only been home for a few hours after clearing the crime scene at the Hardward ranch. As I headed to the kitchen for coffee, a sob came from Johnny's bedroom.

"What's wrong?" I poked my head in. Johnny was still in bed.

"I'm never going to see Sen Vang again," he said, wiping tears from his eyes.

I sat beside him. "I asked her to see about making it possible for us to visit once she gets back home."

"You did?"

I nodded.

"But that'll take forever," he said.

"A few years, yeah, but it'll happen one day. You just got to believe."

Johnny sniffed and rubbed his eyes again. "Sen Vang told me to always remember the good things about Vietnam. Like the *Chim Lac* and what it represents. Hope and peace and prosperity."

I looked at the dresser at the foot of his bed. Its mirror

reflected the colorful needlepoint hanging on the wall behind us.

"Did Sen Vang ask where you got such a beautiful *Chim Lac*?"

"She thought November had made it for me," he said. "You know, because it's like a weaving. But then I told her you brought it home from the Hardwards."

"What did she say about that?"

"She was surprised and said it was even more special because her friend Dao Pham had stitched it."

"Did you take it off the wall for her?"

Johnny shook his head. "No, she saw it hanging up there, but she was more interested in looking at it in the mirror. Like we are now. Sen Vang traced the reflection with her finger and said, 'Ah, she made it in reverse.' Whatever that means."

"I think she meant that because Dao Pham was left-handed, her stitches go the opposite way."

I got up to look at the *Chim Lac* above the bed, then stepped over to the dresser mirror. Like a photograph held up to a looking glass, the image was flipped, swapping left and right. I traced the outline with my fingertip: the belly, the outspread wings, the long tail and beak. The colorful threads—yellow for flowers, green for foliage, blue and white for sky—and a trail of distinct knots arranged inside the mythical creature's body.

And then I saw what Sen Vang had seen.

"It's going to be another long day," I said. "I probably won't get home till very late. Look after Hattie, your mom, and November for me, okay?"

"Uh-huh," Johnny said.

"Don't forget your chores."

"I won't."

"Okay, son. I'll see you later. Love you."

"Yeah, Dad. I know."

I turned off the two-lane and once again dodged potholes on the dirt road leading to the Hardward ranch. I didn't go all the way there. A trio of rigs sat idling at the fork ahead.

I pulled around them, parked in front, and got out.

"No rest for the weary, eh, Orville?" I said, walking back to his vehicle.

"It has been a very busy few days, Sheriff, I will hand you that," he said. "Maybe the busiest since I joined the department."

I looked at the other two deputies. "Everyone know the drill?"

"Squad's ready," Trace Wakefield said.

"All locked and loaded?"

Three heads nodded.

"Let's go to work," I said.

We drove in a convoy down the dirt road. The Big D ranch and the Triple Triangle beyond it came into view. I could feel eyes on me from both, but didn't let up on the gas until I nearly passed the first entrance. Then I cranked the wheel hard and hit the lights and siren.

The three rigs behind me followed suit and we roared in fast. Orville pulled abreast of me while the two deputies fanned out to flank us, forming a solid front line as we raced toward the ranch house. If a fence or a field got run over, well, I had a feeling the owner wouldn't be in a position to bellyache.

The sound of my bootheels clomping up the porch steps made me think of Bonnie LaRue's high heels clacking like a typewriter when she wrote the editorial for the morning paper's lead story on the Hardward murders. If voters wanted real justice, she opined, they should question the motives of the DA and judge who were behind the recall, not the sheriff who'd just proven his mettle twice over.

I pounded on the front door and Dillard's weaselly son, Bobby, answered, but I brushed right past him.

"I got a warrant, Dill," I called out. "You can stand back and let us search, or you can try flushing the evidence down the john. I'd advise against the latter—you'll be the one swimming in the septic tank to fish it out."

Dill Dillard appeared in the doorway of his office. He wore the high-crown gray Stetson creased the way he liked it and smoothed his horseshoe-style mustache the same color with his thumb.

"I got no idea what brings you out here, much less what you're palavering about," he drawled.

"Sure you do, Dill," I said. "All the cattle rustling that's been going on."

"You mean the story in the *Burns Herald* about you catching the sumbitches. Yup, I seen it. Even a blind pig finds an acorn once in a while."

"There's still one acorn left, and according to Red Caldera, it's right in front of me."

Dillard snorted, then guffawed.

"Says the sheriff with, what, how many days' experience? How many hours left before that badge gets plucked off your shirt by the good people of Harney County who showed enough sense to recall your sorry ass? You'll be lucky if Fish and Wildlife takes you back to keep an eye on the bugs and bunnies."

He guffawed again.

"You're right, Dill, I did learn a thing or two the ten years I patrolled for Fish and Wildlife. First time you and I met was at the Hardward ranch. When I asked why you and your son showed up there loaded for bear, you said it was because Harney County was full of diamondbacks, and you showed me your snakeskin boots."

"So what?" he said.

"So, diamondbacks don't live up here. Nearest ones are four hundred and fifty miles away. Only kind we got in Harney are Great Basin rattlesnakes."

I clicked my cheek. "Orville, what's the name of the outfit that's been buying up all the ranches that Caldera admitted he helped drive into bankruptcy?"

"I have the paperwork right here, Sheriff," the chief deputy said. "According to the documents, and as sworn to by the lawyer who drew them up, it is Diamondback Ltd. The address is a PO Box in Burns."

Dill started to sputter. His son, Bobby, made a run for the front door, but Trace straight-armed him and laid him out flat.

Footsteps sounded to my right. It was Jazz accompanied by Manny Hernandez.

"What do you got there, Deputy Flambeaux?" I said.

"This man says he's worked for Mr. Dillard for years," she said. "He has something to tell you."

"In English or Spanish, Señor Hernandez?" I said.

"*Inglés*," Manny said. He looked at Dill Dillard. "That's *Español* for English."

"You don't speak a word of it!" Dill snapped.

"*Sí*, Señor Dillard, I speak *mucho*. That means a lot in *Español*. Understand *mucho* too. Now I speak it to Sheriff Drake about the drawer in your desk where you keep all your papers. You called it secret. That's *secreto* in *Español*. See? Languages not so different."

Manny flashed his missing-tooth grin. "You told Bobby about it right in front of me, thinking I nothing but a dumb Mexican. You know something, Señor Dillard? Who's the dumb one now?"

"Deputy Wakefield," I said. "Cuff Mr. Dillard and read him his rights. And Deputy Flambeaux, do the same with his son."

"Yes, sir," she said.

"Come on, Orville, let's see what's in that drawer this snake in the grass is so anxious to keep secret. My money's on deeds to all the properties he bought after poisoning his neighbors' stock."

The desk was made of oak and big as a bull. I opened the drawers, but didn't find a secret one. I was about to send Trace out to the barn to get an axe, when Orville scooted his wheelchair into the kneehole, rapped on the sides a couple of times, felt around, and, whoosh, a hidden drawer slid open beneath the main one. He pulled out a manila file folder and thumbed through a stack of papers.

"Eureka!" he said.

We kept searching and turned up more evidence, including a checking account, ledger, and handwritten notes from Red Caldera. Two hours later we were ready to march father and son out to the rigs.

"Trace, you take Dill in yours," I said, then signaled Jazz to come close.

"Yes, Sheriff?" she whispered.

"You take Bobby. I got a feeling he's going to spill his guts."

"Why, because I'm a woman and you think he wants to try and impress me?" she said.

"Because he won't be in the presence of his overbearing daddy," I said. "He'll be looking for a way to get out from under him once and for all, even if it means selling him out."

"I hadn't thought of that," she said. "They don't teach that in the police academy manual."

"When I was with Fish and Wildlife, I learned a lot about nature," I said. "But this job? It's human nature you got to know."

We headed down the road and I turned toward the Hardward ranch while my deputies continued to Burns.

The temperature hadn't dropped, and the sunbaked, wind-scoured house and barn appeared more forlorn than the first time I'd seen them. Tumbleweeds caught in the sagging barbed wire and withered hayfields spoke of abandonment; the weight of the sadness that had settled over the ranch felt heavy.

I glanced at the kitchen window where Comrade Minh had threatened Dao Pham with death if she didn't turn over the bejeweled statue of a water buffalo. He was sure she'd taken it from him. I could see it all playing out—how he'd shot her husband when she refused, and how he'd shot her, too, when she swore she didn't have it or know who did. I could also see my own reflection in the glass, the seven-point star on my chest and the words Harney County Sheriff written in reverse.

That made me think of the *Chim Lac* in Johnny's mirror. I recalled the trail of knots Dao Pham had stitched into it—the trail that Sen Vang had seen, too.

I walked past the washtub filled with dried yellow lotuses, through the barn, and along the gully still filled with dead livestock. At the back fence, a row of nine sunflowers bowed their heavy heads.

The first time I'd seen them, I remembered which numbers were lucky in Vietnamese culture and which were not. I'd picked the fourth because it was the number associated with death, and there I found Dao Pham's box of memories.

I'd ignored the ninth sunflower then, even though number nine was lucky and symbolized eternity. Now I looked at the ground in front of the ninth sunflower and saw that the soil had been freshly disturbed.

Despite a day in the hot sun, the dirt was still soft. I scooped it out easily with my hands. Instead of uncovering an ancient figurine made of jade, ivory, and gold, I pulled up a single, dried stalk of a yellow lotus.

Sen Vang had returned last night. She'd left it for me to find —her way of saying thanks for taking care of Johnny and for allowing her to dig up Be Trau and take him home to Vietnam where he belonged. But the message of the yellow lotus was more than that. It was an emancipation proclamation for us both, an invitation to accept that the war was finally over—to shake off the shackles of guilt, remorse, and regret, and get on with the business of living.

I slipped the dried yellow lotus in my shirt pocket and vowed to do just that.

Dusk had come and gone by the time I rattled over the cattle guard. The only light in the house was the yellow one shining from my bedroom window. Icarus it is, I said to myself. But when I opened the door, I found Gemma wearing boots and slipping on a jean jacket.

"Don't tell me you got a call about a sick horse and are taking off?" I said.

"No, I've been waiting for you," she said. "Moon's up, stars are out. We're long overdue for a midnight ride. Giddyap, let's go."

I returned her smile. "I'll saddle Wovoka and Sara."

"Uh-uh, hotshot. With everything that's been going on, we need to let 'er rip like we used to."

"The Triumph," I said.

"And redlining it all the way," she said.

We snuck out of the house hand in hand and fast-stepped to the airfield where I kept the bike. As we neared it, we heard November singing and saw her standing in the moonlight up on the knoll where Pudge and Henrietta lay. Her arms were outstretched, her face raised, her voice strong as she gave thanks to the ones who'd come and gone before her, including True Eyes, Summer Moon, Shoots While Running, and their daughter Breathes Like Gentle Wind.

I kickstarted the Triumph and 650cc's of raw power roared to life. Gemma climbed aboard and tightened her arms around me and buried her chin in my neck. I released the clutch and gunned it, shifting through the gears lickety-split. We sped down a familiar trail and out onto a salt pan as big as a lake and just as flat. A comet blazed overhead and we raced it.

Whooping and hollering, we set all our doubts and fears free. It wasn't death and the devil we were running from, but tomorrow and the next day we were rushing toward.

When we reached the middle of the salt pan, I braked to a stop and we got off. Just as fast, off came the bedroll tied to the back and so did our clothes. As we embraced and joined as one in the light of the night sky, it felt as good as the first time and the last time and all the times in between because what we had together was strong and true—so true that the stars believed it and held us and wouldn't let go.

ABOUT THE AUTHOR

Dwight Holing is the award-winning author of twenty books, including two bestselling mystery series: the Nick Drake Novels and the Jack McCoul Capers.

His Nick Drake mysteries have won the Silver Falchion Award for Best Western, the CLUE Award for Best Mystery & Suspense, and the Laramie Award for Best Novel with Western, First Nations, and Americana Themes. His short fiction was awarded the Arts & Letters Prize for Fiction.

Dwight Holing is a member of Mystery Writers of America, Western Writers of America, and Sisters in Crime where he serves on the board of directors of its Capital Crimes chapter. He lives beside a coastal river in California with his wife and two dogs who'd rather swim than walk.

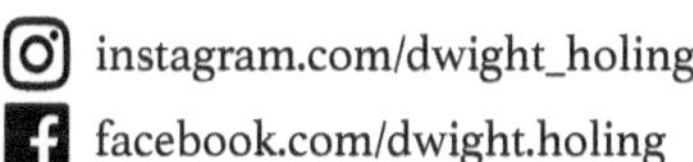

instagram.com/dwight_holing
facebook.com/dwight.holing

ACKNOWLEDGMENTS

I'm indebted to many people who helped in the creation of *The Yellow Hair*. As always, my family provided support throughout the research and writing process.

I'm especially grateful to my advance reader team who read early drafts and gave me very helpful feedback. They include Gene Ammerman, Jeffrey Miller, Kenneth Mitchell, Annie Notthoff, John Onoda, Teresa Onoda, Haris Orkin, and Leslie Wood.

Thank you Emma Moylan for proofreading and copyediting. Kudos to design artist-extraordinaire Rob Williams for designing and creating the cover.

I offer respect to the Burns Paiute Tribe of Oregon, the Klamath Tribes, and the Confederated Tribes of the Umatilla Reservation.

Any errors, regrettably, are my own.

GET A FREE BOOK

Thank you for reading *The Yellow Hair*. Reviews are the lifeblood of books so please leave one on the retailer's site.

If you belong to a book club, consider encouraging your fellow members to choose *The Yellow Hair* or any of the other Nick Drake mysteries for discussion. Contact Dwight Holing directly if you'd like him to join your club's meeting in person or via Zoom to talk about the book, the series, and his writing process. His contact information is on his website where you can subscribe to his free newsletter where he posts information about the crime fiction world plus upcoming book tours and events.

Sign up for his newsletter to get a free book and be the first to learn about the next Nick Drake Mystery as well as receive news about crime fiction and special deals.

Visit dwightholing.com/free-book. You can unsubscribe at any time.

ALSO BY DWIGHT HOLING

The Nick Drake Novels

The Sorrow Hand (Book 1)

The Pity Heart (Book 2)

The Shaming Eyes (Book 3)

The Whisper Soul (Book 4)

The Nowhere Bones (Book 5)

The Forever Feet (Book 6)

The Demon Skin (Book 7)

The Broken Blood (Book 8)

The Thunder Head (Book 9)

The Yellow Hair (Book 10)

The Jack McCoul Capers

A Boatload (Book 1)

Bad Karma (Book 2)

Baby Blue (Book 3)

Shake City (Book 4)

Novels

Hard Blue Empty: A Mystery

Short Story Collections

California Works

Over Our Heads Under Our Feet

www.ingramcontent.com/pod-product-compliance
Lightning Source LLC
Chambersburg PA
CBHW051219130726
47988CB00001B/148